CW00531338

Death always follows

(A Mike Cannon Jumps Racing Mystery)

Eric Horridge

Death always follows

DEDICATION

This book is dedicated to <u>all</u> the peoples of Australia.

We really are the <u>lucky</u> country.

Death always follows

CHAPTER 1

The MALDIVES….Seven years earlier……..

The silver fuselage of the plane shone in the bright blue sky as the pilot banked to make the final approach into Velana International airport, the largest of four international airports in the Maldives. It was situated on Hulhule Island in the North Male Atoll, near the capital, Male. There were no clouds to affect the glorious view the passengers on either side of the aircraft had of the various islands and atolls that stretched across the Indian Ocean.

As the plane drifted lower, the azure waters surrounding the white sands of the atolls highlighted the numerous resorts with their over-water bungalows that stood out like legs from an insect. Boardwalks connecting the various rooms with central arrivals areas, bars and swimming pools.

She looked out of the window and smiled.
"Doesn't it look perfect?" she said.
He reached across her from his aisle seat and looked out at what she was pointing towards. Their heads touched briefly, and he gave her a cheeky kiss on the cheek. She smiled. The wedding and reception two days ago had been the happiest day of her life. Everything had gone as planned. No hiccups, no arguments. The stresses of the previous weeks and months all evaporated on the day. She could not have been a happier bride and Phil had never looked so handsome, so sweet, so loving. She sighed inwardly, now it was time to relax and enjoy the honeymoon.
"Amazing," he replied, "looks just like the brochure."

They sat back in their seats waiting for the *bump* as the wheels of the aircraft hit the runway, it was the start of their adventure, seven days of relaxation. They were looking forward to sleeping, eating, swimming, snorkeling, diving, and Phil hoped, *lots* of sex.

Unfortunately, those hopes died quickly, and only one of them would return home alive.

Two years before......

The lights of the garbage truck pierced the gloom as the truck moved through the quiet streets of the tiny town of Apollo Bay, the southern-most village on the Australian mainland. At 6 am most of the permanent citizens of the village, all 1500 of them, were still in bed or just getting ready for the day.

It was dark, winter had been brutal and still was. Strong winds and rain lashed the truck as the driver moved slowly up the streets, the vehicle stopping every ten yards or so to empty the recycle bins that sat along the side of the road.

Sam Morrison had been up since 4 am. The drive down to Apollo Bay after he had been to the depot to collect the vehicle at the municipal offices, had taken him an hour. He had to drive through the winding roads of Otway Forest, in the National Park, before he could even start his job. A large stainless-steel travel mug now half-filled with coffee sat next to him from which he occasionally sipped to keep himself awake. This was a trip and a job he did every week, alternating the collections from recyclables to organics, today it was the yellow lids, the stuff that people thought could be of use again. Often they were wrong, but that was the responsibility of the company that received the waste. The load that Sam was carrying would be assessed and sorted at their waste sorting plant. The normal waste bins with the red lids were much easier to deal with he thought. Whether the content was right or wrong it all went into landfill.

Sam barely concentrated on what he was collecting, the camera in the back of the truck recorded what went into the hopper. Occasionally he would glimpse at the screen on his dashboard just to check to see if there was anything unusual being thrown away, particularly things that could damage the hopper like bits of metal, old bicycle parts, or other 'hard' rubbish items.

As he stopped to pick up a bin on Cawood Street, just outside the Apollo Bay Holiday Park and before heading left on Casino Avenue, he took a quick glimpse at his screen. The rain and the darkness didn't allow him a particularly clear view of the contents but in the split second that the bin lid opened and the insides disgorged themselves into the back of the truck Sam was sure he saw something he shouldn't have fall into the hopper, a small body. Boy, girl or adult, he wasn't sure, however, whatever it was had been dressed in bright clothing. His first thought was that it was a mannequin but he immediately had doubts. He stopped the truck, leaving the high beams of his headlights shining down the road towards the Great Ocean Road and the aggressively sounding sea of the bay. He jumped down from his warm cab into the rain and wind and ran around to the back of the vehicle, climbing up onto the back bumper and used the emergency stop button to halt the hopper midway through its crushing process. Sam peered through the gloom and then he saw it. A hand, just a hand smashed and bloodied, reaching out as if trying to escape death, death by crushing from the weight of the giant hopper. Sam retched, dropped down from the back of the truck seating himself on the wet road. He immediately forgot about the rain and the wind that whipped at his overalls and soaked his skin. The shock of what he had just seen was too graphic, too evil, and it seared itself into his mind.

The sight of the hand would never leave him.

CHAPTER 2

"How do you say that name again?" he asked.

"Warr-nam-bool," she replied, saying each syllable slowly. "How many times need I tell you?" she said jokingly.

"Well it is an unusual name, isn't it. Not like Sydney, or Adelaide, or even Melbourne. A bit hard to get your mouth around it," he teased. "Anyway, does it mean anything, this….*Warr-nam-bool?*"

Michelle had expected some of these questions once it had been finally agreed with Cannon that they would spend some of the summer, the jumps *off-season* in the UK, Down-Under. He would be helping one of her friends and her husband, a racehorse trainer in Australia to prepare a couple of his horses for the biggest jumps racing festival in the Southern Hemisphere. In addition, and as a sweetener, she had convinced him that there would be a holiday in it for him as well. Being away from Woodstock and Oxfordshire would hopefully mean a bit more sun, less rain, and provide Cannon with the break they both needed.

They had endured a couple of tough years recently, initially financially and then personally. Cannon had been accused of race-fixing by the BHA, and his best horse, *RockGod* had nearly been killed in a bizarre running of the Grand National at Aintree, just eighteen months prior. The horse's owner, Charles Flint, had died by running onto the course to stop *RockGod* from winning the race and ironically was crushed to death by his own supreme equine athlete.

Flint, a successful stockbroker had been hiding secrets about his personal life for years. Eventually, they slowly unraveled to the point of disaster, ultimately resulting in Flint's demise and the suicide of his daughter.

Fortunately, that was all behind them now, however, post his recovery after the Grand National, *RockGod* had been removed from the stable as part of Flint's estate, as the HMRC and other authorities followed up on the mess that Flint had left behind by his death.

Cannon's stable however was ultimately the beneficiary from the events at Aintree. His profile was raised due to the now-famous *incident at the last* as it became known, and owners new and old, began to place more of their horses with him.

Along with his assistant, Rich Telside, they were able to take on some new staff, and increase their capacity to thirty horses. The season just concluded had brought them a total of fifty-eight wins, almost back to where they were a few years earlier. The number of wins was important, but the prize money was what counted most. Owners wanted a return on their investment and Cannon and his team had delivered, an increase in stakes earned above his previous best year by over thirteen percent. Success had helped Michelle win the argument, finally convincing Cannon to take the trip down-under and to experience the Warrnambool festival of jumps racing which included one of the most unusual jumps races in the world. It was a race, an event, that Michelle had *googled* many times in order to provide support for her cause.

Her friend Emily, a former colleague and another school-teacher, had married an Australian many years ago. It was one of those romantic notions that sometimes happen. Emily had taken a year off to travel and *see the world* and had never come back home. She had stayed in touch with Michelle over the years through emails and the occasional phone call. Over time they began to Skype and FaceTime each other. Emily had eventually invited Michelle and Cannon to visit them.

In some ways, it was a quite fortuitous invitation. Michelle originally had no idea that Emily's husband was the first member of his family to get involved in horse racing. Michelle knew that they lived on a farm near a place called *Colac*, somewhere in the state of Victoria, but had little awareness about the area until she tried searching about it on the internet. It turned out that Emily's in-laws, the Brownlows, were cattle and sheep farmers predominantly. Their son, Peter had become a racehorse trainer only a few years previously. The offered holiday/visit was part of a plan/agenda proposed by Emily with two elements. One, to help Pete prepare his horses specifically for the Warrnambool festival and two for Michelle to reconnect with Emily and meet her family. Emily had become more aware of Cannon's success and his increased profile through the Grand National incident and believed that he could help her husband improve his chances of winning the most prestigious race at the Warrnambool meeting.

"Apparently from what I can find, the word Warrnambool originates from the local indigenous Australian name for a nearby volcanic cone. It is interpreted to mean many things *including land between two rivers, two swamps or ample water*," Michelle said after typing a few keys on her iPad that sat on her lap.

"Umm," Cannon replied, "Volcano, hey?"

"I doubt if it's active. Not now," she responded, "seems like it's been dormant for thousands of years."

They were sitting in Cannon's study, the weak April sun shining through the windows. Sunset was still around an hour away at a few minutes to eight. It was dry outside, the April showers of the past few days had stopped, leaving a sky of grey and white cloud, threatening, but keeping their distance for now. The winter had been mild this year compared to the previous year. Storms like Ciara and Dennis and the flooding across the country were now a distant memory. The sight of racecourses underwater and the damage it had done to the infrastructure, not forgetting the impact on the sport generally, including cancelled meetings and lost income during that time had added more weight to Michelle's argument that they should take a break and get away from the stresses of running a racing stable. It had taken her over a year to convince him.

Cannon did not reply to her observation about *volcanos*, he was looking on his desktop computer screen at his training schedule for the horses in his stable. Some new additions were expected in a month or so, some would arrive just before and some just after the trip to Australia. He needed to add them to the plan. Some of the horses he was taking on were novices, with little experience of jumping over fences or hurdles, and a couple of others had *big* race experience and had won some reasonable races. While he was away, Rich would settle those horses that arrived into the routine of the stable, and where necessary begin schooling those novices that needed it.

Cannon still hadn't responded to Michelle's last comment, his mind was elsewhere. She repeated it before tapping him playfully on his shoulder.

"Did you hear what I said?" she asked.

"About the volcano?"

"Yes,"

"Sort of…" he answered sheepishly, "I got the drift of it."

Michelle looked at him, not sure whether to say anything or not. She decided to stay quiet.

"Sorry," he continued, "but we have spoken about this trip quite a lot recently, and it's well….."

"Gotten a bit much?" she interrupted.

"Yes," he replied, "I think we just need to carry on as normal and let the next week look after itself. There is still so much to do here, plus you need to hand over your classes to the substitute teachers. Once we get to Oz or at least get on the plane, then I'll start to believe we are going on holiday."

Michelle knew Cannon was right. Over the past few weeks, she had talked about little else and it was clear to her that despite having convinced him of the need to get away and that it would be good for both of them, he wasn't totally sold on the idea despite his assurances to the contrary.

A *busman's* holiday is never a relaxing pursuit and working with another trainer's horses in a place you don't know is not necessarily an easy task either. In fact, it can cause unnecessary friction, and it was something Cannon was hoping to avoid, not only for his own peace of mind but for his relationship with Michelle. They had been together now for a number of years. While they had not married, they had discussed it several times and it was clear to Cannon that it was something they both expected would happen at some point. They had not got around to it as yet, due in most part to the need to get over the experiences of the past couple of years.

Cassie, Cannon's daughter, who was at university in York had now fully accepted Michelle as his partner. What hadn't yet been tested was how she would see Michelle as Cannon's wife. According to Cannon, it was not Cassie's call as to where he and Michelle took the relationship, but it was obvious to Michelle that Cannon wanted Cassie to accept Michelle completely, not just as a de facto stepmother.

Michelle stood up from her seat. "I'll let you carry on then," she said, nodding towards the screen. "I'll make you some tea, then I'll give Emily a call. She'll have been up a few hours already by now. She and I still have a few arrangements to make. She wants me to take some Walkers shortbread and a few other things from M&S that she can't get over there, so I'd better get cracking on them this weekend otherwise it will be too late."

Cannon looked at her retreating figure as she left the room. He knew he was a lucky man to have her in his life. After he had lost Cassie's mother to cancer he had thought his life would never be the same again. No matter how much distance he put between the present and the past, his experiences as a DI always seemed to come back to haunt him, and losing Sally when Cassie was so young seemed to exacerbate the issue. Michelle had helped ease the pain, helped him begin to forget some of the demons. Unfortunately, the demons didn't always forget him. The Charles Flint incident was just one example of how the past never seemed to remain where it belonged, *in the past*. He hoped that their forthcoming trip would help put most of it behind him forever and that the way forward was going to be easier and more fruitful. That things would become much more positive for them compared with what they had both had to endure in recent times.

CHAPTER 3

"Bloody hell, I'm knackered," he said, "it's a hell of a way to come. I just hope it's all going to be worth it."

They were still sitting in their seats on the Emirates flight that had landed at Melbourne International airport. It was just after 11 pm. The flight had been a few minutes short of thirteen and a half hours, this in addition to the seven hours they had taken from Gatwick to Dubai.

Michelle looked out of the window to her left as the A380 trundled along the airport apron to finally arrive at their gate. Outside she noted the hive of activity as workers moved to their respective stations waiting for the pilot to shut down the engines so that they could begin the loading and unloading process and turn the plane around for the next leg of its trip which was on to Auckland in New Zealand.

"Bet you're glad we're not off to NZ?" she asked.

"How right you are," he replied. "I'm not sure how anyone would even try to do it. Another four hours plus, sitting in the same seat after this leg of the journey, would do my head in."

Michelle smiled, tired but elated to have finally arrived at their destination.

"Come on," she said standing up from her seat, "let's get going as I'm sure Emily doesn't want to be waiting too long. It is late after all and we still need to get our bags, clear passport control and customs. I hear that customs can be very strict as well here, so I hope you've filled in the landing cards correctly?"

Cannon sighed as he watched the human snake in front of him slowly edge its way towards the cabin exit door. It always seemed to go much slower than you expected when you were in a hurry. As they got closer to the door, thanking each of the flight attendants in turn for their help during the flight, many who he observed he had never seen at all during the trip, he felt the cold blast of air coming down the chute and into the plane. It wasn't the air conditioning, but the chill of the Australian autumn evening, nine degrees Celsius. Cannon shivered. He hoped it wasn't a portent of things to come.

The road ahead of them stretched out into the distance like a thin washing line. The car headlights created a ribbon of light piercing the dark. After clearing Customs, Michelle and Cannon had finally been able to meet Emily who had been waiting patiently outside the arrivals hall. It was just before 12:30 in the morning and Cannon was beginning to struggle with jet lag. He was irritated. Michelle and Emily hugged each other in greeting while Cannon stood and waited for his turn to say hello.

"So how far do we have to go still?" he asked politely, looking into the darkness ahead. They were sitting in Emily's car, a Land Rover Discovery. He noted that it was a new car, the latest model. They had been driving for just over an hour and he noticed that Michelle had fallen asleep in the back seat. He tried to keep his own eyes open but found himself struggling at times, drifting in and out of consciousness, his head lolling against the back of the seat or the passenger side door window.

"Another couple of hours or so," Emily replied.

Cannon didn't comment.

"Peter will be waiting for us," she continued, "he said he would be getting up around three to get the milking underway, then he was going to put the horses through their paces."

"I guess I won't be much use to him today," Cannon replied through closed eyes, "hopefully tomorrow?"

Emily looked across at him briefly noting how tired he looked, the sound of his voice making it obvious that the trip had taken its toll. Anyone who had taken flights between Europe and Australia, a full twenty-four-hour trip, excluding any stops or layovers and the added complication of the time difference between the continents, would know how it affected people. Cannon was no different. Despite his age, fitness, and his profession, which included early rises each day, the long-haul flight was playing havoc with his body clock.

"Just relax Mike," Emily said. "I know the road and it's very quiet at this time of night so just close your eyes and I'll wake you when we get there."

It was the sound of the car engine being switched off that woke him. Cannon stretched in his seat, feeling the pressure of the seat belt across his chest and abdomen as he did so. He rubbed his face with both hands in an attempt to wake himself from his dozing. He looked at his watch, pushing the button on it to light up the screen. The time still showed Dubai time. *Useless* he thought.

Michelle stirred in the back seat. She had slept nearly all the way, a four hour plus drive.

Cannon looked out of the front windscreen and then across to his left. The lights of what he guessed was Emily's house were already on in some of the rooms, and away in the distance was what looked like a very large shed. Near to the shed, shadows, black with white blotches of different sizes could be seen standing behind metal fences, metal runs, being readied for milking. The light from the building illuminating the animals closer to the shed doors. If needed someone with a persuader would tap a leg of the animals, encouraging them up ramps. However, most of the cows already knew the drill so encouragement was generally by whistle and calls, the stick seldom used.

Cannon opened his door and felt the cold. Early autumn at 4:30 in the morning was chilly in this part of the world. The lights of the car remained on still, Emily having left them on despite the car instrument panel sending out *pings* to advise the driver to turn them off.

He stretched again, arching his back, then held open the back passenger door for Michelle to climb out.

She passed him a jacket which he swiftly put on. As he did so, he saw a man approach them from the milking shed, the lights from the house creating a silhouette and a shadow across the driveway and on the man's face.

"Mike!" the man said, holding out his hand as he approached Cannon, "finally I get to meet you in person."

Cannon noticed the strong Australian country accent, different from what he had heard on the plane and in the airport. He took the man's hand in his, noting both the size and roughness of his host's hand compared with that of his own.

"Peter, likewise, so good to meet you too," he said. "Sorry if I'm not with it, but it's been a long trip," he continued apologetically.

"No worries mate," Peter replied. "I'm so thankful that you agreed to come and provide some advice, share your experience. I'm sure I'll appreciate all the help you that can give me once you're back to your normal self and are happy to start," he continued. "Let's get you inside and we can catch up later this afternoon. I'd would like to show you around when you are ready."

"Sounds good," replied Cannon, "after you...."

Once Cannon and Michelle had been shown their room and had dumped their suitcases unopened on the floor, they had crawled into bed, deciding on taking a shower later. They slept through until midday.

When Cannon finally opened his eyes, he was a little confused initially. Daylight was streaming around the edges of the block-out blinds that covered the windows. He looked at his watch again.

"Bugger," he said to himself, "still on Dubai time!"

As he began changing the dials to local Australian time, Michelle stirred, opening her eyes and asking the time.

"Just worked it out," he replied, "it's just after twelve."

"In the morning or at night?" she asked.

"Midday."

Michelle closed her eyes, then suggested they get up and shower. Thereafter they should go and meet their hosts properly.

"Must be close to lunchtime for them," she said.

Cannon agreed. He was feeling hungry himself. While they had been well fed on the flights, airline meals were never really satisfying. He craved a proper coffee and a meal that wasn't purely microwaved.

As they spoke they could hear voices in the house somewhere. It sounded like it was either the TV or people in the kitchen talking and knocking crockery and cutlery together as they were preparing food. Emily and Peter had two children, a boy, and a girl. The son, Daryl, 15, from what Emily had advised Michelle when they last caught up on Skype, was away at a school retreat in the bush. Being a private school, they would be away for the whole of term two. At least eight weeks.

It would be Easter soon, with the weather getting cooler, however, his boarding school always took his class away at this time of year. The daughter, Stephanie, was still at primary school. Aged eleven, it was she who they could hear talking, distinguishing her voice to that of Emily and the TV.

Cannon clambered out of bed, shivering in his nakedness. He had undressed and just dumped the clothes he had travelled in on the floor. The jacket Michelle had given him was draped across his still unlocked suitcase.

He walked into the on-suite bathroom and grabbed a large towel to wrap around his waist. Then coming out of the bathroom he picked up a backpack that he used to carry important documents, such as their passports, and his toiletry bag. Once back in the bathroom he started shaving, then he brushed his teeth, and finally took a shower.

"That's much better," he said as he dried himself off while standing at the end of the bed. He noted that Michelle had fallen asleep again. "Your turn now," he continued, kissing her gently on the forehead in order to wake her.

She stirred, opening her eyes again slowly.

"I must have drifted off," she said.

Cannon moved to the window and opened the blinds halfway. The sky was a light blue, clear, but with a breeze blowing through the trees that stood in the immediate vicinity of the building.

"Big house," he said, recalling what he had seen when they had arrived last night. He remembered how far they seemed to have walked from the front door to their bedroom.

"Typical Australian farmhouse I guess," Michelle replied, leaving the comfort of the bed. "*Federation* style I think it's called."

"Well I'm sure we'll get shown around it later," Cannon said. "In the meantime, you get ready and I'll go and say hello."

CHAPTER 4

Breakfast turned out to be a mid-afternoon lunch. Cannon, Michelle, Peter, and Emily now sat together after they had finished eating, enjoying the warm sun that had broken through the clouds of the morning. Cannon had noticed how grey the sky was when he had looked through the blinds after his shower. The sky was clear now and the sun shone brightly into the breakfast nook. Michelle guessed that it was twice as big as their lounge back in England. Open plan living was big in Australia and size and space was something Australia had plenty of, she thought. Stephanie had gone to her bedroom to use her iPad, FaceTiming her friends as she often did during the weekends. The silence that reigned after the last of the coffee was finished was only broken by the sound of birds in the garden and the low calling of the dairy herd that having been milked in the morning were now settled down in a lush paddock some quarter of a mile away from the house.

"How are you feeling now, mate?" asked Pete, "a bit more human, are you?"

Cannon smiled. The sleep, shower, and lunch had worked wonders. The jetlag seemed to have disappeared and he hoped that the *hitting the wall* syndrome that often came with long flights would not eventuate again like it had done last night. He expected that time would tell.

"Feeling much better," he said, looking across the table at his host.

Pete was a big man, standing at six foot three in his socks, broad-chested, and with huge *farmer's* hands. He had lived on the land, either with his parents and now with Emily, all his life. While there had been ups and downs over the years due to droughts and bushfires since he had acquired the property from a very wealthy favourite uncle, the farm was essentially the same as when it was first bequeathed to him.

The only exception and this was due to Pete wanting to pursue another interest, was the building of stables for his racehorses. Predominantly, they were his own thoroughbreds that he had bought to train and race for himself. However, once he had qualified for a trainer's license he had managed to get a few clients during the past few years. Many were locals. People who believed he was able to deliver some return on their investment. The horses he had in his charge were not really city grade, though occasionally one would pop up and show some spark and he would take them to the metropolitan tracks like Flemington or Caulfield, and occasionally to Moonee Valley. Unfortunately, most of them lost their *spark* when racing in the city and he reverted more to the country meetings where he could challenge for the country cups. It was due to his experience with the slower horses that he decided to look at those he could potentially convert to jumpers, *steeplechasers,* or *hurdlers.*

The season in Victoria started around mid-March each year and ran through to the latter part of August. The schedule for the coming year, excluding trials, was for approximately sixty races, including 40 steeplechases and 20 hurdle races over that period, with total prize money nearing four million dollars. Most of the racing was in the western part of the state, its home being Warrnambool, and the richest race of the season being the *Grand Annual* steeplechase to be held there during a three-day mid-week carnival in May.

The race alone had prize money of $350,000, nearly 200,000 pounds, a huge amount considering the size of the field, which was normally between twelve and fourteen runners. This compared with forty runners at Aintree in Liverpool, for the English Grand National where runners raced for total prize money of one million pounds. The winner there earning just over half the pot. Cannon had been surprised at how much money there was on offer in the Australian race as he had thought that jumps racing in the country was on its knees. He had read that a few years previously there was talk of banning the sport altogether, due to a number of horses being killed or badly injured during some races. As it was, he knew that jumps racing was only legal in Victoria and South Australia and that despite improvements in safety for both horses and jockeys through the use of better-designed jumps, there was still a cloud over the whole sport. Any further deaths or serious injuries would likely put pressure on the authorities to ban the sport altogether. It was a constant concern for all those involved and a partial justification for Pete to seek help from Cannon. While some other trainers were willing to provide guidance and support, Pete was cautious. There were always vested interests and in an industry with few players the bigger the stable, the more likely their success. Most jumps trainers also had a yard full of runners who raced on the flat only. It was the only way to survive. Pete fortunately was diversified. He had the farm, his dairy cattle, however, his interest in jumps racing was seen by many as just a hobby.

He did not see it quite that way. He wanted to be the best trainer he could be. He sought out help when necessary, but he was cautious with whom he approached. Cannon was someone he believed he could learn from, and it was a great opportunity to have Michelle and Cannon visit. For Pete, to have a runner in the Grand Annual would be an enormous thrill, to have success in the race would be even better. It wasn't about the money, it was about the race itself, one of the top three races of Australian jumps racing. The distance of the race officially listed as *about* 5500 metres. The estimation being due to several sections of the race being run in open paddocks with little or no fences. The race is the longest horse race run in

Australia on a public racecourse. There are 33 obstacles, more than any other steeplechase in the world. Horses run clockwise, and counter-clockwise at various points of the race. The race is unique in that when re-entering the racetrack itself after racing through the open paddocks, horses turn left on the first lap and right on the second. Knowledge of the course and how to save a horse's stamina are vital to the chances of horse and rider. First run in 1872 it was known as the Warrnambool Handicap Steeple until 1877, then the Grand National Steeple from 1878 until 1881, then reverted back to the Warrnambool Handicap Steeple until 1894, and finally, it became the Grand Annual Steeple in 1895.

"Well if you are up to it," said Peter, "let's take a walk down to the stables. You can let me know what you think of them."

Cannon looked across at Michelle, who nodded imperceptibly. The gesture indicating that she was okay for him to leave her for a while. She and Emily had some catching up to do and both would be glad if they had time alone to do so.

"Sure, no problem," Cannon said, "I'll just get my jacket and I'll be with you in a sec."

"Good-onya," replied Pete in a laconic style, indicating a laidback persona. "I'll meet you outside once you're ready," he said.

Despite the sun still shining, the mid-afternoon breeze kept the temperature down and Cannon was pleased to wear a jacket that he had specifically brought with him. He knew that by being in the Southern Hemisphere he was heading back into winter, just as the UK was heading into spring. The temperature difference though wasn't as stark as he had expected. It was warmer than at home! As they walked towards the stables, Cannon asked why Pete thought he could help him improve a crop of jumpers in such a short visit? The carnival in Warrnambool was just over two weeks away.

"And how many do you have?" he asked.

"I have ten in work, in total," was the reply.

"Jumpers?"

"No," answered Pete, "five jumpers, chasers, and hurdlers. The rest are my flat horses."

Cannon was quite surprised. He knew that Pete had a small string but didn't expect it to be so small. Thinking about it though he knew that it wasn't Pete and Emily's livelihood. As far as Cannon went, in his mind what Pete had, *was* a hobby. A serious hobby perhaps, but a hobby, nonetheless. *A nice position to be in*, he thought. He kept his view to himself, but he could understand other trainers thinking the same, no matter if Pete thought differently.

When they arrived at the stables, Cannon was impressed. He hadn't expected what was now in front of him. The building was huge. There were

18

three stable blocks with ten stalls in each. Set in a u-shape, but not touching each other and with a yard in the middle allowing for horses to walk around before and after exercising. Pete pointed out a large heated and well-lit fourth building, which he said included Tack rooms, a Feed room, a Medical room with facilities to manage any injuries to riders, a Vet's room packed with scoping and other instrumentation as well as an indoor horse-walker. There was also a pool for horse recovery and strengthening. This final building along with the others made a square.

"This must have cost you a few quid?" Cannon said, whistling at the size of each individual stable and the quality of each. "These buildings only look a few years old."

"They are," was the reply, "but doing what I've done here has been worth it. Horse and jockey welfare are vital for the jumps game to continue here, so I wanted to make sure every base was and is covered. By looking after the horses, you get a better result, a better outcome. The same is true with the jockeys as well, in my view."

Cannon nodded in agreement.

As they walked into the first of the three stable blocks, Cannon asked,

"Do you have a favourite horse?" noting that his own favourite, *Rockgod*, was now no longer with him after the *Charles Flint* affair.

"Actually, I have a couple," said Pete. "*Wings of Dawn* is my best jumper and *Montego Girl* my best flat runner. The latter is a five-year-old mare that has won six times around here, including a couple of country cups. *Wings of Dawn* has won three steeplechases so far, but mostly races worth about $30,000 each. Winning a race like that pays about $18,000 a time."

"That's not too shabby," Cannon noted, "and any horse that wins six races can't be too bad either, likewise the trainer," he continued. Smiling, he said, "The owner must be pleased?"

Cannon thought he saw colour rise in Pete's cheeks, but decided not to say anything. He waited for Pete to reply. While he did so he wondered how the system worked in Victoria. It didn't appear to have as many restrictions about grading horses like there were in the U.K, and it seemed like there were a limited number of runners in jumps racing across the state. Maybe that was why *any* horse seemed to be able to run in *any* race?

Pete eventually responded to Cannon's question. "I'm the owner," he said eventually, "of both the horses I mentioned....so yes I'm very pleased, and very lucky."

Pete indicated they should move on. They walked through the three buildings with stables in them. Cannon, despite himself, inspected nearly every horse and where possible chatted with some of the track riders he was introduced too. He noticed that many of them were not originally from Australia and despite working as riders for Pete in training the horses, they also worked for Pete as stable hands.

As the tour progressed they eventually stood together just in front of the fourth building. Given the cold of the afternoon, which was now becoming more noticeable as the day moved towards evening, the heat emanating from within the building was inviting. Cannon was hoping to get out of the cold and stamped his feet as a gesture, a subtle message to Pete that he would prefer to be inside and warm rather than stand outside in the cold to talk. The late afternoon sun was now low in the sky, it would be dark in less than an hour. The *show and tell* of the facilities had taken much longer than Pete and Cannon had expected.

"Unfortunately, I'll need to be off in a minute, Mike. Cows to milk." Pete indicated "I'll need to get over there a-sap."

"No problem," Cannon replied, "will it be okay to look around?"

"Of course, mate, go ahead. I'll see you back at the house. I should be there in about an hour and a half. About six," he said looking at his watch.

"Great," replied Cannon. "I'm hoping to see your jumps and track facilities tomorrow. If they are half as good as what I've seen this afternoon then…" he let the meaning of his message drift. Cannon was aware from conversations with Michelle that Pete was uncomfortable talking about how lucky he was to have a family that had set him up for life. Cannon could see the humility in Pete, it was a trait he was beginning to admire.

"You will see tomorrow that they're not the best and I'm happy for you to give me any advice you can about improving them," Peter answered, pointing back over Cannon's shoulder. "They are about a fifteen-minute drive away, near one of my larger dams."

Cannon considered this for a second. A fifteen-minute drive? The size and scale of Pete and Emily's property was now becoming clearer in his mind. It was a big operation, jumps racing was just a part of it, but not the main game.

"OK, see you later," Cannon said.

He turned to enter the building all the while watching his host walk away. He noted Pete reach for his phone, looking briefly at the screen then making a call.

Once inside Cannon looked around with a tinge of jealousy at the quality of the contents. The building was quiet, however, he could hear a voice somewhere and on occasion the whinny of a horse. The building itself and the facilities within it were impressive. Inside the Tack room, new racing gear was everywhere, neatly stacked. Lugs, winkers, blinkers, saddles, racing bits, and much more were all laid out on shelves or hooks.

As he wandered through the room he noticed the complete lack of any security measures in relation to the equipment. It looked like the door to the Tack room didn't even have a lock. An honesty system seemed to be the go and immediately he struggled with the concept in his mind. A small book with columns in it asking who had been in the room, when and for how long was lying on a small table. It seemed to mean a 'self-policing' policy was in place and from Cannon's point of view was a little naïve. All it seemed to do was to allow for an individual to let the reader know that he/she had been in the room at a particular time and date. What it did not do was to provide any information about who had been in the room but who had *not* written anything in the columns. Effectively this was like giving someone carte blanche to be alone (or even with others) in the room without anyone ever knowing of their presence.

Cannon shook his head and looked around. There was no CCTV or any other security system anywhere to be seen.

Leaving the Tack room and entering further into the building through another door, he found himself in a small passage where he noticed the voice he heard previously getting a little louder.

A few metres away to his left he saw a large glass panel, a viewing window. He stopped and peered into what he realized was the Vet's room. It was enormous. Inside he could see a woman inspecting a horse's leg, a girl of around eighteen or so, held the animal's head to keep it calm. Cannon watched as the woman, whom he assumed was a Vet, ran her hands up and down each leg. He knew she was feeling for *heat*, an indication of any lameness, inflammation, tissue, or tendon damage that the horse may be suffering. Finally, she appeared satisfied and nodded to the girl. The youngster took hold of the reins that had been tied to a tall pole and swiftly turned the horse around walking it in a slow languid circle. The Vet watched as the horse relaxed, almost jig jogging as it moved effortlessly around the room.

"Okay Karen," Cannon heard the Vet say. "He's fine. Take him back to his stall, I'll see him again tomorrow."

"Thanks, Deb," the young girl replied smiling, "much appreciated."

Cannon remained watching as the Vet pressed a green button attached to the side of a table and noticed a metal wall at the back of the room rise up like a remote garage door. It rolled over and over itself exposing a large empty gap. Once completely open, the horse was led outside into the slowly encroaching darkness and taken away back to its stable. An outside light which had automatically come on when the door opened, illuminated a blue or black SUV parked about ten metres away from the door. Cannon assumed it belonged to the Vet as apart from the Land Rover that he and Michelle were driven in to the farm the previous night, he had not seen any other near the building. The Vet pressed the button again and the door slowly closed.

Cannon found the door to the room and entered quietly. She had her back to him.

"Hello there," he said.

She turned around to face him. somewhat taken aback by his unexpected presence.

"I'm sorry if I caught you unawares," he continued, apologetically. "Mike Cannon," he explained, pointing towards himself and offering his hand, "just on a visit to see Pete and his family. He was showing me around the place but had to leave to go and check on his cows. I was just wandering around trying to take in the facilities. Very impressive!" he gushed.

"Deborah Ryan," she replied, before rubbing her hands on her jeans, apologizing for doing so, before taking his. She indicated the dust that drifted in the air, floating in circles and caught by the lights of the room.

"No problem," Cannon replied, "I deal with horses every day. I understand what it's like working with them, especially keeping them fit, well and calm. You did a good job from what I can see," he said, referring to how easily she was able to work on the animal without it appearing to be in any stress from her examination.

"Thank you," she replied, accepting the compliment. "So, you are the trainer Emily has been telling me about," she went on, "the one who was involved in the Grand National fiasco just over a year ago?"

Cannon flushed slightly. Not sure if her comment was a statement of support or criticism. He let it pass.

"Yes, that's right," he answered. "There's a whole story behind that, which I'm not sure was covered very well here in Australia, but it's over now and I'm here on holiday, *sort of*," he continued, indicating to her that he wasn't intending to sit with his feet up while staying on the property. "I'm working with Pete, helping out with his jumpers, trying to improve their chances in the Grand Annual. I'm particularly looking forward to the race which I believe is quite spectacular?"

"It is," she replied, "although not quite on the same scale as Aintree."

Cannon acknowledged her comment with a nod of his head.

For a second there was a silence between them, Cannon used it, making an initial assessment of her. First impressions were often right. His time in the police and his experience over the years had mostly stood him in good stead. He tried not to, but it was now in his nature, an innate desire to understand people. What drove them, their ambitions, their motivation.

Deb Ryan was no ordinary Vet as far as looks were concerned. She was tall, nearly five feet ten, (about one, seventy-eight metres), wiry with long limbs. Apart from jeans, she wore a dark blue cardigan, with a sky-blue shirt underneath. Trainers, now slightly muddy with long term use, finished off the outside. He wondered if he would ever get to know the inside? She had long dark hair tied back with an elastic band, allowing her full face to be seen.

Cannon noticed she had dark green eyes, slightly downturned. Her nose sharp, which suited her long hairstyle and a longish chin. Her colour was warm, not pallid like many people in the U.K. who suffered from a lack of sun.

He found her attractive.

She broke the moment.

"Well I'd better get on with things," she said. "I just need to tidy up here, let Pete know about the horse and then I'll be on my way home." "

"Do you live far away?"

"About twenty-five minutes or so," she replied. "I have a surgery just on the outskirts of town. My house is attached to it."

Cannon nodded, gesturing around the room where tack, bottles, scrubs, and other materials lay and needed to be put away or disposed of. "Well, I'll leave you to it then," he said. "So nice to meet you, Deborah, I'm sure I'll see you again during our stay."

"I'm sure you will," she replied, a warm smile on her face.

Cannon turned to leave, asking as he did so about the horse that she had been working on.

"Oh, that's *Core Intelligence* a sprinter that belongs to one of Pete's clients. He's been off the track for nearly eight months now and we are just about to start light training with him again. Pete wanted an assessment so that he could let the owners know."

"I see," replied Cannon, reminding himself that in Australia there is no real let up for flat racing. The *season* is all year round. The jumps racing season is just a subset, run in parallel during the early Autumn and Winter months. "It looks like he's in good hands," he went on, "so let's hope the owners are pleased with the progress."

"I'm sure they will be," she replied. "He's a bit of a hack, won a couple of mid-week races but will never be a group horse. Once fit again, he's likely to be set for some of the higher value country races. Unfortunately, there aren't too many of those, but I think the owners run the horse more for the fun of it than the money."

Cannon looked at his watch, he was starting to feel a little tired. It was now just before six pm. The encroaching darkness outside that he had noticed when *Core Intelligence* was taken outside through the rolled-up door had crept in and was now affecting the chemicals in his brain. He and Michelle had only been in the country for less than a day, jetlag was the obvious cause. He said his goodbyes and left the building in search of Pete, dinner then bed.

CHAPTER 5

Fifteen nautical miles off the coast of Apollo Bay, the container ship MSC Walton slowed slightly on its course so as not to cause alarm with any of the local authorities or coastguards monitoring ship movements in the area. Despite the slowing, the ship continued on its way heading eastwards towards Adelaide. It would then carry on to Fremantle in Western Australia before sailing out across the Indian Ocean and onto Antananarivo in Madagascar, before finally heading for Mombasa. The sea in the Bass Strait was calm, the all-enveloping darkness solely lit by the ship's lights reflecting on the gentle ocean swell. The new moon had come and gone. A full moon was due in two weeks. Despite the pressure rising, cloud covered the sky. It was ideal for the drop.

The Captain gave the order and the package went over the starboard side. A splash as it hit the water the only sound to be heard other than the rumbling of the engines sitting within the belly of the giant ship. The two crew members who helped get the package ready watched as it slowly drifted away from the hull. A beacon installed with a GPS transmitter set at a very low frequency was attached to the base, the underside of the skiff that held the contents.

It was all that anyone on board needed to know.

The package would be collected within the hour.

The skiff would then be sunk.

The fishing boat, the *San Marino,* had been at sea for two hours when the package was eventually picked up by the crew. It was collected and hauled over the side, then hidden below. The *San Marino* would be back in Apollo Bay harbour at least an hour before dawn broke, the *additional* cargo, now hidden, would be removed when the harbour was quiet. Between leaving and returning, the *San Marino* would have filled its hold with Snapper, Rock Lobster, Squid, and Whiting.

CHAPTER 6

The small village of *Forrest* is a forty-minute drive inland from Apollo Bay. Renowned for its sixty-odd kilometres of bike trails, walking tracks, and horse-riding facilities, it is aptly named, sitting within the Great Otway National Park, an oasis of temperate rainforest, waterfalls and huge redwood trees.

Anton Singer and Brendan French were regulars. They knew most of the bike trails intimately, trying out the easy or the hard ones depending on the day, the weather, or whether there were too many other people around, *blow-ins* from the city who only visited once and never again.

While Cannon and Michelle were struggling through the next day of their visit, after another night of tossing and turning, Anton and Brendan chased each other along the *Yo-Yo* trail, the furthest of the fifteen tracks away from the main road to Apollo Bay. It was also one of the hardest trails to race, one of the reasons why it was so quiet. It was how they liked it.

Anton, aged twenty-six, was a trainee doctor. Brendan, slightly older, a physiotherapist. Trail bike riding was a way of de-stressing, clearing the mind while challenging themselves physically. Keeping their bodies fit was important to both of them and they threw themselves into each run they made on the various trails. At times it seemed they were indifferent to the dangers as they sped around sharp turns and over steep hills, which was ironic given their respective professions.

Rushing around a tight bend just 500 hundred metres from the end of the trail, Brendan saw the *snake*. It wasn't common that cyclists and snakes met. A tiger snake, roughly five feet long was sunning itself in the middle of the track. Brendan screamed a warning as he braked hard to avoid the reptile, the vibrations of the cyclist's wheels having disturbed it, its head now standing six inches above its coiled body, ready to defend itself if necessary. Anton just a foot behind didn't hear the warning, and he smashed into the back of Brendan's bike. Both men slid along the path as the impact of bike on bike, sent them both hurtling to the ground. Anton catapulted over his handlebars.

They each hit the ground hard, winding themselves, Anton smashing his shoulder on the hard-compacted soil, Brendan knocking his head against a rock on the side of the track.

Through the visor of the helmet that had protected him from any damage to his head, Brendan looked up to see the snake's tail curl away as it slid off into the bush, its yellow and black stripes merging into the undergrowth.

After taking a few deep breaths, he sat up. He felt the roughness of the track through his cycling gear, padded lycra shorts under loose-fitting cotton shorts.

"Shit, that was close," he said turning to Anton, "how are you doing?" he asked.

"What the fuck happened?" said Anton.

"Snake. Didn't you hear me call out?"

"No, was too busy concentrating on catching you."

"Are you ok?" asked Brendan, noticing Anton trying to manipulate his shoulder in a rhythmic circle.

"I'll be fine," came the reply, "but he won't be...," Anton replied.

He pointed towards Brendan's left.

Brendan turned around. The skeleton was almost fully intact. It lay just under a large tree fern, disturbed by Brendan's fall. Surprisingly, from what they could see of the skeleton there had been little predation. The body was naked, and what was left of the skin was dry, yellowed. The eyes were gone, dark holes now. It was clear though that the body was that of a man.

How long the body had been hidden or lay where it was would be something that would need to be established. Likewise, the cause of death. Having seen cadavers as part of his training, the sight of a dead body didn't worry Anton. His biggest concern was mobile coverage to report what they had found. The snake was forgotten.

CHAPTER 7

Inspector Andrew Bruce, or *AB* as he was known, didn't like standing around in the bush. He was a city policeman. He had arrived from Melbourne. Looking at the spot where the body was found was an exercise in showing intent. An intent to support the locals, the *country* police. It was something his boss, David Thatcher, had insisted he did.

The area had already been cleared, the forensic teams had done their job, the scene had been scoured, and the necessary photographs had been taken, Bruce was there however…*showing intent.*

It was just before midday. The drive from the city had taken three hours.

"Second time in two years I've been out this way," he said. "Still haven't been able to spend enough time on the first case," he went on, "the body in the dump truck, Apollo Bay."

Leading Senior Constable, Samantha, '*Sam*', Cromwell said nothing. She knew *AB* well, she liked him. They had worked together for the past year. Cromwell knew of the case that Bruce referred to, but it was a touchy subject. The local police in Colac believed it was a case in their patch, and it was, however, they just didn't have the resources to focus on it. They had initially taken on the investigation but given the lack of progress and personnel changes due to the investigating officer being booked off sick for mental health reasons, the case was escalated up to the Geelong Operations unit. Unfortunately, they too had limited resources available to them. Eventually, the case ended up on AB's desk. Over the past year, the investigation had moved from a priority, then scaled back due to Bruce giving it no attention at all. The file was pushed around within Bruce's team, but progress was slow. A country murder no matter how it came about should have been given the necessary attention. It wasn't. Eventually, in time, it slipped through the cracks.

Nobody was working on it. Until now.

The body on the track was sparking everyone back into focus. Bruce now held the mantle. It was his job to solve both cases while keeping the locals on side.

He looked around him at the width of the track, the bush on either side, wanting to understand where and how the body had been found.

He asked himself silent questions. As he did so he was also conscious that he was looking for any snake activity, any movement. He hated snakes and frankly didn't like the bush much either.

Bruce had a list of things in his head that needed answering. He pondered these as he nodded to Cromwell to advise her that he had seen enough. He started walking back to their car that they had parked at the end of the trail.

The most obvious question that needed answering was who the dead man was?

Secondly, how he had died and how the body had ended up beside a cycling track, miles from anywhere?

During the trip down to Forrest, Bruce had been able to discuss the situation with the local Police chief, Seth Cusscom, who had been gracious enough to call him on Bruce's mobile, and who had thanked him for his participation and help. Cusscom had relayed some of the detail about the case that they had been able to gather so far. It was limited.

Bruce was told that there was no sign of trauma on the body other than decomposition, and speculation was that the man may have died from natural causes, such as a heart attack. This was still to be verified by the Forensic Pathologists, Cusscom had said.

While Bruce pondered the possibility of natural causes and noted that it was an option, he was not convinced. Surely if that was the case then some form of alarm would have been raised at the time if the individual hadn't turned up at their place of work or had contacted family or something…?

Surely the person would be known to someone, he thought?

This was a consideration that he and Cromwell had discussed during the journey down from Melbourne.

Other theories that Cusscom relayed to Bruce, included one that the body was that of a hiker who had encountered a snake, been bitten and died.

That also seemed unlikely as the deceased had nothing with him to suggest he was hiking.

Around the immediate area where the body was found, Cusscom had advised there were no items that one would expect a hiker to have with them. There was no sign of a backpack, there were no water bottles in the immediate area of the body either.

The question remained, how was it possible that the body had lain where it was for as long as it had?

From what Bruce had been advised, the body had no means of identification on it either. No wallet, no credit cards, nothing. Why was that?

More concerning was how long the body had been lying in the undergrowth. *Trying to get a date of death would be very difficult,* Bruce thought, knowing however that the forensic scientists and pathologists would enjoy trying to fathom it out.

"What do you think Constable?" he asked Cromwell as they reached their car.

"I'm not sure Sir," she answered formally, "I think we have a bit of a mystery here."

"Agreed," he said, "but I guess it's nothing new. It's our job to find the answers. I just wish it wasn't out here," he went on, indicating the trees that towered around them.

As AB climbed in then closed his car door, he sighed to himself realizing that being out in the country looking at this type of case, meant that his career had stalled. He was a career policeman, yes. A divorcee with no children. Married to the job, his wife of a couple of years could not compete with or accept his irregular hours, *his total commitment to the cause.* She wanted children. He wasn't ready.

He thought he would progress further up the ranks more speedily than he had. There were reasons why he hadn't and he knew what they were. Instead, he focused on doing the job. Working the city predominantly. Being out here in the bush and being asked to keep the locals happy confirmed his suspicions. He was a good cop, but he wasn't going anywhere fast.

CHAPTER 8

The horses ran towards the obstacles in pairs. The sun had risen an hour earlier taking the chill off the morning. Cannon watched as both rider and horse cleared the jumps.

Compared to his own charges at home, the animals were being asked to clear fences that were much smaller, much easier, and safer. This was a requirement placed on them by Racing Victoria and the ARJA, the bodies that oversee jumps racing in the state. A few years previously there was an outcry by several community groups, including the RSPCA amongst others, because of a number of deaths on racecourses. Particularly prominent were those during jumps races. The sport was nearly outlawed.

Fortunately, sense prevailed, but not before changes were required of those involved. The jumps, especially the hurdles, were to be constructed of wood with a soft yellow synthetic brush rather than natural brush that was previously used. The steeplechase fences were likewise constructed from artificial components, including high impact cushioning foam and molded birch, so very different to those in the UK where natural birch was used.

"I think both of the horses are brave enough," he said, his breath turning into vapour as he spoke, "but the jocks are a little tentative. They are taking off much too soon and that's causing the horses to land awkwardly. Also, I think they are riding too quickly into the hurdles," he went on. "They are too keen to get over the jumps and not being careful enough with rhythm and pace. Horses need to be relaxed and confident when they are meeting an obstacle. I hope the jocks are easier when racing over bigger fences?"

Pete held his binoculars to his face, following the two horses *Binge-Eater* and *Striped King* both owned by him, as they headed towards and cleared the next flight.

The training facility that Pete had built was impressive and well-constructed. An eight hundred metre section of a nearly two kilometre grass track, which had two sets of jumps running parallel to each other. One with four hurdles and one with four steeplechase jumps on it. The course was used by the flat runners as well. There was plenty of space for them to use the balance of the track to train on, including the inside of the jumps section along the running rail.

Cannon watched on. While he was impressed with the bravery of the horses in Pete's care, both those that Pete owned himself and those he trained for others, he was quite concerned about the quality of riding. The riders themselves were, in his opinion, too small to be riding Steeplechasers and Hurdlers. These horses needed better control, more strength in the saddle, he thought. He noted that both riders seemed dark-skinned, *aboriginal* perhaps? He would ask later. Pete interrupted his thoughts, eventually answering Cannon's question.

"I guess it's because we have such a limited number of races and even fewer high-weight jockeys here compared to the UK, it's inevitable that we don't necessarily have the same quality," Pete said, acknowledging Cannon's comments. "However, we do have a few good Irish jocks out here that ride both flat and jumps and they are pretty good," he continued, "I use one of them myself, Tony Carey."

"I've heard of him," replied Cannon, "came out here a few years ago I recall. How is he doing?"

"From what I understand, he's doing okay, but had a bit of trouble in recent years with his personal life and his career. Got divorced a few years ago having had an affair with a girl at a stable he was riding for. Then about fifteen months ago he got involved in a bit of a betting scandal with a trainer he was associated with. I think he was suspended for about three months. Apparently betting on races he wasn't involved in but had insight from the trainer about how the horses were going. It may have been one of George Sormond's runners from memory. He's the other trainer in this area."

"And we all know," said Cannon, "betting on races by jockeys is not allowed."

"Precisely," Pete said.

Pete raised his binoculars again, watching as the two horses they were focused on completed their circuit and were then eased down by the riders. They allowed their mounts to canter slowly over a distance of about two to three hundred metres around the track before they came to a steady walk.

While he watched, Cannon considered what Pete had said about Carey. No matter where you are in the world, he thought, money, opportunity to gain advantage was always there. It was no different in Australia than it was in the UK, Ireland, America, or anywhere else where gambling was allowed. Someone was always looking for an angle. What was it about the human psyche? He had endured much during his time in the police force and in some ways even worse since he had been out of it. He had hoped that the trip down-under was going to be easy, a break, a rest. He was visiting at the request of Michelle and as a guest of Pete and Emily. He was there to advise, to help, to teach, anything other than that, was outside of the agreed remit with Michelle. He was going to enjoy the experience while here, the hospitality. He had no intention of getting involved in anything else.

Cannon offered Pete some advice.

After having spoken with the two riders about their techniques, Cannon asked them to take the next two horses and do another circuit. It involved jumping the hurdles, not the chasing jumps yet.

He would ask one of the jockeys to exercise *Wings of Dawn* over the larger fences separately. It was the horse being readied for the Grand Annual.

The sun was now higher above the horizon and the lights from the farmhouse were no longer shining out into the darkness. The horse's *Flimflam and Operator Please* were ready, having been warmed up with a half-mile canter around Pete's track.

"Okay, off you go," Cannon said to the two jocks waiting for his instructions. "Remember what I told you. Keep relaxed, trust in the horse, and let him trust you. Get a little closer to the fence before you ask him to go with you. You both need to be in unison, together, you are basically *as one*, not two separate entities flying through the air," he continued. "Not only does it look awkward, unseemly, but it puts both of you in danger of falling or being unseated. Remember what I said. The correct position is that you form a straight line from your shoulder, through your elbow and knee and down towards the ball of the foot. There should be a bit of room between your body and the horse's withers."

The riders noted Cannon's comments, but also believed they were pretty reasonable jockeys anyway and didn't need too much advice, especially from a *Pom*. Cannon was aware of this and tried to be subtle. He didn't want to get them offside nor indeed upset Pete's existing arrangements with them. After all both men had been riding for several years. No longer jockeys who could race often, but they did have experience in racing and while weight issues predominantly had curtailed their careers as leading *hoops* they were still jockeys. They rode out each day, they worked for the stable, they looked after the horses. It was their life, their passion.

Sometimes they were transitory, sometimes they stayed in the same place with the same trainer for years. Pete had been lucky. While he didn't have a large stable, he did have a large business and many of those he relied upon to ride and help train the horses, especially those who raced on the flat, also helped with other duties across the farm. It was mutually beneficial.

Cannon and Pete watched as *Flimflam* and *Operator Please* were taken through their paces. Cannon noted how the two riders adjusted their posture slightly from the way they had originally met each fence. They seemed to have more time to get themselves ready to meet the jump. The horses raced together clearing the flights of obstacles. Cannon and Pete watched through their binoculars.

Cannon smiled to himself as he watched the riders seemingly float across the obstacles, landing with momentum on the other side, the horses picking up the *bits* in their mouths, excited, and ready for the next jump. Maybe it was the quality of the horses compared to what he saw originally but

Cannon felt a surge of pride in himself. He was all about the equine athlete and how to get the best out of them. Helping Pete in any way he could was worth the smile he could feel crease his own face.

Cannon knew that success and failure were never far away in this game. He had been lucky to have good horses in his stable but good horses didn't always mean good times. Nothing could be taken for granted. He thought back to the recent past. Thank God he had Rich to *mind the fort* while he was away. Without his assistant trainer, he would be lost.

Wings of Dawn, known to everyone in the yard as W.O.D or just *Wings* was a brutish animal. Cannon had not had the opportunity to see him until Pete had arranged for the horse to be brought out for exercise. Having been cooped up in his box until the others had completed their work, W.O.D was full of energy, kicking out, jumping up on his back legs, and generally making a nuisance of himself.

"He only allows Jamie to ride him, particularly here at home," Pete nodded towards the man holding the reins of the large bay animal, patting the horse's long neck and talking quietly to him, calming him down. "On the track, we've used a few jockeys in the past," he went on, "but he seems to have settled in recent times with one of the younger jockeys, a guy called Christian Counter. We've booked Christian to ride him next week, a last hit-out for the horse before the carnival," he said.

Cannon had forgotten about upcoming races. He had been focused on the carnival. He was excited about what he would see, how things worked, and given he was on holiday, he was looking forward to relaxing in the atmosphere of the occasion.

W.O.D was nearly seventeen hands high, approximately 173cm tall, measured from the ground to the highest point on the withers, the ridge between the shoulder blades of the horse.

He had an extremely intelligent eye and a very beautiful head, a small star almost perfectly placed in the middle of his forehead.

"He's got an amazing confirmation," Pete highlighted, "it's a pity he is not as quick as he looks, as on looks alone he would have been racing on the flat making much more money than he does now."

Cannon smiled. He knew that looks alone didn't win races. The horse needed to have a will, a desire to win. If looks were the only determinant of success many a horse would have visited the winner's enclosure on that basis alone. In jumps racing in particular, success came about through desire, a willingness to push through barriers, to compete, to be brave.

Cannon thought back to a race in 2017, the Cotswold Chase at Cheltenham where *Many Clouds* winner of the 2015 English Grand National and *Thistlecrack,* the favourite in the race and an unbeaten horse at that point in time, met for the first and only time. *Clouds* refused to let the *Thistlecrack* win the race. After a bruising trip, both horses jumping the final fence together, the horses exchanged leads until the very last yard, both straining to win, both following their instincts. Sadly *Clouds,* who won the race, collapsed and died of a pulmonary embolism shortly after the finish.

Turning towards *Wings,* Cannon looked him up and down as Jamie, his rider and minder climbed aboard with assistance from Pete, ready for his exercise.

Wings did indeed have a great confirmation. It should have made him a much better racehorse. Sadly he wasn't quick enough to race on the flat, as Pete had mentioned, but he was brave and he would run all day. *Staying* horses, those with stamina, and good jumping technique were what you needed in steeplechasers. Cannon noted that *Wings* had balance, his frame was well proportioned. His bone structure showed that he could take the jarring of jumps racing. He was not too light, and he was athletic.

"I'm keen to see him go," he said, noting that it was this very horse that was the reason for Cannon and Michelle's visit. *Wings* was the catalyst. The next couple of weeks leading up to and concluding at the carnival in Warrnambool, ideally successfully in the Grand Annual, were what it was all about. Cannon hoped he could help Pete achieve the goal, but first, he needed to assess *Wings* and see whether the horse had the will to win.

CHAPTER 9

Bruce lay back on his chair, his feet positioned on the side of his desk. White melamine, Ikea.

He was back in his office. Another long drive completed, back to Melbourne.

He was trying to reacquaint himself with the body in the *garbage truck* case from nearly two years ago. He stretched his back. He had been sitting for hours. The office outside his own was quiet. What a way to spend a Sunday he thought? At least he had some spare time to relook at the file while he waited for the initial findings to come through from those pathologists examining the skeleton found in the bush in Forrest.

Empty cups, white plastic, courtesy of the office Espresso machine and a tube of a hundred disposable cups attached to its side, were strewn around the floor. Some sat within a basket given to him to keep such detritus in one place, others lay on top of the desk, occasionally being threatened by Bruce's feet to be kicked across the desk and onto the floor.

Bruce hadn't eaten all day. It was coffee or nothing at all. He was beginning to feel the effects of having no food. The caffeine from the coffee kept him alert, but the lack of food was impacting him differently. His sugar levels were dropping, and he felt that he may be getting the *shakes*.

The late afternoon sun was dipping into Port Philip Bay and clouds were building. Rain was expected over the next few days across Melbourne. Unusually for this time of year, the weather was coming from the North. It meant it would be unseasonably warm in some parts of the state, notably the North East, and despite the rain, the temperature for the next day or so would sit at around 20C as opposed to the normal average of between 15C and 17C. Bruce didn't expect it to last.

He continued to turn through the pages, conscious that as he read, his mind was beginning to wander. He needed to focus. He needed to eat.

He picked up his mobile phone, ordering a *Nasi Goreng* from a Malaysian restaurant on Elizabeth Street. *Forty minutes* using Deliveroo he was told.

Looking at the graphic pictures of the deceased, the body itself having been badly crushed, made him wince. He had seen many bodies but the sight of a smashed torso with a bloodied head, its features completely destroyed, flattened into a mass of hair, teeth, and skin was something he was not keen to see too often.

He stared at the pictures again. The body had been dressed in jockey's silks. AB recalled that the silks had no meaning, that they were not 'live'. They were not used by anyone as owners, they were more a *fun* pair. A joke. Some sick joke at that, he thought.

Holding one of the photographs in his hand, he turned it around to look at the back. It was blank, there was no narrative, nothing to indicate who the individual was. He scanned through a few more before finding what he needed.

"Timothy Hedge," he said out aloud, reading the name associated with the body. "Timothy Hedge?" he repeated, trying to recall from memory what he knew about the victim.

Unable to do so because his mind continued to wander due to too much caffeine, he scanned through the file before finally finding the detail that he was looking for.

A small black and white image was attached to a single sheet, the official report. The picture was a passport photo, taken when Timothy Hedge must have been around twenty. It showed a young man with dark hair, soft eyes, and a cheeky grin just sitting below the poker face that he needed to control for the photograph. *Authorities didn't like smiles on official documents.* Bruce looked at the picture again. It was sad he thought. Hedge was dead within six years of the picture having been taken. The passport that he must have been applying for being valid for ten years, having outlasted him. Bruce recalled that Timothy Hedge wasn't the brightest pin in the cupboard, that he had made some bad choices. Choices that ended up with him being killed, murdered. But why and by whom? He also recalled why the investigation slowed, eventually stopping completely. Resources. Priorities.

Bruce knew that he was part of the problem. It was *his* case and he had let it slide. He reached for another coffee cup, but the contents were cold. He swallowed it anyway. He realized that he also needed to swallow his pride in investigating *country* cases and get on with policing them.

Clubbed to death, was the conclusion made and stipulated in the report. Bruce was unsure how the experts could come to that conclusion given how the body was mangled in the garbage truck, but he accepted it. *Clubbed to death* meant murder.

He took a mouthful of rice. Deliveroo had been on time, forty minutes.

It was dark outside now, and as he ate he saw his reflection in the office window that looked out over the city. He looked at the man looking back at himself.

Overweight, underpaid, and alone, he thought to himself. A career policeman. A good one, but someone not politically astute. Something you needed to be to get to sit with the Premier, have lunch with the MPs. It wasn't for him. He knew he was never going to become Chief Commissioner, no matter how many years he would serve. He was never going to achieve the higher ranks, but he also knew that it wasn't what he wanted. He wanted to serve, *uphold the right* as the motto said on the badge. After twenty-six years he knew his place. Part of that place was to solve the murder of Timothy

Hedge along with the body on the track. He would however have preferred that both cases were city-based rather than in the bush.

CHAPTER 10

"I think he's a pretty good horse," said Cannon. "Do you think Counter is a good enough jockey to ride him next week?"

They were back in Pete's house, sitting in a small alfresco area open on one side of the building and looking out towards the west. The sun had set and the lights from Colac bounced on the horizon, creating a semi-circle, a halo effect above the distant tree line. Occasionally a cloud would drift across the sky, causing the light to dim or even disappear for a while.

"Yes, I think so," he said. "He's riding just above minimum weight next week, on Thursday," he went on. "Counter is quite light so *Wings* will be carrying a little bit of dead weight in the race, but we'll see how that goes. See how he handles the trip."

"I assume we are going to watch?" asked Cannon.

"Yes of course. The race is at Terang about 70 kilometres from here. The only thing on the calendar after that is the Warrnambool trials."

Cannon nodded.

"Oh, and thanks for the feedback and the help this morning," went on Pete, "I think I learned a lot…. I hope you had a good day afterwards?"

"Yes, we did," replied Cannon, "it was great to wander around and see the place. Michelle is really impressed," he continued.

"Glad to hear it, mate," Pete replied, "Emily had been a little nervous before you got here. She thought I may be a little too *country* for you, a bogan. She was especially worried about what *you* would think about the setup and whether I was justified in asking for your help. Must be a *woman* thing," he said.

Cannon laughed. He let the sexist reference to Emily go. He understood where she was coming from.

Maybe Pete still had elements of the old Aussie idea of Sheila's and people acting larrikin like saying fair dinkum, true blue and g'donya within him due to the way he was brought up, but Cannon saw him differently, saw him as a farmer in the first instance and a racehorse trainer secondly. As he did during his career as a policeman, a senior detective, Cannon felt he could read and understand people's motivations. So it was with Pete. They had hit it off almost immediately and Cannon was pleased that he could be of help.

The wine and the coffee offered by Emily were finished, so Cannon and Michelle headed off to bed. They were being spoilt by their hosts.

"Not sure where I am going to hide all these extra pounds I'm putting on,"

Michelle said, snuggling up into Cannon's arms. "We've only been here a few days and I feel like I've not stopped eating."

"Me too," complained Cannon, "but that's the problem being on holiday, we just eat and drink."

They lay quietly, a single globe set into a cylindrical shaped lamp sat on a bedside table to the right of Cannon. It gave off enough light for them to see into each other's face without too much shadow. It was just before midnight and the house seemed extraordinarily quiet. There was no sound from outside. The expected rain, a short shower, had not yet been forthcoming, so there was no sound from the raindrops hitting the roof. The sky was still clear. The wind from the north dying as it crossed the coast.

"It's a bit cold," Michelle said.

"Umm," he agreed, "it's a clear night and winter is on its way, but we'll be home by the time it gets really cold here," he continued, considering whether to talk or sleep. He decided to talk. "I know we've just arrived a couple of days ago and I'm just getting over the jet-lag, but at this stage I'll be sad to go home. There is so much to see, we've come such a long way and we've got such a limited time to fit things in. Maybe we could extend the stay?"

Michelle perched up on one elbow, exposing her shoulder. She looked down at him and smiled. "Mike Cannon!" she said mockingly. "Am I hearing you correctly?" she asked incredulously. "Do I hear you saying that you are willing to leave the stables at home under the control of Rich for a little while longer than we had planned?"

"Yes," he replied, "I am. I spoke with him this afternoon while you and Emily were making dinner. Everything is fine currently. He sent his regards."

Michelle lay back in the bed looking up at the ceiling. For a second she lay quietly, then sat up, rolled over, and kissed him on the mouth. He pulled her close, his right arm wrapped around her waist. He caressed her hair.

"You know we can't do this right now," he said, "it's a bit awkward. It's too quiet."

"I know," she said, smiling, "maybe another day?"

Cannon shook his head and turned out the light. "No, how about now?" he asked.

"Can you be quiet?" she said

He touched his forehead against hers.

"Yes," he said.

They were quiet.

CHAPTER 11

"According to the report I've just received," Bruce said, "it looks like our victim, the body on the track, starved to death."

A murmur spread across the small room. The audience he was addressing easily fit inside it.

"Forensic Anthropologists," he continued, 'bloody rippers!"

He was back in Colac at the local police station. He had arranged for an incident room to be set up and he hoped that between himself, Cromwell, and the two constables and single admin support staff he would be able to get somewhere on the case. Cusscom had been helpful in letting Bruce have three of the local staff, at least for a short while, and Thatcher had been keen to give Bruce enough rope to be able to work 'closely' with the country. Bruce knew that Thatcher would use progress on the cases to continue to make favour with those higher up. Thatcher was ambitious like many others and the politics of personal growth came from the successes made in the field.

"It seems from what the Forensic Anthropologists have been able to establish from their investigation," he said, "and I am paraphrasing now, they have established that our individual on the track was small, male and from analysis of the teeth and bones had a diet that was similar to what a jockey would eat."

"Do they think the individual was a jockey Sir?" asked one of the Constables.

"That's what *we* need to establish but they have given us something to think about. At the moment we can't be sure," answered Bruce, "but the evidence seems to suggest something like that. Apparently from their analysis, the individual was certainly an adult, fully grown, so we can rule out the body is that of a child."

The Constable, Jim Alworth, nodded in response to Bruce's comment.

"So, what's next?" asked Cromwell.

"Good old-fashioned detective work," he answered. "Door knocking, the usual bag of questions. Let's see what we can come up with."

"Was there no DNA on the body that was useful to us?" asked Cromwell.

Bruce had been through the report several times. The only DNA that was useful was mitochondrial DNA in the bones and teeth of the victim and that is normally used to confirm relationships with living or deceased relatives. As the report had mentioned, if a relative, living or dead, of the deceased, is NOT on the collective databases held by the AFP for law enforcement purposes, or the National Criminal Investigation DNA Database (NCIDD), which was established back in 2001, then it is impossible at this stage to match the body to anyone. This may have been the reason why nobody came forward at the time the person went missing.

"There was nothing particularly useful in the report to us, unfortunately," he said, "so it's back to basics"

"Bugger!" exclaimed Cromwell.

"There is one bit of light on the horizon though,"

Cromwell and the rest of the team sat up.

"What's that?" she asked.

"I managed to convince Thatcher that we needed a bit more work done if we are to crack this case," he said, "so I asked if they could get one of the Forensic Anthropologists to scan the skull and see if they can build it up for us."

"Like facial recognition software does?" interrupted Alworth.

"Yes, although facial recognition software matches a *reading* of sorts against a known DB. What we are looking for is a face that we can use to see if anyone knew the victim. Apparently, despite all the technology it's difficult to build a face from a skeleton and match it to a face on a database. The face that is built is just a guess, its static, the lines on the face can't move. Unfortunately, it's going to take a couple of weeks to finish the job, so we'll have to continue as normal. As I said, it's back to *good old-fashioned police work*."

"And what about the other case, Timothy Hedge?" asked Cromwell.

Bruce referred to a folder that each had been given but none had yet had reason to look at.

The admin person attached to the team who had produced the folder, Jane Twilden, was very thorough. She sat at the back of the small room and acknowledged Bruce with a slight nod of the head and a glimpse of a smile.

"We know Hedge was murdered. We know he ended up in the garbage truck. What we don't yet know is the obvious reason, why? As you know, how he was killed is clear, straight forward. Unfortunately, and it's my fault," he continued, "the investigation stopped months ago. This was because of other cases in the city, I moved my focus to those and this one *got left on the shelf*," he acknowledged.

"You'll see in the folder that there are a few statements from various people we spoke to at the time. Some who knew Hedge, some who were aware of him and some who worked with him a for a while."

"What did he do?" asked Cromwell, "for a job," she added.

Bruce looked into the folder, to remind himself of how Timothy Hedge made a living.

"Seems he was a bit of a transitory worker. Worked in stables, did lots of odd jobs in the odd factory in the region, painting, labouring, but mostly spent his time around the local horse racing fraternity."

"Then one assumes he would have been well known by the trainers, the jocks etcetera?"

"Yes, it appears so, but no one really knew him on a social level. From what I can recall reading in the statements at the time, most of those spoken to just emphasized the fact that he was a bit of a loner."

"Yet someone smashed his head-in, dressed him up in jockey silks, and dumped him in a dustbin that would ultimately ensure his body was crushed."

"Exactly," replied Bruce, "and it's our job to find out who."

Cromwell gave a whistle, the Constables in the room moved uncomfortably on their chairs. Two cases, both very different yet both leaning in a particular direction. The area they needed to cover was large. The people they needed to talk too were country people, honest, forthright. They knew they would have to re-read the statements, visit the same folk again. Some of the statements were almost two years old now, especially those regarding Timothy Hedge. The consensus between the locals in the team, the Constables, was that they understood why the city policemen, Bruce, in particular, had let the Hedge case be de-prioritised. When there was little to go on, and success seemed unlikely, cases like that of Hedge were put to the bottom of the pile. The leadership of the force, even in the country, wanted results.

"It says here, Sir, that Hedge's body had been cleaned before it was put into the dustbin," said the second local Constable, Emmanuel Bossin.

"Yes, you are right," replied Bruce. "From what the experts were able to deduce, there was an attempt to remove as much DNA material as possible from Hedge's body. It was washed thoroughly, scrubbed apparently, even the hair was washed. It would appear the silks were put on with gloves and then the body was again blow-dried as if to get rid of any strands of material still on it that were potentially useable by forensics."

"And was there, Sir?"

"No Emmanuel. That is what has made the whole thing challenging. Little to go on. Despite the detritus from the body being in the truck. We thought we might have some luck with the shampoo used on the hair and the liquid soap used to clean the body, but they are just normal everyday soaps that anyone could have in their bathroom. The report shows that the analysis done even struggled to lock down a specific brand."

"So, we are almost back to square one Sir," Emmanuel said.

"Yes, unfortunately we are," Bruce replied, "like looking for a needle in a haystack, and one put there two years ago."

CHAPTER 12

Terang Racecourse, known as the Flemington of the Bush, is lined with spacious turf picnic areas for punters and a historic-looking grandstand almost the length of the straight. Despite its vintage look, it hosts some of the best modern-day facilities within it. A straight of four hundred metres allow punters to easily discern how the field of runners are positioned as they charge towards the winning post.

It was expected that *Wings of Dawn* would race well. Over the past few days, Cannon had been given free rein to work with the jockeys and the horse. Strictly speaking, Pete was still the trainer, but he had other things to do on his farm, so he let Cannon take over. Once the sessions were finished, Cannon would ensure that Pete got a full rundown on what he'd done with the horse and riders. Cannon filmed most of the work on his mobile phone and then shared it privately with Pete. No YouTube.

The sessions had improved *Wings'* confidence as well as that of the riders. Cannon hoped that Christian Counter would see the improvement in the horse and would take advantage of it.

The race that *Wings* was entered in was a 4000M chase over twenty-two chase obstacles. There was a field of ten, *Wings* was the third favourite.

Inside the parade ring, Cannon and Pete met with Counter prior to the race. The day was cool, but the sun was shining and there was a gentle breeze from the east. The wind would be drying out the track which had been watered overnight and again in the morning to improve the *going* to give it a more a good 4 or 5 rating.

Wings had travelled well and looked keen to be getting on with things. As he paraded around the ring the three men watched the animal jig on his toes. As the owner and *trainer*, Pete was particularly excited. A total purse of $30,000, or the $18,000 which the winning owner got, wasn't to be sneezed at. It was a precursor to the big one at Warrnambool.

Pete did the introductions to Counter.

"Christian, this is Mike Cannon. He's a trainer in England and is here on a working holiday. I specifically asked him over to help me with *Wings* in particular. You may not know but a couple of years ago Mike had a Grand National runner that was interfered with while competing in the race by people running onto the track, and which resulted in the race being abandoned."

"Yes, I recall," answered Counter.

"Well he's been helping me over the past couple of days with *Wings* and he believes that the horse is now more confident plus a lot fitter than in previous races. That confidence improving the horse by a length at least, over every jump."

Cannon held out his hand and said, "It's a pity I wasn't able to meet you earlier, I've been using the local lads to school the horse. Working on their technique on take-offs in particular. Trying to get them to be bolder. Jumping at the right time. Not too early as they were previously. I think it's helped the horse as well. He seems more confident at the jumps. I think he's worked out exactly when to take off, even before the jockey knows."

Counter listened intently.

"We've won a few races together," he said, "but I'm not so sure he's ready for the big ones yet particularly at the carnival next month. Having said that I'm not down for the ride anyway just yet."

"Well let's see how he goes today," responded Cannon. "I hope you will be pleasantly surprised."

The bell to mount was rung and Cannon gave Counter a lift-up onto *Wings'* back. The animal was bigger than most of his rivals in the race, and the improved fitness that Cannon seemed to have been able to instill in the horse seemed to ooze from the horse's demeanour and overall attitude. He seemed to be intimidating his rivals.

From the grandstand, Cannon and Pete watched as the all maroon silks of *Wings* walked around the back of the starting stalls.

Cannon found it fascinating that jumps races in Australia all began in the same starting stalls as flat races. In the UK jumps races used a flagged in starting approach. All runners brought into a single line by a flagman allowing the starter to let the horses race once he was satisfied that they were more or less in a straight line and a fair start could take place.

The horses for the race were quickly loaded and sent on their way. The small crowd on the course let out a cheer. There was an initial bit of scrimmaging for position by the field as they approached the first jump but by the time they did so, the horses seemed to have settled into a rhythm.

Wings raced comfortably covered up on the inside of the field, positioned just less than halfway. He sat around sixth spot as the front runners encountered the first obstacle.

As the leaders hit the first fence, two of them went down. Two fallers at only the first obstacle, one of them the favourite, a grey horse. Cannon watched the carnage happen, seeing the jockey on the favourite had taken off way too early to jump the obstacle, the horse's back legs hitting the fence which resulted in the animal becoming unstable and landing in a heap. The failure to land properly brought down the second horse which had been travelling right behind the grey. The favourite's jockey hit the ground, immediately covering his head with his hands as the rest of the field cleared the fence.

Once clear the fallen jockeys stood up, feeling their bodies for bruises or worse, broken bones. Fortunately, neither had any such affliction. The only thing dented was their pride. Falling at the first jump, in front of the crowd meant a short walk back to the weighing room, but an embarrassing one at that. Fortunately, both horses also had no injuries, and both stood up without assistance. Having no jockeys on their backs, their instincts from the training kicked in and they stood silently waiting for their grooms, their *strappers*, to come and collect them and take them back to their stables.

While they did so, the rest of the field, now down to eight continued to race. Within the next ninety seconds or so they would be back where they started from and with another twelve fences to jump.

Cannon trained his binoculars on *Wings* who was now sitting fourth. The field was slowly beginning to string out. Cannon was impressed with Counter's riding. They were clearing the obstacles with ease and Counter was giving the horse a great ride. The jockey had the horse just on the flanks of the second favourite.

As the field cleared the third last fence, *Wings* had moved up to third, then almost immediately upon landing Counter made his move. He gave the horse a kick in the belly and a quick whack on the flanks with his whip and the horse accelerated. Within seconds he had hit the front, leaving his closest two rivals behind in his wake. By the time he reached the penultimate obstacle, he was four lengths ahead of the second-placed horse. Cannon could see that horse and rider were enjoying themselves. They cleared the second last fence with ease. The crowd cheered as *Wings* hit the finish line ten lengths ahead of the second horse, being eased down.

Pete was delighted and shook Cannon's hand vigorously.

"Mate, I don't know how you did it but that was fantastic," he said, "bloody amazing. I'm stoked."

Cannon just smiled. "Let's go and lead him in," he said.

"Mr. Brownlow?" Bruce asked.

"Yes," Pete replied, "can I help you?"

They were standing just inside the winning box *Wings* having been taken away by his strapper for swabbing after the race. It was mandatory that all winners needed to be tested for any illegal substances that they may have in their system that may have influenced the outcome of the race.

Pete and Cannon were leaning on the fence awaiting Counter to complete his duties with the media about the race, and then they had planned to retire to the bar to have a small celebratory drink before heading back home. The horse would be brought home in a shared horse box trailer by a local driver who took horses around the state to the various meetings.

"Inspector Andrew Bruce," the man said, holding out his hand for Pete to shake and then showing Pete his warrant card. "Oh, and this is Constable Alworth." he continued, nodding towards his colleague a step or so behind him. Both men were in casual clothes, which Bruce was used to, but Alworth, not so. "Can we have a word?"

"Sure," responded Pete, "I guess the bar will do. It's not a particularly busy day. Will that work for you?"

Bruce nodded.

"Oh, and by the way," continued Pete, "this is Mike Cannon, he's helping me with the training of my runners. Particularly getting ready for the carnival at Warrnambool in a few weeks. He's here as a guest of mine from the UK. He's a relatively recently retired policeman, DCI if I recall?"

"D.I." interrupted Cannon, "retired quite a few years ago now," he went on, trying to make light of Pete's comments and hoping to keep a low profile about his past. That was over now. Despite recent events, he was now back in the habit of training racehorses, not solving mysteries.

"Nice to meet a fellow cop, albeit one now retired," went on Bruce. He held out his hand again and the two men shook warmly.

After Pete and Cannon had spoken to their jockey about the race, Counter went off to weigh in and Pete led the way to the bar. It was quiet, so it was easy for them to find an empty spot while still being able to view the track through wall-to-ceiling windows along one side of the bar area. Once their drinks were ordered, the two policemen settling for tea, and Pete and Cannon a beer each, Bruce apologized for the rather unconventional approach of meeting on track but advised Pete the rationale behind it.

Cannon sat silently, observing. Once their drinks had arrived he sipped his beer, taking in the detail of the conversation. A lifetime of listening and analysing what and how things were said began to stir at the front of his mind. It seemed he never let go of his experiences. Despite himself, he felt he was slowly being dragged into the conversation.

"Do you remember a couple of years ago, there was a body found in a garbage truck, in Apollo Bay, a man called Timothy Hedge?" asked Bruce.

"Yes, I do recall that," answered Pete, "I think you even may have questioned me about it at the time."

"Your memory is pretty good, I have your statement here with me," replied Bruce, turning to Alworth who produced the document from a folder he was carrying.

"I can't remember what I said then, it was a long time ago, and I don't think I would have any more to add to what I said at the time."

"You are probably right Sir, but we have relaunched the investigation due to new that we have received, and we are following up new leads."

Cannon picked up the lie straight away. His instinct told him that there was no new evidence really, that the police were starting all over again. The reason why was unclear. Cannon could surmise. Perhaps something else had happened in the area and that had sparked another look at the Hedge case?

"Okay, well happy to help if I can," replied Pete. "What would you like to know?"

"Well let's start with Mr. Hedge himself. How well did you know him?"

"I didn't really, he was a bit of a loner. He worked for me around the farm at different times. Sometimes with the lambing, sometimes with the cows. Feeding by shifting hay bales, the milking, that type of thing. Occasionally he would work with the horses, mucking out, helping with feed, and very rarely he would walk the horses, give them exercise."

"And over what period of time was this?" asked Bruce.

Pete gave it some thought before answering.

"I'd guess over a year or so, eighteen months maybe."

"Did Mr. Hedge ever stay on the farm while he performed his duties?"

"No, I think he either stayed with friends, family, or in his own flat, but I can't be sure. We never really talked about it. He came to work, did what he was asked to do, and then left. I paid him cash, as he wanted, at the end of each week and that was that."

"Cash?"

"Yes, it was the best way of making sure he pitched up to the end of the week. Once he got paid, sometimes I didn't see him for weeks or even months after that. He wasn't the most reliable I have to say, nor indeed was he the smartest either. But he did work hard and once he got the hang of things he could be left alone to get on with them."

"When did you last see him?"

"Oh, that must have been two years plus ago now. He last worked for me about three months before I think his body was found," said Pete. "But how does this move things along. If there *are* new leads I'm not sure where I fit in."

Bruce coughed into his hand. Cannon picked up another lie, he knew that the Bruce was fishing.

"Do you know who else Hedge worked for?" Bruce asked.

Pete thought about this for a few seconds. Cannon sipped his beer again, watching Bruce as he waited for Pete to answer.

"I'm not sure," he said. "He may have worked for anyone in the district, to be honest. I don't recall as it was a good while ago now. I think he worked for Walt Grovedale on his farm for a while, plus he may have done some stuff for any of the three Vet practices in town as he loved working with animals, and maybe even worked for George Sormond, the other trainer in the area, but I'm guessing now.

Bruce looked at Pete's statement from two years previously. Looking for consistencies, inconsistencies. There was nothing obvious.

"Thank you, Sir," he said. "I have already spoken with Mr. Grovedale this morning and I do hope to speak with Mr. Sormond later today. I see he has a runner in the last race, but I'm not sure if he'll be on the course for just the one race. He may well have sent a stable rep."

"I think you are probably right. George can be a bit of a bludger at times. Especially when he has only one horse running at a meeting. It's a long way from Colac to Terang."

Bruce smiled. Distance in Australia was a given. The drive from Melbourne to Colac never far from his mind.

Not one to sit and say nothing, Cannon had held back his own thoughts until the end of the interview between Pete and Bruce.

Eventually, he asked Bruce the question he been dying to ask. "Could I ask what has prompted the renewed look into Mr. Hedge's murder since the investigation seems to have stalled a while ago? Is it anything to do with the races, especially the upcoming carnival?"

"What makes you think that, Mr. Cannon? Or can I call you Mike?"

"Mike's fine," replied Cannon.

"Well...*Mike*...we think there may be a connection between Mr. Hedge's death and the racing community in the area. You may not know this, but Mr. Brownlow is definitely aware of it, so I am happy to share it with you," he continued. "Mr. Hedge was found in the garbage truck dressed in jockey silks. He wasn't a jockey but was a pretty small man. So, we think it odd that he was dressed in that way. We found no DNA evidence on him at all. The body had been thoroughly washed from head to toe. The silks that were put on him were done so with great care. Someone went to a lot of trouble to make sure nothing was left to chance."

"Sounds odd to me too, thinking about it," interrupted Cannon, "frankly though it's a clue as well isn't it?"

"How do you mean?"

"Well, why would you do that unless you were trying to send someone, let's say the police, down a rabbit hole. Trying to imply something that was an untruth?"

"Maybe a double bluff?" replied Bruce.

"Maybe."

"Anyway, we needed to speak again to those who may have dealt with Mr. Hedge around the time of his murder. Something else has popped up in the area which we are looking into and we wanted to see if there was any connection."

"And is there?" asked Cannon.

"It's too early to say, but by revisiting what happened to Mr. Hedge we just want to keep an open mind."

"I'm sorry Inspector," jumped in Pete. "I'm not sure what else I can add, other than what I've said already. Maybe George can give you a bit more information if you see him later this afternoon, but I can't recall anything else about when Timothy last came to work for me other than what I've already told you."

"I understand. Well, thank you anyway. Oh, and well done with your horse today. That was quite impressive. Good luck in getting him ready for the Grand Annual at Warrnambool."

"Thank you," replied Pete, looking at Cannon. "Mike here has been a big help. In just a few days he has worked wonders. Even the track riders have felt more confident in their work with *Wings* and my other jumpers."

"Perhaps I'll have a couple of *bob* on him when he goes around next?" said Bruce. "Which reminds me, did you ever have a jockey or track rider disappear on you about a year ago?" he asked.

Pete thought about this for a second.

"No, not that I can recall," he answered. "Most of my track riders have been with me from the beginning. Why do you ask?"

"No particular reason. Something has come up though and we were just seeing if it rang any bells with people in the area."

Another bending of the truth thought Cannon. It was clear that something else had happened and Bruce was trying to see if it was linked to the Hedge murder.

"No, sorry," Pete repeated, "I can't add anything else."

"Okay well thank you for your time," Bruce stated, " and thanks for the tea."

"No worries."

"And nice to meet you too Mr.Cannon, sorry…Mike!"

"Likewise, Inspector. Good luck with your enquiries. Seems like you have a couple of challenges on your hands."

Bruce smiled inwardly. So far, every individual they had spoken to about the Hedge case had little to relay other than what had been stated nearly two years previously. No one had seen anything. No one had known where Hedge had disappeared to. Where he had gone? Who he had met? Someone must have known. Someone had killed him. But why? What had a drifter uncovered that had resulted in his murder?

Bruce and Alworth said their goodbyes and they went off looking for George Sormond.

"How odd," said Pete draining the last of his beer and putting the empty glass back on the table that they were sitting at. "It's been two years since I last spoke with the police about Timothy Hedge, and I'm not sure how they would ever expect me to remember anything else about someone I hardly knew that I hadn't already told them at the time."

Cannon knew why Bruce was now asking such questions. He surmised that either Bruce had got a kick up the backside about lack of progress with the case from his superiors or something else had happened in the area and Bruce felt there was a connection of sorts. He guessed it could be a combination of both. Similar things had happened to him when he was in the *Force*.

"What do you think about his last comment?" asked Cannon.

"About the track rider or jockey that just disappeared?"

"Yes."

"I don't know anything about that," Pete replied, "what do you think?"

"Not sure to be honest. It just seemed a little left field that's all. Anyway, it's not my business. I'm here to help you win this big race in just less than a couple of weeks. It was a great start today though, don't you think?"

"Yes, it was," replied Pete a big grin on his face. "Drink up, I've finished mine. Let's get home before it gets too late. We've got an hour and a half's drive, at least, ahead of us and I want to check the milking is underway before it gets too dark," he said.

"Fine with me," answered Cannon. His work done for the day, he was keen to get back to the farm and check on *Wings* when the horse had returned. He wanted to see how the horse had pulled up. How the legs had handled the trip and the jumping on what was fairly hard ground when compared to that his own horses raced on in the UK. He knew they bred them tough in Australia, but they needed to be sound as well. As he had seen already, *Wings* had great conformation but was still required to race over long distances and jump over a large number of fences, and any horse no matter how good could always injure itself. He found himself becoming attached to the horse and the thought of racing in the Grand Annual was beginning to excite him.

CHAPTER 13

It was easy to drop the package into the sea. The *San Marino* had been early, waiting to pick it up. Further out to sea at twenty miles due south of Apollo Bay, slightly to the northwest of King Island the MSC Globe let the lines go that were holding the cargo in a small raft.

The package was safely stored by the time the small fishing boat entered the Apollo bay harbour.

Sitting in the Bayleaf café just on the Great Ocean Road in Apollo Bay, the skipper of the *San Marino* chatted quietly with his guest at the table. The café was quiet as most of the diners who had come in for breakfast had left. Of the dozen or so tables, only three were still occupied.

"I think we'll need to slow down for a while," said the fishing vessels captain. "There are too many parcels to handle. We need a bit more time between shipments."

The visitor took a napkin and dabbed it on the chin highlighting softer hands than those of their seafaring colleague. "Agreed," came the reply. "I'll make a few calls. I'm not sure what is on its way, but I will try and see if we can intercept it. Perhaps use another route?"

The captain of the *San Marino* finished his coffee and brushed off the remains of a croissant from his ribbed jumper. Standing up, he thanked his colleague and quickly left the café. He knew that his visitor would ensure that things would slow down a little. They had a good business between them and didn't want to jeopardize it. They knew the local police were too busy with domestic matters, traffic fines, local disputes, the occasional break-in to be concerned about. The police seldom investigated what was happening in the harbour. They relied on self-regulation and for the few vessels operating out of the place to *do the right thing* and to be honest and be good citizens. It was known broadly that most of the fleet in the harbour, other than the recreation sailing boats belonging to the local sailing club, were from long-standing families. People who had lived in the area for twenty years plus.

What the captain of the *San Marino* needed to be cautious of was the rumour around the town that Detectives from the city had re-opened the case of the body in the garbage truck from two years ago. The captain hoped that it was the only thing they were focused on.

CHAPTER 14

"Did you find out anything else?" asked Bruce.

"No nothing at all," replied Cromwell. "It seems like no one can recall anything about Timothy Hedge other than he was just a drifter. Seemed to go from job to job as the mood took him."

Bruce sighed. He was becoming frustrated.

The team, as it was, the four of them plus Jane Twilden were the only resources allocated to the two cases and Bruce knew it wasn't enough. To try and solve both would be almost impossible with such a small team. He needed a slice of luck.

It was early morning and the team was sitting in the situation room trying to come to terms with what they had been able to establish so far. It was very little, indeed bleak. Just like the weather was outside, cold and grey, the mood was inside the room.

"And what about our body on the cycle track?" Bruce asked.

"Even worse," replied Cromwell. "Constable Bossin and I couldn't find any individual who knew of anyone disappearing so suddenly. It seems like the mystery man is exactly that, a mystery."

"Jesus Christ!" exclaimed Bruce. "We are getting nowhere fast, are we? No one knows anything about either of the two bodies. No one knows anything other than what we gathered two years ago about the Hedge case, and in relation to our victim in Forrest no one knows bugger all about that as well," he raged. "Gee that pisses me off. Someone knows something, we just need to find out who that person is, or who those persons are. People just don't die without someone knowing about them," he concluded.

"Well happy to go through the list of those who we spoke too and compare notes," Cromwell said, "maybe you can see something I can't."

Over the next few hours, they poured over the statements that Cromwell and Bossin had been able to gather from the people they had interviewed. The detail was very similar to those that Bruce had been able to collate along with Alworth. As they compared notes they had a small breakthrough. It was a statement from one of the three Vets in Colac taken two years previously. The Vet had mentioned that Hedge had worked with him for a short while, a few years previously. That Hedge loved working with animals and that he would help with the cleaning of cages, feeding, and generally labouring at the practice. These were things they already knew from earlier conversations, but at least it was consistent.

"What's this Vets name?" asked Bruce.

Cromwell checked the statement detail.

"Max Optin," she replied once she had found the information.

"Did you interview him yesterday?" Bruce asked.

"No, we didn't. His practice was closed."

"Okay, well let's see him tomorrow. Maybe he can fill in a couple of gaps for us?"

CHAPTER 15

"How was your day?" asked Michelle.

Cannon and Pete had arrived home around four in the afternoon. Pete had gone off to supervise the feeding of his sheep and the start of the milking process for his cows and had asked Cannon to check on the horses down at the stable block. Only *Wings* had raced that day, but there were a few of his horses due to race over the coming weeks. Flat runners to race at Hamilton, Stawell, Mortlake, and Ararat in the Western part of the state.

Pete had two of his other jumpers, *Flimflam* and *Binge-Eater* also being readied for the carnival. They both needed to race and trial before the meeting, so Pete wanted to get miles into their legs before the upcoming races. They were accepted to race in Donald, Casterton, and Horsham. Pete hoped Cannon could help decide which races to go to once the fields had been published.

"I had a great day," Cannon replied kissing her on the lips. They were in the kitchen. Emily was outside bringing in, then sorting out the day's washing. Stephanie was in her room. Cannon noticed that Michelle was becoming familiar with the layout of the house and was beginning to feel at home. From what he could see, she was making pies of various sizes.

"Chicken, for dinner, plus a couple of others to be put into the freezer," she said. "A bit too cold outside for a barbecue according to Emily, so that's why we're having one of these tonight," she said.

Cannon nodded. With the nights drawing in, something he hadn't expected to encounter, he realized that life on such a big farm, in Autumn and Winter could be hard at times. The cold surprised him as well. On Pete's farm, there was always so much to do. His own place wasn't in the city, but it was in Oxfordshire. Rural, but not isolated.

As he stood by a counter-top watching Michelle work on the dinner, he listened for other noises. It was quiet. Very quiet. Even the lowing of the cows from the milking sheds couldn't be heard despite some of the windows in the room being slightly open. The stillness, the fading light seemed to hold him for a second.

His mind wandered. He had a small team at home but there never seemed to be enough time for everything that needed attention either. Having had the opportunity over the short time that Michelle and he had been visiting to see the extent of the farm that Pete and Emily were looking after, he had to admire them. Running such a large farm, and especially the training of racehorses in addition to the rest of the business that Peter had responsibility for, was hard work. Cannon didn't think that he could ever manage such an enterprise. He guessed that Emily was more than happy to allow Michelle to bake for them. He also realized that Pete was very happy giving Cannon free rein as well with the horses. Both of them were sharing the bus, he thought. Both he and Michelle were together on a busman's holiday. He smiled to himself. It could be worse, he thought. At the very least today's race showed that he was adding some value. He hoped that Pete could see that.

"*Wings* won easily," he went on, happy to share the good news, "and we met his jockey, a real competent young rider. I was very impressed with him."

"That's great, I assume Pete was happy?"

"Yes, he thanked me for helping him with the horse in particular, but later on thanked me more broadly for helping with the others."

Michelle smiled.

"How about your day?" he asked, "what have you been up to?"

While Michelle continued with making dinner, Emily returned from the laundry and began helping her with the rest of the ingredients for the meal. Fresh vegetables from their own vegetable patch, as well as potatoes grown on the farm, that had been stored in a large kitchen pantry, were inserted into various pots for cooking once the pies had been put into the two kitchen ovens to bake.

"Well," Michelle said. "Emily took me into Colac and we had a walk around, looked at the shops."

"Don't tell me," he said, "but did you see anything worth buying?"

Anticipating his question, she had a ready answer.

"Well, I did see a couple of things I liked, yes, but decided to hold off. Emily and I will be going into Geelong next week, where we might find something to wear at the carnival, so I want to save some money for that."

Cannon nodded. He understood how Michelle thought about spending money on the right things, not just anything. It was a big part of their relationship. She was a teacher and despite her working at a Private school, budgets were always tight there. A bit like running a racing stable. Staying afloat was just as hard as producing winners on the track.

Cannon admired how she knew how to plan, prepare, and with limited resources always seemed to come up with the right answer, the right solution. It was one of many things he loved about her. Resilience, tenacity, were words that he found described her well. He was a lucky man.

Above the now increasing noise in the kitchen as various bowls, dishes, plates, cutlery were pulled from out of cupboards and drawers and placed on the dining room table or into the dishwasher Cannon heard Michelle say, "While we are in Warrnambool, Emily and I won't attend all three days if that's okay? I want to have a look around the place. I'm thinking of the middle day if that suits you?" she asked. "I see they have a few attractions in the town that are worth a look at. A maritime village with a famous light and sound show, plus we may go and have a look at Port Fairy, just up the road. I believe it's a lovely spot."

"Whatever you want to do is fine with me," he said.

"Good," she answered, smiling back at him. "You see Emily," turning towards her host, "even cynical ex-policemen can be loving and generous with their praise and support."

"You're a lucky woman," Emily responded, "and you've done well to find such an attractive man," she said teasing him. Cannon blushed. He thought back to his and Michelle's lovemaking the other night. Had they been as quiet as they thought?

Over dinner, the conversation moved from the issues on the farm, through to the days' success at the races. Eventually, the matter of Timothy Hedge was brought up. Pete mentioned it to Emily and asked if she could recall anything about him.

"Not really," she answered. "wasn't he the guy that came and went every now and then. Sort of went *walkabout* as the aboriginals say?"

"That's right. If you recall he ended up in a garbage truck in Apollo Bay, murdered. Two years ago."

Michelle turned towards Cannon, who hadn't mentioned the conversation he and Pete had shared with Detective Bruce. She shivered.

"Wow," she proclaimed. "Mike, it looks like wherever we go something always follows us like this."

Cannon put up his hands in mock defense. "Sorry my darling, but this is something that happened two years ago. Not my doing," he smiled, "though I did find the whole conversation somewhat disturbing as to why it had taken so long for the case to be reopened."

"Me too," said Pete, "it was as if something else has happened and the boys from the city have been dragged back out here to look into it."

"I agree."

Cannon thought back to the conversation in the bar. He felt then, and his instinct was telling him now, that something else had caused the shift in activity. That there was something else slowly building. He looked at his hosts. They were good people. Surely they were not involved in any way with what the police were now investigating, Hedge's disappearance and his ultimate death? Were they?

CHAPTER 16

"How can I help you, Inspector?" Max Optin had asked when they had been formally introduced in the reception area of his practice. The Vet acknowledged his young receptionist Tina and had thanked her for calling him to the front desk.

They were now sitting in a small office at the rear of the Vet's practice, which was situated on Skene Street, three streets away from Lake Colac itself. Sounds of dogs barking in a backroom echoed along a short passage.

Bruce, Cromwell, and Optin managed to fit into the small space that the Vet used to manage his patient records and issue accounts using a very old laptop computer and associated printer. Optin was obviously focused on the reason he was in practice, the animals. Bruce looked around the room, noticing a well-worn chair standing in the corner. It looked like the man slept at the practice if necessary. Optin confirmed it. Old fashioned values contrasting with modern-day expectations.

"Yes, occasionally if needed, I will sleep here," he said, rather more cheerfully than Bruce would have expected. "Sometimes the animals need care at various times of the day, particularly at night, so I often sleep in the chair. It's easier than going home," he stated.

Technology related to the modern world, outside of veterinary science did not sit well with Optin either. They were a necessary evil but not one he enjoyed using. The only item that was relatively new that Bruce could distinguish was the Vet's mobile phone. Something that in today's world one couldn't be without, especially a 24-hour available Vet.

Bruce looked the man up and down. It was hard to establish if he was sixty or seventy, but Bruce was of the view that if anyone could recall Timothy Hedge it would be Optin. After all, Optin's practice had not moved in nearly thirty-five years so he should be able to recall someone who helped around the place just a few years previously.

"Firstly I'd like to thank you for your time," Bruce said in response to Optin's question, "and I hope we won't take up too much of it, but we are here to see if you could help us concerning someone who used to work with you, a few years back."

"Oh?" enquired Optin.

"Yes. Timothy Hedge. You do remember him?"

"Indeed, I do."

"And you know he was found murdered."

"Yes, such a sad situation," Optin responded sympathetically, "he was such a gentle soul."

The empathy shown by Optin was tangible. To Bruce and Cromwell, there appeared genuine sadness in Optin's voice.

"Just for the record, and I'm pretty sure you confirmed this a couple of years back when you gave your initial statement to the local police, could you look at this picture and confirm your understanding that *this*," he pointed at the photograph that Cromwell had removed from a folder, "is Timothy Hedge?"

The Vet picked up the image and put on a pair of glasses attached to a piece of string sitting loosely around his neck. He peered at it closely, seeming to take an age to respond.

"Yes, this is Timothy."

"And when did you last see him?" asked Bruce.

Optin thought about the question for a few seconds.

"As I think I said in my statement, I last saw him about a month before he seemed to have disappeared," he replied. "The local police came to ask me about him but never indicated why other than they were trying to find out his movements. It was only when I saw in the local paper a few weeks later that he had been found dead that their visit sort of made sense."

Bruce looked at Cromwell. They shared the view that vital time had been lost by the local police between the finding of the body and the investigation into Hedge's movements starting.

"And again, for the record Mr. Optin, what did Timothy do for you when he worked here?"

"Basically, he acted as a *gofer*, a cleaner, he did most things asked of him. He just seemed to love being around the place. I needed assistance at times as this place can get rather busy as you can imagine, so I needed someone to help me with the load."

"And how was he employed?"

"How do you mean?"

"Well, was he a formal employee? A casual? What?" jumped in Cromwell.

Optin took a deep breath before replying. "He was a casual. Paid by the hour. Cash, which was how he wanted it. He was never a formal employee.

"Nice and convenient!" retorted Cromwell. "No real records to be kept," she said.

"Look, Sergeant."

"Senior Constable," Cromwell advised.

"Senior Constable," Optin repeated with a nod of the head, "Timothy didn't only work for me. He did odd jobs for all the Vets in the area here. I also know he worked on some of the farms as well. He got about quite a lot, plus I think he claimed welfare as well."

"Did you tell all this to the enquiring officer," asked Cromwell, "when you initially gave your statement a couple of years ago? From what I can see there is nothing mentioned anywhere which you have just stated or asserted."

"No, I didn't," replied the Vet, "at the time I wasn't aware that Timothy was dead. The police were only asking about his movements. I didn't want to get him into trouble."

"About what?"

"Him claiming welfare when he was working for me and others."

"And those others were…?" enquired Bruce, leaving the question open.

Optin sighed. "As I indicated already, he worked for all three of the Vets in the area at various times, plus he may have worked for others in the towns along the coast, Warrnambool, Portland, Port Fairy anywhere. He seemed to disappear at times and then without fanfare suddenly pop up on your doorstep."

"And you took him on again?"

"Yes, why not? It was always nice to see him, and he knew what I needed from him. The relationship was symbiotic. It worked both ways. If I had no work for him I would let him know and he would tell me how I was able to get hold of him when I needed to." Optin looked at his mobile phone sitting on a small desk. "I would call him and when he could, he would be here."

Bruce considered Optin's reply, finally asking, "You said he worked for other Vets in the area. Who would they be?"

"We have two other practices in Colac, both of whom are much bigger than mine. Their practice names and addresses are easy to find. I concentrate as you can see on domestic animals, dogs, cats, rabbits, guinea pigs, that kind of pet. I have done so for years. Most of the larger animal care, such as horses, sheep, cows have been treated by the others. That's not to say I haven't worked with larger animals in the past," he continued, "but it's just that I don't have the energy anymore. I'm a widower you see, my wife passed away six years ago. She used to help me in the practice whenever I needed her. Reception, that type of thing," he said. "I've concentrated on the smaller pets predominantly as I've gotten older. Must be at least fifteen years since I last worked with anything bigger than a fat, overweight Labrador," he chuckled.

Bruce could see that Optin had now shared all he knew about Timothy Hedge. He wished that there had been more detail in the initial statement that Optin had made, but he understood now why certain information had been left out. It showed compassion.

"Well thank you Mr. Optin for your help," Bruce said, "but at this stage, I don't think we will be interrupting you again. Certainly not in the short term."

Despite Optin's age, he smiled, sheepishly, his face apologetic.

"I'm sorry Inspector if I did the wrong thing at the time. I just wanted to do right by Timothy."

"No worries," replied Bruce. "We'll see ourselves out."

The two policemen left the office. Once outside Bruce turned to Cromwell. "We need to have a chat with the other two Vet practices," he said. "Let's get some lunch first and then see if anyone there knows about Timothy Hedge."

As he spoke his mobile rang. He looked at the number before answering. He mouthed the words to Cromwell as to who was calling. It was his boss, Thatcher.

"Bruce," he answered.

"AB," came the reply. "just thought I would give you a call to find out how things are going?"

"With what Sir?" Bruce responded, "the Hedge case, the body in the bush, or the overall relationship with the local coppers here?"

The sarcasm in Bruce's voice was not lost on Thatcher.

"All of the above," Thatcher said.

Bruce sighed but gave a brief breakdown of the status. "It seems that Seth…"

"Cusscom?" interrupted Thatcher.

"Yes Sir. He is generally happy with the progress we have made so far, especially with us taking some of the strain away from his own team and despite us taking a couple of resources away from him as well." Bruce replied. "It seems the locals have a couple of investigations that they are pursuing that they would normally need all their resources on, but given the circumstances, they are happy for us to follow up on an old case like that of Hedge. Indeed, they are happy to let us handle it through to the end, even though it means taking a couple of their people away from them."

"And what about our body in the bush?"

Bruce rolled his eyes at Cromwell, indicating to her that Thatcher was becoming a pain with his questions.

"Bit more of a challenge Sir. We haven't had much time to look into it, but we will. We've been trying to find out more about Hedge."

The line was quiet for a second. Eventually, Thatcher said. "We've got a bit more information from the forensic team about our dead man on the track," he said. "Seems like he wasn't from around here."

"Sorry Sir, what do you mean?" asked Bruce.

"We think he may be an immigrant. Possibly from the Philippines, Singapore, or Malaysia."

"And this helps me how? Sir."

Thatcher didn't reply immediately. Finally, a chuckle came down the line. "I'm not sure myself to be honest, but I'm sure you'll work it out Bruce. It's why I pay you the *big bucks,*" he said. "I'll email you the latest report. Enjoy your stay down there. Give Seth my best."

Bruce closed his phone. He was hungry. Turning to Cromwell he said,

"Lunch, my shout. I'll fill you in over a coffee."
If Thatcher was going to be a prick then at least Bruce would make it worth his while. Expenses would be on him.

Once Optin had seen Bruce's car drive away and he was sure there was no sign of the policemen returning, he picked up his phone and made a call. "We need to have a chat," he said.

CHAPTER 17

"Hi Dad! How are you?" Cassie asked, her face staring back at him from his iPad. FaceTime was great he thought as it cost you nothing especially if you had an unlimited data service with a local provider. He hadn't asked but Cannon guessed that Pete would have ensured he had the best communications around. When Michelle and Emily used to talk over the weeks and months before they arrived there never seemed to be any issue.

Michelle was in the lounge room chatting away with Emily. Stephanie sat at the dining room table doing some *homework* on a laptop. Michelle, being a teacher had looked at what Stephanie was supposed to have been studying. Geography was the answer. She had originally thought from what she could see that Stephanie was playing games, probably with classmates, rather than working. She was right but she decided not to say anything.

"I'm fine," Cannon replied to Cassie. He was sitting on the bed in their room. "What time is it now there?" he asked. It was just before ten PM local time and given the recent changes to clocks for daylight saving Cannon wasn't clear if he was ten or nine hours ahead of the UK.

"It's just before one in the afternoon," Cassie replied. "I'm just about to get some lunch. I have a meeting with one of my Profs. at two o'clock."

"That's good to hear. What's the weather like in York?" he asked. As he spoke he realized that it was always one of the dumb questions everybody seemed to ask when they were talking with someone in a different part of the country or overseas. Particularly the British. The weather being a key part of most people's day, it seemed. Things happened or they didn't if the weather was good or bad. Rain, snow, wind all influenced what people did, how individuals reacted. It was also an odd question because the information was readily available through various apps on a smartphone, an iPad, or most connected devices. Cannon looked at the screen, conveniently ignoring a couple of weather apps that Michelle had loaded already.

"It's quite mild today," Cassie replied. "About eighteen degrees. The sun is shining so it's almost t-shirt weather."

Cassie turned the screen towards a window allowing Cannon to see the sun streaming through the window of her student apartment.

"Looks lovely," he said. "And how *is* the studying going?"

Cassie was now in the final year of her undergraduate degree in Law. It seemed to Cannon that she was heading in a Human Rights direction. He was very proud of her, but he knew that any post-graduate course she may want to study cost money. He hoped she realized that it was likely incumbent on her to get a scholarship or another student loan if she decided to study further. After the loss of *RockGod,* the stable was surviving and results improving but being flush with success didn't always convert to direct cash for the stable. For owners, yes, perhaps. So, survival was the key. Thank God for the loyalty of Rich and the rest of his staff, thought Cannon.

"It's going well," she answered. "Only a couple of months to go now."

"Yes," he said, smiling back into the camera, "it's amazing how quickly time goes. Anyway, what's up?" he asked.

"Nothing," she replied somewhat sheepishly. "just wanted to see how you are enjoying Australia."

Cannon wasn't taken in.

"Come on Cass, I know you better than that. Is it money?"

"No," she replied. "It's Samuel."

Samuel? Cannon thought. *'sWho's he?* It was not a name Cassie had ever mentioned since she went back to University after last year's Grand National. In fact, she had spoken very little about what she had been up to other than her studying. Even when she was home for Christmas she was very quiet about her friends.

Eventually, Cannon asked the question. "Samuel?"

"Yes."

"What about him? And anyway, who is he?"

"He's a fellow student."

"Law?"

"Yes," she replied. "He's a few years ahead of me. He's a Post-Grad now but we've become good friends."

"And?"

"Well he's from Cape Town, and he's asked me to go with him on holiday there after exams."

Cannon did not know what to say. For a few seconds he forgot that he was on a screen, Cassie could see his thoughts on his face.

"Dad?" she queried.

Cannon eventually asked the question he dreaded. "How long have you known this…*Samuel?*

"Oh, about a year, maybe fifteen months," Cassie replied nonchalantly.

"And how old is he?"

"Twenty-nine."

Cannon was almost apoplectic. "Twenty-nine?" he spluttered. "Cassie you're not even twenty yet! "

"I know Dad, but I like him."

"I'm sure you like lots of things Cass, but …"

His voice trailed off as he considered what to say. His daughter was a young woman now, not a teenager anymore. The teenager who went off to University had grown up. She was independent she could make her own decisions.

"Dad!" she interrupted, "can I just say something?"

"Of course," he replied, wondering what was coming next.

Cassie took a deep breath before saying. "Dad, it's not what you think."

"And what am I thinking?" he asked, knowing that she would have worked out what he was inferring.

"That I'm sleeping with Samuel?"

"And are you?"

"Dad!" she replied, "I'm going to ignore that. It's not something I'm going to answer."

"Okay," he said putting his hands up in defeat, almost letting the iPad fall off his lap. "I give up. Sorry."

The silence between them seemed to go on longer than the few seconds it took for Cassie to speak again.

"Dad," she said. "Samuel asked me to go with him to South Africa to see if I really want to study Human Rights law next year. Part of the course includes studying and working overseas. He thought that by going to see the country and the way things operate there, it would give me a better perspective."

"But you said you *liked* him,"

"I do, but we are just friends Dad."

Not with benefits, Cannon hoped.

"Just friends," she repeated.

Cannon took a deep breath.

"So, are you asking me for money to support you on this holiday?" he said.

"No. I'm just looking for your advice," she answered.

Cannon noticed the tone in her voice. It had changed. He realized that he had disappointed her. He saw the tears well up in her eyes, glistening in the light through the window shining into her room. He was twelve thousand miles away from her. She was on screen asking for support. He swallowed deeply.

"Go on," he said eventually.

"I just wanted to know what you think about the prospect," she asked. "I've never been to Cape Town nor anywhere else in Africa," she continued. "Samuel says that despite the various reports you hear every now and then, Cape Town is still a reasonably safe place to go."

Cannon had no real experience of Africa. His police work never really took him away from the UK. He knew about the issues of South Africa, the past, the challenges, the poverty in many places, the corruption. He felt uncomfortable about the prospect of Cassie wanting to visit but he understood that it was a part of her future. A decision now that could affect both of them forever.

"So where would you stay, on this *holiday?*" he asked.

"With Samuel, *naturally.*"

"Oh."

"Plus, the rest of his family," she quickly added. "It seems they live in a place called Bishops Court. Very swish I understand. It's not that far from the Kenilworth racecourse you may like to know. Samuel's father used to be a doctor in the army. Now he's in private practice. They have a pretty big house and….."

Cannon started to relax but couldn't help interrupting her flow.

"Does the family know about this?"

"Yes," she replied, "I have spoken with Samuel's mum and dad a few times already. They assured me that I would be well looked after."

There it was, he thought. A done deal already. She had outmaneuvered him. She had got all her ducks in a row. What she wanted was affirmation, not direction.

He knew he was defeated.

"Okay," he said, "just as long as you promise me that you won't come back married…or worse…." he let the comment slide.

Cassie beamed. Her eyes that just a few minutes previously had shown tears, now showed excitement.

"Thanks Dad," she gushed. "I can't tell you how excited I am."

Smiling back at her, he said, "I can imagine. However, you need to get through the rest of this year before you go anywhere, so I hope the courses…"

"Modules…" she interrupted.

"Yes, modules. I hope they are working out for you?"

"I'm doing fine Dad," she answered. "Doing really well."

Finally, he had to ask about money. How much it would cost to get to South Africa.

"Don't worry Dad it's covered,"

"By Samuel?"

"Yes… by Samuel's family."

Cannon felt a little aggrieved but decided not to say anything. His contribution to the visit was just an obligatory, *yes,* and a *wave goodbye.*

Was there anything else she would need? he thought.

How long would she be away for?

Where was her passport?

He couldn't stop his mind racing but kept everything to himself. He knew she would work things out. He just needed to take a step back. To give her space and to give himself time to process what he was hearing.

Having little else to say, the weather having been discussed again, Cassie let Cannon know that she had used up a half an hour of her lunchtime and that she needed to get on. She needed to get a sandwich and get over to her Professor's office before 2 pm. They signed off, Cassie's face disappearing from his screen in milliseconds. He took the earphones that he had been wearing out of his ears and placed them on the bed next to him. Rubbing his face, he sighed. It had been a long day. Tomorrow he hoped to spend more time working with *Flimflam* and *Binge-Eater*. Training horses was his game.

CHAPTER 18

Bruce looked at his notes. He was half-sitting on the table in the incident room. The meeting with the two other veterinary practices had provided very little new information from that they already knew. Timothy Hedge seemed a misnomer. He didn't seem to fit any criteria that was particularly onerous as far as they could tell. When it came to acting as he did, perhaps committing minor fraud regarding his employment status and the claiming of benefits that he wasn't really entitled to, he was hardly a mastermind, thought Bruce.

"So, what do we know?" he asked, "anything….any takers?"

The room remained quiet. Between Bruce and the other three, they had uncovered very little by talking with the other Vets. Both practices had used Hedge at times to do the *menial* work, but neither of them had anything of value to add.

He was frustrated.

"We need to find out where Hedge went when he went walkabout," he said, "he must have gone somewhere!"

"Family perhaps?" said Alworth, in hope but without conviction.

"Maybe. But where are they? From looking up the Centrelink records a couple of years ago he didn't indicate any next of kin, and from what we've been able to check from the births, marriages, and death register he had no direct relatives at all. Even his fixed address at the time seemed a bit dodgy."

"Why was that, Sir?" asked Alworth.

"Why what?"

"Why was it dodgy?"

Bruce indicated the folder that he had put on a chair next to him. He was getting angry, not a trait that he was used to expressing. Sighing he asked,

"Have none of you read the report? The statements? You've all had copies of it for a few days, I was expecting a little bit more understanding of the situation by now," he complained.

"Sir," Cromwell jumped in noting Bruce's demeanour, "I think we just need to take a step back on this issue of Hedge and what he did and how he did things."

"How do you mean?"

"Well let's have a look at the statements we took today. It's been two years since Hedge's death. We know he was a loner, and we know he worked for the two Vet practices at various times. We also know he ended up in Apollo Bay in the back of a garbage truck."

"Yes I get that Constable," replied Bruce, "but how does that help the investigation?"

She was quiet for a second, then said. "I think someone is lying."

"About what?"

"About Hedge. I think someone knows more than they are saying."

"And what makes you think that?"

"Because…" she began.

Bruce immediately interrupted her. "Because you *think so,?* Because it's in your *water?*" he continued sarcastically. "We haven't even been able to establish a motive, a reason *why* Hedge was killed yet," he continued, "and we are now two years on. I think we need to get some perspective here. We need facts, not theories!" he exclaimed.

It was as if the air had been sucked out of the room. Bruce's tirade took its toll. Cromwell asked for a ten-minute break. Bruce agreed.

She stood on the pavement of Queen Street in the late afternoon sun. The cases heard at the Magistrates' court next door to the Colac police station had concluded. A few people milled around outside the courthouse, but most had gone home. Not being a smoker, Cromwell walked on the spot, wrapping her arms around herself to keep warm. It would be dark in less than an hour.

Bruce appeared at her shoulder.

"Sorry," he said.

Cromwell looked at her feet. She noticed the scuff marks on the toes of her shoes and the cracks between the bricks making up the pavement. Having worked with Bruce for a little while now, she knew his background. She knew he was a good policeman and she knew how passionate he was about finding solutions to cases. He wanted to crack every one he worked on. She understood the frustration he must be feeling. A big-city policeman in a small country town trying to solve two cases with limited support. The expectation that he and she could find the answers was immense.

"That's okay, Sir," she said. "I get where you are coming from. I just think though that we may need to take another look at our approach."

"In what way?"

She nodded towards the door of the police station as a man entered its lobby looking for someone to talk to. Looking for the charge officer, the charge desk. Looking to report a car accident perhaps?

"Everyone who comes here has a perspective about things. They come here for a reason. That reason is not always real." she said. "Sometimes, many times, the real reason they come to us is because it is easy to deflect a problem, make a statement, tell a lie, bury the truth such that we can be sent off in the totally wrong direction."

"And you think that's what's happening in the Hedge case?"

"Well Sir, it just seems impossible to me that nobody knows anything about Hedge. It is just too....convenient."

Experience told him that she was right, somewhere there were clues. They just needed to find them.

"Okay, it's getting late now, but first thing tomorrow let's have another look at the statements. If you are right Cromwell, then we need to find the inconsistencies," he said. "In the meantime, I'll see you inside."

Cromwell smiled.

"Maybe we can have a drink later?" he said as he opened the door into the building.

"Sure...Sir," she said in reply, "I'd like that."

CHAPTER 19

Cannon had woken early. The cool evenings that he and Michelle had considered pleasant, were about to change. It was about to get colder.

The day had started with a wind blowing from the west. It was soft but it gave notice that the day could be expected to develop into a dirty evening. The sunrise in the morning had been spectacular. The high-level cirrus clouds over the sea would move over Melbourne later. The *relative* warmth caused by the north winds blowing from the centre of the country during the past few days had now been replaced. For the next few days at least, the expectation was for rain.

He ignored the full breakfast that Emily had offered, grabbing himself a piece of toast and an apple as he left the house. He pulled his jacket around himself to keep warm from the early morning chill, Pete having already left the house to carry on with the milking. Cannon walked silently towards the stable block. In the early morning light, he stepped cautiously along the road towards the stables.

He had left Michelle fast asleep. Over the jetlag now, his body clock settled, he found himself feeling so much better, his mind sharper. During the night he had the best sleep he had had for quite a while. He was feeling relaxed, but something had started to bother him. Something that had been said didn't add up. He had no idea what it was, but it was there. Maybe he was imagining it?

The prospect of improving the fitness of *Flimflam* and *Binge-Eater* and even that of *Montego Girl* excited him. He was in his element. It was what he was good at. He smiled to himself as he entered the barn.

In the back room the staff, the stablehands, and others were already hard at work and they acknowledged him as he walked towards the stall of *Wings*. Cannon was on a mission. He was part of the team now, albeit a small one, and in just a relatively short period of time, he had become someone who the rest of the team trusted, someone who they could work with. He was impressed by the way he had been embraced into this small community of people. If this was a microcosm of the way Australia as a country accepted you, he was slowly beginning to understand the *Aussie* way.

It wasn't what he wanted. It wasn't what he needed.

Binge-Eater lay on the ground, his off-hind leg shattered.

The horse's rider held its head trying to keep the horse calm. Trying to comfort the animal the best way he could.

The accident was just that. Two horses jumping fences together, one rider less confident than the other. A rider sending a message through his legs, his request to the horse underneath him. Jump!

The horse jumping, early, too early. Smashing a trailing leg on the fence. Unseating the rider, and both hitting the ground hard, the horse breaking a leg.

"Try and keep him still," Cannon said.

Binge-Eater was still trying to stand, despite some of the bone in the leg having pierced the skin.

"Where's the Vet?" the jockey asked.

"On her way, I think. I hope!" replied Cannon.

"I hope she gets here quickly the poor horse is in a lot of pain,"

"I know, I know," Cannon repeated sadly. He also knew what would happen next.

Debra Ryan administered the final dose of barbiturates, pentobarbital, having sedated *Binge-Eater* earlier with xylazine to relax the horse.

Cannon and Pete watched on. It had taken twenty minutes for the Vet to arrive after Cannon had called Pete to tell him what had happened.

While waiting, Cannon had watched as *Binge-Eater's* jockey cried. He was close to tears himself at times. He had seen death on a racecourse before. He had his own experiences. He didn't want to see any more.

Flimflam had been led away and was now resting in his box. It was late morning, the sun was hidden away behind a skin of watery grey clouds. The rain was coming soon. The wind was slowly increasing in strength. Blades of loose grass blew around their feet as the small group stood around the carcass of an animal that just a few hours previously, was training to race in the next few days.

"You can't blame the jockey," Cannon said, "It was just one of those freak accidents that can happen at any time."

Pete was quiet. It was the first horse of his that had needed to be euthanized.

"What happened?" he asked.

"Basically, it was just bad luck," replied Cannon. "Both *Binge-Eater* and *Flimflam* were jumping over the hurdles, not even the chase fences, and somehow *Binge-Eater* took off way to early at the jump and caught a trailing leg on the fence. He landed and smashed his off-hind leg. Any other time he may have got away with just the fall. Today…"

"And *Flimflam?*"

"The horse is fine. He's been put away now. I didn't do anything else with him, so he hasn't had much exercise at all. I sent him straight back to the stables."

"Okay," said Pete sighing deeply, "thank goodness for small mercies. It's just as well the horse was mine and not one of the other owners," he said. "It would be a real nightmare if this got out."

"What do you mean?" asked Cannon.

"Well, technically Mike you don't have a license to train out here. I just don't want people, the racing authorities, to think that I absolved myself of responsibility by giving the training responsibility of my horses to you. I could lose my license and could face a fine if it became known. I should have applied for a Visiting Trainer's License for you. It would have been so much easier."

"That's true Pete, but let's not worry about that for now. I'm sorry if I've put you in a spot. I'm more than happy to stop if you think that's best," he answered.

"No, no, it's fine Mike," Pete replied, "I'm just a little shell shocked if I'm honest. I know these things occur but when it does happen to you, well it's a bit hard to accept."

"Tell me about it," Cannon replied, thinking back to the Grand National.

"I'll arrange for the carcass to go to the knackery," Deb Ryan said. She had not spoken until now. Rather concentrating on the horse that she had just euthanized. She had watched how the light had left its eyes, the breathing slowed, and the end come.

Pete nodded.

"Thanks, Deb," he said, "much appreciated. Do you need any help?"

"No," she answered, "I'll be fine."

Arranging for a horse transport to take the dead horse to the local knackery wasn't something Debra Ryan did every day, though it was not unusual. She and other Vets in the region were called to treat horses as necessary. Births, deaths, and injuries were all part of life.

Deb Ryan was good at what she did. She was respected and it was why Pete used her more than the others, especially treating his own racehorses. Her reputation in helping to get equine athletes back on the racecourse almost preceded her. She had an affinity with them and that was why she was often the on-course Vet at various race meetings in the region.

In any one week, she would be at the applicable track at least twice. Each race meeting required to have a Vet present to ensure that the horses racing that day were fit and healthy. The Vet would always be at the start of each race, available to consult with if anything had occurred pre-race that a jockey felt was impacting his or her mount. This could include a horse arriving lame at the starting stalls, having noisy breathing, feet problems, a bad action, or even the horse just being cranky. These were just some of the issues an on-course Vet needed to contend with. Much of what went on at times like these were not visible to the race going public, who were generally too far away from the starting gates. Sometimes if the TV cameras at the course were focused on the start, it was occasionally possible to see what a Vet may be required to do. The wider TV public at home would often have a better view, but generally, the activities behind the starting stalls before a race were of little interest to anyone. It was all about the race. Most of the meetings Deb Ryan attended were local. Country meetings. Occasionally she was required to travel to a picnic meeting and every now and again a metropolitan meeting but that was very rare.

In addition to checking out the physical condition of each race's participants, she would be responsible to obtain the necessarily required swabs of those horses winning a race. Where a club also chose to test other runners in the same race she would procure the swabs or blood samples required. These were necessary to ensure the integrity of the sport.

While dealing with racehorses which to her was the most fulfilling part of her job as a Vet, many of the animals she dealt with in any one week, included cats, dogs, mice, rats, rabbits….pets, that often when they couldn't be saved from injury or illness she would need to euthanize. Most belonged to households. Occasionally they could be strays or animals injured or found on the road that were lost or had no microchip within them to determine who owned them. If she did need to put a domestic animal down it was normally taken away afterwards by the owner. Children, parents doing so to arrange their own burial, and to grieve in their own time.

Unfortunately, taking away a 500kg horse wasn't easy. It required specialized equipment. In addition, there were formalities to be undertaken. Racing Australia needed to be advised of *Binge-Eater's* demise by lodging a *Death Notification Form*. Deb Ryan's cause of death certificate would then allow the horse to be de-registered and the carcass disposed of properly.

Pete knew she would handle everything. He took one final look at what was previously one of his racing hopes, *Binge-Eater*, then walked away. He headed towards the house, shoulders down.

"He's taking it pretty hard."

"I can see that," Cannon replied, "I feel that I've let him down."

She looked at him noticing the seriousness on Cannon's face. This was only their second meeting, but she was beginning to like him. Cannon showed empathy towards people and animals. It was a trait that she always thought worthy in a man.

"I don't think you should feel that way. These things happen."

"True, but when you are entrusted to look after someone else's horse as a trainer, I think you have both responsibility and accountability to ensure its safety and well-being."

She could not argue with his position, instead saying, "It was an accident. You yourself made that point."

"Yes, you're right, it could have happened anytime. At least the *jock* is okay, though I guess a little shook up, and *FlimFlam* is none the worse for wear. So that's a positive," he said.

Ryan looked at Cannon again, then she took out her mobile phone from one of her jeans pockets. She turned away as she spoke into the mouthpiece, walking away from him in slow circles as she arranged for *Binge-Eater* to be collected.

"They'll be here in about half an hour," she said once she had made the necessary arrangements. "I think it best if you go back to the house and have a chat with Pete. Leave things with me and I'll sort everything out here."

Cannon looked around. There was just the two of them. The day had started out positively but now any thought of working with *Montego Girl*, which had been the plan once he had finished with the jumpers was now long forgotten.

He looked up at the sky, the weather was changing. Rain was on its way and the wind was gaining strength. It was going to be a wet afternoon. The cold and the wet were better for horses that ran in jumps racing, he thought, as it made the landings on the softer ground so much better on the horses' legs.

It was a pity that the rain was going to arrive too late for *Binge-Eater*.

Silently he walked away from her, his thoughts to himself. He headed towards the house.

CHAPTER 20

He realized he was being myopic. Focusing on one case. They needed a breakthrough.

"Let's have another look at the statements," he said, "especially those we took yesterday, and let's compare them with what they said previously."

Cromwell, Bruce, and Alworth sat at the table in their makeshift situation room. Bossin and Twilden were arranging coffees.

Fortunately, Bruce had been left alone by his boss that morning. There had been no calls from Thatcher and Bruce was glad for it. He had nothing to report back on, so not having to have a conversation with Thatcher was good news.

There were only eight statements to read through, and these were spread across the three veterinary practices in the town, plus a farmer, another trainer, and Pete Brownlow. Bruce had studied them overnight as he sat in his hotel room. Dinner with Cromwell had been quick, Thai, from *Mango-Thai* on Murray Street.

Five of the personal statements that they reviewed were compared against those of two years prior. They included all the Vets still practicing in the town plus those trainers that Hedge dealt with in the time just before his murder. None of the individuals concerned had anything to add to that that they had been able to recall two years previously. There were no inconsistencies or any changes to what was asked at the time and that asked in the latest interviews. The other three statements they checked were from people who were not even living in the area when Hedge died but who knew of him.

"I can't see anything unusual in here," Bruce said, "what am I actually looking for? I think we are wasting our time."

Cromwell sat back in her chair raising her hands above her head, frustrated. "There must be something here," she said.

Bossin and Twilden came into the room and distributed the coffees.

Bossin looked towards Alworth to judge the feeling in the room. Alworth shook his head imperceptibly, allowing his colleague to sit at the table without commenting. It was the best thing to do.

"Alright," Bruce said. "Let's go back to basics. The first thing we need to do is rule out those we believe had nothing to do with Hedge's murder. Those that had alibis."

"All of them seem to have alibis, Sir," responded Alworth. "Each other! It seems like everybody we have taken a statement from has the same story. Almost a mirror or a copy of the others' statements."

"What did you say?" asked Bruce.

"I'm just saying, the statements all seem very familiar."

Bruce took a deep breath. Was it possible that there was collusion between the locals? Did they know what had happened to Hedge but were hiding something? If so what? Why? It didn't make any sense.

She read out the names. "Walt Grovedale, George Sormond, Deborah Ryan, Max Optin, Peter Brownlow. All of them had some dealings with Timothy Hedge in the past," she said, "and every one of them has indicated in their statements from two years ago, and repeated over the past few days, that they know nothing about his murder."

"And you think one of them is lying?" Bruce asked.

"Yes Sir, I do. Or at least someone is."

"And you've drawn that conclusion based on…?"

"Perfection," she answered.

He looked confused.

"Everything is just *too* perfect," she continued. "Maybe it's intuition, maybe it's something else, but I sense that somehow the statements have been compromised. It's as if everyone who gave a statement had already agreed on what to say, what to write. They all seem too clinical. The words used are almost exactly the same in each."

"Maybe, but perhaps it's because the questions asked were the same to every person?" he replied. He was getting tired of the conjecture.

"No Sir," she replied, "I think there is a cover-up somehow, and all or some of these five," she pointed to the documents spread out on the table, "know more than they are saying."

"That may be, but it's not getting us anywhere," he said. "At this stage, we have no evidence to that effect. Hedge could have been killed by anyone. What we need to find out is a possible motive, the why, then we can work out the who."

Bruce had to admit that he and the team were clutching at straws. In the two years since Hedge's death, nothing new had occurred, no new evidence had raised its head, and now the principal suspects, according to Cromwell's *gut instinct*, were protecting each other.

He looked at her skeptically.

He needed something! In almost complete desperation but being hopeful of progress elsewhere, he asked if there were any new developments regarding the body in the bush case.

Nobody responded. They had been focused on the Hedge matter. Bruce was growing even more impatient.

"Well let's have a look at what we know," he said. "Firstly, from initial DNA tests and physical analysis of the skeleton, we've been advised that the body seems to be of someone, a male, of Far Eastern, Malaysian or Filipino, descent."

"A tourist perhaps? Or a backpacker? Someone who had no friends or family here?" asked Bossin.

"It's possible. That would account for no one coming forward at the time of his disappearance," replied Bruce, "however one thing that doesn't seem to make any sense, is the fact that the victim starved to death."

Cromwell jumped in. "Maybe that's the answer, Sir," she said. "Maybe there was *no* crime. Maybe the man went hiking, somehow got himself into trouble, fell where he did, and he couldn't walk or crawl out and slowly died of thirst and lack of food?"

"That's not a bad theory Constable, but what about his clothes? What about a phone? We didn't find anything like that near the body. Also, what about any hiking gear, a backpack, a water bottle, and why particularly was he on *that* track? There are so many questions about this matter. It doesn't make sense," he replied.

"Is it possible the body was found by someone and the clothes stripped off them. Stolen along with anything else, like his boots or shoes, his phone?"

"And then the body hidden away again?"

"Yes," she responded. "It sounds callous, but it's not impossible."

Bruce mulled it over. He wasn't convinced but he was happy to consider it.

"I think, we'll have to pay the good people of Forrest another visit to see what they know," he said. "In the mean-time, I think we need to try and find out where Timothy Hedge was living just before he ended up with his head smashed in. It's clear that he moved around a lot and that he didn't have a *fixed* address as we know it." He pointed towards the folder that contained a copy of the report drawn up by the local police force, two years ago. It had been used by Bruce as the starting point of *his* own investigation at the time. The report provided little of value other than the comment by the local police in Colac querying the fact that Hedge's body had been found some seventy kilometers away from where he was known to hang out. The greater Colac area was where he *lived*, they believed. Apollo Bay, where he was found dead, was not his *patch*. So why was he there?

The police had been unable to trace his movements for the weeks prior to him being found in the garbage truck. According to those who he worked for, those who had given statements, he did have a mobile phone, but the police investigation into its use had found little about it. They had the number of the phone, and triangulation tests had been tried on it to determine where Hedge may have travelled to. The results were unsuccessful, unclear. The reception between Colac, Forrest, and Apollo Bay was poor in certain places. Even getting a 3G service at times was a problem. It was eventually established that the mobile phone had been turned off for some considerable time before Hedge was found dead.

The phone itself had never been found, however.

Bruce turned to the team. He wanted to stir them up a bit. Get them going. He wondered if Cromwell's theory had some merit. He decided to run with it, after all, he had nothing else to go on.

"In the light of what we know, which is very little currently, I think we need a stronger, more direct approach," he said. "Constable let's see who we can ruffle. If you are right, someone might blink. So, it's about time we put some pressure on. Let's see if something gives. Kicking the can down the road has got us nowhere, so let's stir things up a bit! Let's create some doubt as to what we know. The FUD factor," he continued. *"Fear, Uncertainty, and Doubt.* If Cromwell is right, then we may have set the scene for something to happen. If there is collusion regarding Hedge's death, then it's possible, if you excuse the metaphor, that over the past few days we may have put a cat amongst the pigeons, and someone may crack," he went on. "It may not work but we need to try something. I'm getting pressure from the City and I don't want the local country coppers, present company excluded," he said, nodding towards Alworth and Bossin, "thinking that we are not helping them either."

The room was quiet for a while. Everyone knew what Bruce meant, what was inferred, and hidden within his words.

Shape up or everyone is out.

Cromwell eventually thanked him for listening and considering her theory.

In reply he said. "Bossin, you and Cromwell are off to Forrest tomorrow. Alworth, you are with me. We are off to Apollo Bay."

CHAPTER 21

The rest of the day had been difficult. From lunchtime onwards, Cannon had spent it sitting in a lounge chair, ruminating.

In just a few days *Flimflam* and *Binge-Eater* should be racing he thought. It was something he was struggling to come to terms with. *Flimflam* was still an acceptance at three upcoming meetings as was *Binge-Eater,* but sadly *Binge-Eater* would now be scratched, permanently.

Was it because of him? His advice? Should he be doubting himself?

The afternoon had dragged. There had been silence throughout the house. Even Stephanie appeared to tiptoe about the place when she moved from the kitchen and back to her room. She spoke in whispers to Emily.

CHAPTER 22

Max Optin's body was not a pretty sight. It was mangled. One of his legs had been completed severed from the torso, and it lay several metres away from the rest of his trunk.

The head lay at an odd angle to the rest of the body, twisted so that the back of the neck was facing forward, resting on the chest. Blood had oozed from the cavity that had opened up when the forehead had been hit and was sliced apart. It and the brain matter had now dried.

Optin's eyes were still open, his face now permanently set in a grimace. The horror of his death etched across his features.

It was just after nine in the morning. Bruce had been about to leave for Apollo Bay. Cannon had gotten over his *funk* of the previous day after he and Pete had spoken about things during the course of the evening. They had been about to start training the two horses, *Flimflam* and *Operator Please* together.

The phone call about the body had been made to Pete by one of the farmworkers who were out preparing the fences for that morning's exercises. It was just before dawn, around six-thirty, when he found what was left of Optin.

"Run down," Cannon said to Bruce.

"*Mowed* down more likely. Looks like he had no chance."

Cannon scanned the ground. It was light now, but still grey. Pete had gone off to make sure the ambulance and the scene of crime team that was expected soon would be able to access the training area when they arrived. They were coming from Geelong. It was where the closest team resided.

The tracks of the tyres used by the car that had torn Optin's body apart were clearly visible on the soft ground. Overnight rain had allowed the tracks, the skid marks, to be embedded in the ground. The tracks leading away from the farm were also visible.

"The forensic teams will find this very useful," continued Bruce, pointing at the divots, the mud spatter. "It should be easy to track the type of car used. The tyre impressions are very clear," he said.

"What puzzles me," Cannon replied, "is why he was out here at all? Who was capable of getting him to come out so early in the morning to this part of the farm, the actual jumps training area? And on what pretext?"

"All good questions, Mike," Bruce said. "Hopefully we'll be able to get some answers soon."

Cannon looked at Bruce. A current policeman and an ex-cop standing together at a crime scene. Cannon found the experience confronting. It wasn't what he had hoped for. Death always seemed to follow him, he thought. Death of a racehorse yesterday. Death of a man today.

Bruce took his mobile phone from a coat pocket. The chill of the morning necessitating the need to wear a coat now. The weather had begun turning towards winter. He dialled a number, waited, then asked the question as to where the SOCOs had gotten too?

Cannon listened to Bruce's request for information.

The answer appeared to satisfy the policeman.

"The SOCOs should be here shortly," he said.

"I guess I need to give you some space then?" Cannon replied. "I'm less a witness and more of a hanger-on."

"Actually Mike, I think you're likely to be more than that. As this investigation unfolds I think you may be able to help me more than you think."

"How do you mean?"

"Well, I didn't expect anything to happen so quickly, but I think when we followed up with new statements over the past few days about the Hedge case, we may have stirred a hornet's nest."

"That was the case you mentioned when we met at Terang? When you were asking Pete about Hedge and if he knew what had happened to him?"

"That's right. Constable Cromwell had a feeling something might happen," he said, looking at Optin's body which was still lying where it was found. Bruce considered covering it with his coat but decided not to disturb the area immediately surrounding the body.

"Intuition?"

"Perhaps…"

"And how do you think I am going to help?"

"I'd like you to keep your eyes open for me," Bruce said, "around the farm, at the track. Somebody knows something, and they may let something slip about what's *really* going on," he answered.

The sound of a car and an ambulance coming up the track from their left silenced their conversation.

Cannon realized he was being dragged into something. The past….

The dreams he tried to forget.

Twelve thousand miles away from home didn't take away what was in his head.

And what was in it now was just beginning to form a shape.

The crime scene tent was quickly constructed. The immediate area around the body was being preserved. Photo's taken. Soil samples removed, tyre impressions collected. It would be a long day in the field. Training of the horses was impossible.

Cannon left Bruce to deal with the investigating teams and he returned to the house.

Once Bruce was satisfied that the SOCOs in their white suits had started with their work which would last all day, he made the call to Alworth. They needed to get down to Apollo Bay.

CHAPTER 23

"It was his own car?" queried Bruce.

"Yes," replied Cromwell, "we found it burnt out in a paddock a couple of miles away."

Bruce seemed incredulous.

He and Cromwell were sitting in the situation room back at the Colac police station. She updated him with what had occurred since the body of Optin had been removed after the SOCO team had concluded their work.

Bruce and Alworth had returned from Apollo Bay. Alworth now having gone off duty leaving Bruce to consider what they had been able to glean from the statements they had taken during the day. It was after 7 pm and it had been a long day. The drive to and from the *bay* after finding the body of Optin had been a bit of a distraction. While it gave Bruce time to think, what he had not realized until now was how Optin had been possibly duped to his death? Cromwell's update provided clarity in some way but also added a level of complexity. There were too many unanswered questions.

Even subsequent mobile calls to the leading SOCO, Richard Juno, about the crime scene, had resulted in a level of confusion. Apart from the body and the tyre tracks, there was very little to go on. The vehicle used to run down the Vet had been found but it was now just a shell. It had been torched and there was little DNA evidence available from it.

"So that would mean the killer was likely with Optin originally? That they knew each other, and Optin was willing to go with whoever it was to the training ground at such an early time this morning."

"Yes, it would appear that way."

"Using his own car?" Bruce continued.

"Yep."

"So, whoever it was with Optin, the killer, clearly had planned what he or she had intended to do. Optin's car being torched means that the killer or killers had a plan to remove as much evidence from the car as possible, as soon as possible?"

Cromwell said, "If you were Optin you wouldn't expect to be run over by someone you knew, especially using your own car."

"Agreed," replied Bruce. "So, do we have any timelines? Do we have any details about people's movements yet?"

The Constable scanned a summary of what she and Bossin had been able to establish from their initial enquiries since Optin's body had been found.

"We met with the other Vets during the day plus we had a conversation with George Sormond. We haven't spoken with Walt Grovedale as yet, but what is interesting is that the burnt-out car was found on his property which borders on that of the Brownlow's. The car itself though had been hidden in a bit of a gully so the fire couldn't be seen from the Grovedale's house. Apparently, Grovedale has been away for a few days in Queensland looking at buying into a stud farm up there. His wife thought the smoke from the fire was somebody burning off."

"How convenient," replied Bruce.

"From what we can speculate, Sir," she said, "It would appear that Optin drove to the training track with his killer. Someone who he knew. From there that individual murdered him and then drove off with his car, subsequently setting it on fire and leaving nothing but a shell. Obviously, the intent being to destroy as much evidence as possible through the torching."

Bruce thought for a second about the crime scene.

"Footprints? In the mud? Any?"

"The SOCOs have done what they can so far. They've taken tyre and shoe imprints, photographed the entire area, taken necessary soil samples, but they did highlight that whoever was with Optin, took great care to try and eradicate most of the shoe imprints. We were lucky to get some partial prints apparently. We have a tread type from the shoes but not a complete set. Size *and* print still need to be worked on to get a better picture."

"Any initial thoughts?"

"At this stage, I hadn't wanted to speculate until we had spoken, Sir," she answered. "but the shoe prints we have, are all on the small side. I think they may belong to one of the riders, a jockey perhaps?"

"And did we get anything from the site where the car was found?"

"Not really Sir," she answered. "Whoever did this, knew exactly what they were doing. They knew exactly how to get rid of anything incriminating."

"Such as…?"

Cromwell started to count on her left hand. Reeling off a list in her head.

"One," she said, "The footprints. Of little use to us currently, both at the murder site and the place where Optin's car was found. Two, the accelerant used. There was no sign anywhere of a can or canister that was used to transport it. From the initial investigation, we now know it was petrol. It could have come from anywhere. The SOCOs believe that they can identify the type from an analysis of the remains of the car. Something to do with exothermic oxidation reaction," she said looking at her notes, "however that will take some time."

"And this helps…how?" he asked.

"It doesn't in the short term but may help in the long term," she replied. "*but* we have another problem."

"What's that?" he asked, his stomach beginning to growl. He hadn't eaten since he and Alworth had bought a scallop pie at lunchtime from the bakery on the main street that ran through Apollo Bay, The Great Ocean Road.

"How the killer got away."

"Meaning?"

"There was no sign of another vehicle at the site where Optin's car was torched."

"Perhaps it had been parked somewhere else?" he replied.

"That's possible, but we managed to get some local resources from the police station here during the day, to help with a ground search," she said, giving a slight nod of her head to the four walls of the room, "and we found nothing in the immediate or wider areas, despite the ground being soft."

"What about prints?"

"Hardly anything at all Sir. The only thing we could find were bicycle tyre tracks."

"Bicycle?"

"Yes Sir. It might sound strange but it's possible the killer or killers rode off on a bicycle after burning out the car!"

Bruce could only admire the ingenuity of it all.

"A bicycle?' he repeated.

"Yes."

"And have we looked yet as to who may own bikes around here?"

"It would appear *most* people do," she answered. "In fact, everyone we have spoken to has at least one. Seems like it's quite a popular pastime, riding. It will be almost impossible to find a tyre tread on a single bike that matches those at the crime scene. Most tyres on bikes sold these days are exactly the same, unless you have or ask for, a unique set."

Bruce sighed. He understood where Cromwell was coming from. He thought of the other case they were struggling with, trying to resolve. *The body on the track.*

Not being too far from Forrest and the many cycling paths and tracks it was well known for, many people in the area, Colac and surrounds were likely big users of bicycles in one way or another. Bruce knew that being out in the country and away from busy roads, meant the locals would very likely use bikes as a key part of their daily recreation. Cromwell was right. It would be almost impossible to trace a tyre tread to a single bike.

Cromwell continued, interrupting Bruce's thought process. "Seems like every month there are cycle races between Forrest and Apollo Bay, through the Otways," she said. "It's almost like a mini Tour-de-France. The roads are apparently full of lycra-clad pensioners at times," she said facetiously.

He threw out a speculative question, expecting a negative answer.

"Any ideas about the type of bike we are talking about?" he asked. "Road? Off-road?"

"It's way too soon to say, Sir. However, as you know getting rid of a bike is quite easy. It can be dumped anywhere, even taken apart," she answered. "The bike used to get away from the scene could be in bits by now. Could even be at the bottom of a dam."

"How many sets of tracks at the scene are we talking about?" he asked.

"At least ten. Some very different from others. The track that the car was on is used regularly for training and racing by a local cross-country team. Mountain bike racing!" she clarified. "Also, it's used by BMX riders as a starting point for a regular monthly 5-mile race. It seems Grovedale, used to ride in races years ago but can't anymore due to back issues. He suffered the injury about 7 years ago. It left him hospitalized for a while. He was born and bred here, inherited well, and has been a highly successful businessman. Apparently, he wants to get into horses now, train them. He's interstate currently looking at stud farms it seems. That's what money can do for you," she said, "lucky bastard!"

Bruce smiled inwardly. "Anything else?" he asked. "What about timing? Have we been able to find out people's movements during the day? Surely someone, for example, a neighbour noticed that Optin was in his car so early this morning? Especially if he was seen driving with someone else?"

"That's the problem."

"What is?"

Cromwell sighed. "Optin was a Vet. He got called out at all different times of the day. So, when his surgery was closed, he would take calls after hours and travel to wherever he needed to be to treat the animal. Remember he said he often slept at his surgery as it was easier for him not to go home."

"Yes, but he also said he didn't really treat large animals anymore, he was too tired, remember. He said he hadn't worked with anything larger than a labrador for years."

"Yes Sir, I know."

"Which means he wasn't expecting to be asked to work on a horse or maybe another animal at all? Perhaps he thought he was being asked to help someone he knew. To be a kind of back-up?"

"We don't know if that was the case," she answered, "but if he knew the killer, which we think he did, then the killer would have known Optin's physical capabilities. Frankly, it doesn't make sense. I think the whole idea of going to the training track was a ruse. I think Optin and his killer were meeting for another reason altogether."

"But why there?"

"I'm not sure, Sir. I can only assume that Optin was convinced by his murderer to drive out to the training track, possibly under some false pretense?"

Bruce considered this.

"Yes, that's possible, especially given the time of day," he answered. Then it dawned on him. "So, if he was with someone, someone he knew then you may be right Constable, perhaps Optin thought he was meeting that person to discuss something else? Meanwhile whoever killed him had planned to do so and had set everything up in advance?" he said.

The constable stayed quiet.

"If that is the case though," Bruce said aloud, "Why go to so much trouble, and for what reason? What possible motive could there be?" he questioned.

They sat in *Oddfellows* on Gellibrand Street, a short walk from the police station. Bruce had decided on a draft beer, Cromwell water.

They had eaten in silence for most of the meal, acknowledging the waiting staff with a thank you when the food was delivered to their table.

Eventually, she had to ask. "How did it go down in Apollo Bay? Did you find out anything?"

Bruce drank the last of the beer in his glass and wiped his mouth with a napkin.

"To be honest, not very much," he answered. "We had the same issue there has we have here. Two years is a long time. Very few people can remember the Hedge incident."

"What about the owner of the house in whose rubbish bin the body of Hedge was stuffed?"

"Gone."

"Gone?"

"Yes, sold the house. Moved interstate. The current owner uses the place as a holiday home now. Lives in Melbourne most of the time."

"Shit," she said, rather more loudly than she had intended. Some of the remaining diners looked around to express their displeasure at her language. The restaurant was still quite full despite the time. It was nearly 9:30. Bruce was beginning to yawn.

"Anything else?" she asked. "Did anybody in Apollo Bay know Hedge at all?"

"Yes, a few people did, though I don't expect too much to come from what they said. We took their statements and I've asked Alworth to verify the detail against what we collected previously. He should be able to give me something tomorrow."

"I guess it's better than nothing," she replied.

"Maybe. Time will tell," he said, yawning again.

"You look tired."

"I'm buggered to be honest," he replied. "It's been a very long day. I'm no use to man nor beast tonight, I just need to get a few hours sleep. Hopefully in the morning, I'll be a little brighter," he continued. "At the moment my head feels like it's about to burst."

Cromwell called over the waitress, asking for the bill.
She paid it with her own credit card.

CHAPTER 24

The day had dawned, grey and wet. The wind had risen, and the temperature dropped. The training track was still a crime scene and neither man nor horse was allowed anywhere near it. While the scene would be protected Cannon was pleased that it was someone else and not him that now had to deal with investigating what had happened to Optin. He knew from his background that some crimes could be solved easily. He doubted this one could be.

He stood at the window of the lounge room. He held a large cup of tea in his hand that had already gone cold. He had not taken a sip from it since he had made it for himself in the kitchen. He had been thinking about the murder of Optin and was lost in his thoughts when Emily and Michelle came into the room.

"Do you want the racing on?" Emily asked.

Cannon didn't reply. He remained standing, staring outside the window. Rain splattered against the pane, a soft drumming effect.

"Sorry Mike," she repeated a little more loudly, "but do you want the racing channel on?" she asked again.

Cannon turned around, facing both the women. He flushed.

"Oh, yes, thanks Emily," he said, "are you sure it will be okay?"

Michelle walked up to him and gave him a peck on the cheek.

"Mike, Emily wouldn't offer if she didn't think it was alright."

"I know darling," he responded, "but I'm beginning to feel that we've brought Pete and Emily nothing but bad luck since we got here and that perhaps we are in the way."

Michelle sighed.

Emily picked up the remote for the TV and pressed a button on the handset. The TV came to life and a Lifestyle program came onto the screen. She quickly pressed a few buttons and changed the program to the racing channel.

"Here you go," she said, holding out the remote to Cannon, "enjoy yourself. We're off...."

He was surprised. In fact, he was confused. A murder had taken place on Pete's property, yet neither Emily nor Pete seemed concerned in the slightest. Now it was just before lunchtime and even Michelle seemed to have put what had happened to Optin aside.

"Where are you going?" he asked.

"Into Colac," replied Michelle. "It's Stephanie's birthday next week and we wanted to get her something. I hope you don't mind Mike, to be left on your own for a while?" she asked.

Cannon nodded towards the window. "Will you be okay, it's a bit wet and wild out there," he said, the sky now dark, grey, muddy.

"We'll be fine," Emily replied, "I'm driving," she laughed, looking at Michelle. "I'm used to looking out for kangaroos on the road," she teased.

Michelle had indicated her concern about driving on roads that she was unfamiliar with. Being in the country increased her worry. Her concern for the wildlife in the area, especially if she had been required to drive at night or in poor light was palpable. She knew about the 'roos, but the wombats, echidnas, and other marsupials like possums, wallabies, and koalas being active in the night-time and possibly being on a road when she was driving worried her. She had made both Emily and Cannon promise her that they would drive during their stay.

"Okay," he said, "have a good time. See you later."

Michelle asked him if he needed anything, but Cannon just shook his head.

"No, nothing at all. I think I just need to take a load off," he replied, trying to sound relaxed for Michelle's sake. He wasn't comfortable at all, the past few days had shaken him. What he had expected from the trip wasn't what he had experienced so far.

From the highs of arriving safely in the country through to *Wings'* win, then the accident with *Binge-Eater* through to the murder of Max Optin it all seemed overwhelmingly familiar, and that was without Cassie's decision to go to South Africa. He decided to warm up his tea in the microwave and watch some racing, after all, it was partially why he was here. He knew Pete was out working on the farm somewhere, but he didn't feel it would be appropriate tagging along with his host, particularly given what had happened to Optin. All thoughts of working Pete's jumpers were now forgotten.

Cannon knew that tomorrow would be different, life carried on…at times he wondered how, and why things happened as they did….

As he sat down to watch the racing from Pakenham he felt the familiarity and the comfort of just watching the races. He could feel how 'just watching' was starting to ease his muscles, relax his mind. At some point he nodded off for a while, on the screen race 3 from the course was nearly about to start and he realised that he must have fallen asleep for about an hour. The race itself was a non-event, the favourite winning by over two lengths. However, just before the start of the race, the commentator referred to one of the horses that had reared up in the stall and needed to be vetted. He noticed then that the Vet for the day was Deb Ryan. The horse that had reared, *Time Traveller* had gashed itself on the metal sides of the stall and Cannon could see blood ooze from the skin torn from a shoulder. He knew what the decision would be and soon the on-course announcer made the necessary statements to those on course and those watching from home that the Vet had ruled the animal out from the race. Cannon smiled to himself. Ryan was a good Vet. She knew how best to treat animals, he thought. Although to be fair, any Vet worth their salt would have made the same decision.

Outside, the sky began to darken even further and the vision from the Pakenham racecourse seemed to show that the wet weather was beginning to reach there as well. The racing would continue despite the wet but the course itself could be downgraded from its current *Dead* status down to a *Slow* one. To a large degree the wetter and softer the track, the better for jumpers, but for flat racing, it was not ideal. Some horses could handle the wet and slippery conditions, but many could not, and those that didn't, found themselves not only disliking the elements but some of them almost refused to race.

Cannon made himself lunch while he continued to watch the TV. He didn't really like watching flat races but given it was the bread and butter of Australian racing, he was slowly beginning to warm to it.

Racing from another small town in South Australia filled the gaps between the Pakenham racing. Race four passed without incident though again Deb Ryan was called on to *Vet* another horse just before the running of the race. She passed the horse fit, Cannon noticing her pat the horse on the rear offside rump as encouragement.

Just prior to race 5 the weather at the Pakenham track had deteriorated and the rain was quite heavy. The jockeys had started to put visors onto their racing caps which allowed them much better vision during the race. It protected their eyes from mud spatter and other detritus kicked up by horses racing ahead of them. One of the jockeys jumped from his mount, *Spirit Level* at the starting gate, and spoke with Deb Ryan. The horse, at her request, was held by the reins and led away by a handler, taking it a hundred metres from the starting stalls. The handler encouraging the horse to trot alongside him, while Ryan watched on to assess if the jockey had good reason to be concerned. It would be dangerous to race a horse whose action, effectively how the horse was moving, was now unnatural. The danger of falling or interfering with other runners was a real possibility during a race, especially if the horse had an internal injury, one which was not evident initially. It was clear to Cannon from what he could see from his TV screen that the jockey was concerned about the horse. The commentator on the TV made the observation that the horse's best runs were on drier ground and it was possibly uncomfortable with the way the track was beginning to get softer, deteriorate. Cannon continued watching as the other horses stood still in the starting stalls. Eventually, vision returned to the Vet and the horse she had been asked to look at. It appeared that Deb Ryan was comfortable with the fitness and the mindset of *Spirit Level* and passed the horse fit to run. The jockey remounted the horse and the handler proceeded to move it towards its starting stall. Once again Deb Ryan gave the horse encouragement with a tap on the rump. It seemed to Cannon that as Vet, she was earning her money this particular day.

The race was run with the favourite finishing third and despite a good battle with the second favourite, *Tomthethumb,* a 14 to 1 shot, got home by a head. *Spirit Level* finished a tailed-off last.

Vision on the TV turned to the excited owners of the winner. Cannon walked to the window just as Pete came in through the kitchen door complaining about the weather.

"I thought you would be happy with the rain?" Cannon asked.

"I am," Pete replied, "especially given the fact that we have an upcoming race for *Flimflam* in the next few days, but in relation to the farm it makes a right bloody mess," he continued. "Everything seems to take longer to do, even the cows take their time walking up from the fields at milking time."

Cannon couldn't agree more, his experience with some of his horses at home confirmed Pete's view. The one advantage was that Cannon only had a stable to run, not a complete farm.

Pete removed his coat and headed towards the kitchen, asking Cannon if he wanted another hot drink.

Cannon declined. He followed Pete into the kitchen.

"What are you watching?" Pete asked.

"Oh, the racing from Pakenham," he replied. "I see Deb Ryan is the Vet on duty today. Looks like she's had a bit of work to do already."

"No surprise there," Pete said. "With this weather, some of the horses racing probably should have been scratched, but you know what owners are like?" he asked with a smile on his face.

"Yep," replied Cannon, the local colloquialism readily noticeable to him. What had happened to "Yes"?

The next and penultimate race from Pakenham was about five minutes from start time when Pete and Cannon moved back into the TV room to watch.

The field of twelve runners were already milling around near the start. Once again it was announced that the Vet was being asked to look at the action of another horse, *Royal Mint.* The horse itself was one of the main chances in the field. The same procedure as used with *Spirit Level* in the previous race was followed. On the TV the vision shown was poor. The rain had gotten much stronger and was whipping almost horizontally across the track. Cannon was surprised that the balance of the meeting had not yet been abandoned, but he knew that the locals loved their racing and that a bit of wet weather wouldn't put them off so easily.

Royal Mint seemed to satisfy the requirements needed by Deb Ryan to allow the horse to race and it was announced that the horse had been passed fit to run. Once again, the jockey mounted the horse, and Cannon and Pete watched Ryan patting the horse on the rump, then rubbing her hand along its flank to provide comfort and encouragement.

The race began but it was soon clear that *Royal Mint* was struggling, finishing a distant second last. It seemed like Deb Ryan didn't always get it right.

CHAPTER 25

George Sormond enjoyed being in his lounge.

The house in which it sat was beautifully furnished, the sign of a wealthy man. It sat at the end of a long drive that snaked across a series of paddocks that surrounded the building. The driveway to the front door was over a kilometre long and ran from the main road towards Geelong up to the house itself where it terminated in a ten-car parking area. On the eastern side of the property stood the stables that held a large number of horses that Sormond trained. The house itself was finished in high quality coloured brick, modern, and covered a floor area of over two hundred and fifty square metres. The furniture inside was contradictory to the building's exterior. It was large, bulky, comfortable, reminding one of the early nineteen twenties. Heavy brocaded curtains in a deep mauve framed the windows of the lounge room that they sat in. Genuine oil and watercolour racing paintings covered the walls on two sides, and a wall unit filled with trophies and awards adorned another side of the room. A cream carpet under a heavy wooden coffee table completed the picture.

"Another Bundy?" Sormond offered.

It was just after midday. The rain from the previous day had not let up and the cold front had now hit the area hard. Racing was still on, but neither Sormond nor Pete had any runners.

"No thanks," replied Cannon, who wasn't a rum drinker but had found he had enjoyed the drink offered by Sormond.

Pete however was happy to have another, and Sormond agreed to join him. Cannon noted that the warmth and calming effect of the dark amber liquid gave Pete a more noticeable glow. It was the first time in the past couple of days that Cannon had seen his host relax.

They were just less than two weeks away from the carnival and the interruptions to their planning for the event had been causing Pete to lose sleep. They had discussed where things had gotten to the previous evening. The loss of *Binge-Eater,* the halt on training, and the murder of Max Optin were the only topic of conversation between them. It was why they were now sitting with Sormond.

Once Pete and Sormond had settled down again with their drinks Cannon asked the obvious question and the reason why he and Pete had asked to meet with the other trainer.

"I assume the police have been in touch, George?"

"About Optin? Yes," Sormond replied. The trainer was a big man, at least 125 kilograms, and had the girth to match. At just shy of six feet tall he appeared more round than tall. His hair was silver-grey, thick. He had a bulbous nose, blue-veined and red dry skin. Cannon had noticed that his hands were small for such a big man, but according to Pete, Sormond was able to work wonders with his horses. He had a reputation of being able to calm any horse, especially those that were highly strung, nervous, or just irascible. Pete also let Cannon know that Sormond had been on his 200-hectare property, training locally for the past twenty years or so. Sormond was also well known in the area for his training exploits and his drinking. Divorced many years previously he did what he wanted when he wanted to. He had support from a team of people who had worked with him for many years. His housekeeper, Mary McKenzie kept the place neat and tidy, which was just as well.

"They came to see me the other day," he continued. "Interviewed me and asked me what I knew about Optin."

"And do you…did you, know much about him? Or why he would go out to the training track that day?"

"Other than him being a Vet we used years ago, then *no* is the answer. I haven't used him for a long time due to him no longer looking after larger animals. I generally use Deb Ryan or someone from the other practice if I need someone to look after one of my horses."

Cannon considered this.

"Before Optin's death, the police were asking us at Terang about a man called Hedge, did they speak to you about that?"

"They asked me about the poor man when they came to see me. I remembered him ending up in the back of a garbage truck a couple of years ago. Shocking!" he said. "He worked for me on occasion, but he was pretty much a loner. He did a lot of menial jobs for me, nothing special really."

"From what Pete has told me," replied Cannon, "it seems like everyone who knew him had the same view."

"Well then, we are all in sync. I'm not sure how I can help the police any more than I have. I told them all I know about Hedge and that's somewhat limited," he responded, "but we don't know what we don't know and that's the only thing I can say about it."

Despite his friendly demeanour, it seemed to Cannon that Sormond was concerned about something. "Maybe Walt Grovedale can tell them something about the man that I can't?" he continued, "but as far as I'm concerned the police now know everything I knew about Hedge."

They sat silent for a few seconds. Pete finished his drink. Sormond looked off into space.

Cannon looked at both men then decided to change the subject.

"How are the horses going?" he asked, trying to sound neutral.

"Not bad," Sormond replied, "not bad at all," he repeated. "I've been lucky this past couple of months," he said continuing, "I had a winner at Terang, on the same day that your horse *Wings of Dawn* won, and I've had a bit of success elsewhere as well. Two weeks ago, I had a winner at Cranborne which meant that I had beaten my previous season's record for winners. So overall things are going okay, and the *cattle* are racing really well, except for one of my mares," he said somewhat sadly. "It's a horse called *Angel Transforming* who has been suffering from tendinitis. She's being stall rested now and treated with ice-packs and we have tried to immobilizer her, just in case. The owner has been getting me to run her way too often and despite me telling him what would happen he refused to listen and now she's injured. She's a very good horse though."

"Is she a jumper?" Cannon asked.

"No, not really…at least not yet."

Cannon was a little quizzical. "Not really?" he asked.

"Well, she's a little slow on the flat. I told the owner that and eventually he accepted my position, that she could be a better jumper than a flat horse. Running her in races, just because you can, didn't make sense to me so I told him to think it through and if he didn't like it then he could take the poor horse away. I hope when she recovers she can do much better over the jumps…..I think she can." he concluded.

"Hurdles or the big stuff?"

"Probably we'll start with the hurdles but if that's too quick for her then we'll try the bigger fences, the steeplechase," he answered. "She's quite smart, tough but she'll need to learn how to jump."

"And that's all the issues you have so far?" Cannon asked incredulously, almost jealously. Cannon knew that with a settled stable it brought results. What Pete and Cannon were experiencing at Pete's yard was not ideal.

A crime scene on the training track and the weather beginning to change was not conducive to great preparation for the carnival, and before that the necessary trials.

Cannon was aware that Sormond had at least two runners in the Grand Annual and one of them *Chesterman* was in with a very good chance. The horse had run second in the previous year's race. Cannon knew from Pete that Sormond had a stable of thirty-six horses, of which twelve were racing on the jump circuit and he understood from Pete that *Chesterman*, in particular, was one of the biggest rivals to *Wings* in the Grand Annual. To hear the horse was well and had no interruptions in its' preparation for the race wasn't exactly what they had hoped to hear.

CHAPTER 26

"Did you ever meet Timothy Hedge?" Bruce asked.

"Yes of course I did," answered the man, "he did some work around the harbour at times, so yes of course I met him, knew him."

The two men stood on the wooden deck of the Apollo Bay Fisherman's co-op, looking out over the harbour. The rain had eased during the morning, but the swell of the sea had not. Deep green waves crashed over the edge of the harbour wall sending plumes of spray into the air. Gulls squealed, not moving, gliding on air pockets, hovering on the breeze.

The cold front that had brought the rain and freezing fog in the morning had arrived with a vengeance. It had passed through the town during the early hours leaving an angry ocean. The boats in the harbour skipped up and down as the swell through the heads sent waves in concentric circles across the basin.

Bruce had turned up his collar to the cold. He and the other man, a sailor, stood under a leaky umbrella. Bruce believed he was being tested. If he wanted to chat and ask questions then it would be on the other man's terms.

At least I'm not on a boat being tossed around, Bruce thought, looking at the seven or eight boats being pushed around within the harbour walls.

"Which one is yours?' he asked pointing to the various vessels.

"None of those," the man said. "Mine's still out there. The *San Marino.*"

"Bloody hell mate, isn't it a bit rough now to still be fishing?"

The man considered the question. It seemed undignified to answer.

"We're fisherman," he said, "it's what we do, come hell or high water…we fish."

Bruce noted the passion in the man's voice.

"So, tell me, Mr. Henderson," Bruce asked, "do you recall the last time you saw him? Hedge I mean."

Henderson procured a frown on his forehead, thinking. "It must have been well over two years ago now, I think he did some work on my boat," he replied. "From memory, wasn't he found dead in a garbage truck?."

"You have a good memory, Mr. Henderson. Yes, it was about two years ago." Bruce replied.

Henderson smiled. "It's a small place Apollo Bay. Not a lot happens, so when an incident like that occurs, it's sort of burnt into everyone's psyche," he answered. "You don't forget that type of thing easily."

"Umm," Bruce responded.

Henderson wasn't sure if the reaction from Bruce reflected doubt or something else. He remained silent.

As the men stood looking out at the bay, clouds swamped Mariners Hill to their left, a mist enveloping the highest part of the hill that overlooked the town. The rain continued to grow in intensity.

Bruce shivered. He wondered how Alworth was getting on. The Constable had needed to check a few details from some of those who lived in the bay and who knew of Hedge at the time of his murder. It seemed that most people had limited dealings with him.

"Maybe we can go inside the building?" Bruce asked, pointing at the small office and shed that made up the co-op.

"Sure," replied Henderson, turning to show the way, walking ahead.

"All I can say Inspector is that Timothy Hedge was a bit of a trouble-maker. I'm not sure how he ended up dead, and at the time I felt really sorry for him when his body was found in that truck, but it didn't surprise me that he came to a *sticky end*."

They had moved towards the back office of the co-op. The area, a shed with a cement floor smelt of fish, both fresh and cooked.

Large cardboard boxes, sealed, were stacked up on top of each other alongside one wall. The writing on the box suggested the contents were local crayfish and crab, destined for an overseas market like China.

Bruce was happy to be inside but a little taken aback by the comment Henderson had made. When he and Alworth had followed up and reviewed the statements made by those from Apollo Bay who had known Hedge at the time of his death, none of them had mentioned that Hedge had been anything but a loner, not someone who would make trouble.

"What do you mean, a troublemaker?"

"Exactly that," Henderson replied. "Somedays he would arrive at our boat or even here at the co-op while we were working, and demand that we give him something to do. Anything. Work that he could be paid for."

"And how often was this?"

"It varied," Henderson replied, rubbing a hand across his face. "Over the years, it occurred many times. Eventually, it became a bit of a joke."

"Why was that?"

"Well because people initially felt sorry for him, but he didn't do himself any favours. He used to upset a lot of them."

"How…?"

"By being a pain in the arse, if you really want to know."

"So much so that someone wanted to murder him?" asked Bruce directly.

Henderson remained silent for a while before responding.

"I'm not sure about that Inspector. Being a pain is one thing but….." the fisherman's face contorted, and he shrugged his shoulders signifying how uncomfortable he was with the discussion.

Bruce wanted more. The generalities that Henderson had referred to were not enough. He wanted specifics.

"So, what did he do then? If he was a *pain*?" Bruce asked.

The fisherman thought for a while, looking Bruce straight in the eye, finally suggesting that what he had to say was his own opinion and that he believed would add little of value to the police investigation.

"I'll be the judge of that Mr. Henderson," Bruce said impatiently, "just tell me what you know."

Henderson turned his face away as he spoke. "We always thought that Hedge was a bit strange, ever since he popped up here," he said. "He just arrived one day, came to this very harbour and asked for a job. Had no CV, no experience of working on a trawler, nothing. Just arrived and started to make a nuisance of himself."

"Nuisance?"

"Yes, you know, just hung around, watched what we were doing while we were setting up the boat, preparing the nets and the lobster pots, that type of thing. He was always asking if he could help."

"And?"

"We ignored him at first. We didn't need any more crew, so we just let him sit there and watch. It was up to him if he stayed."

Bruce nodded, encouraging the conversation. "And this was how long ago?"

Henderson took a breath before continuing. "A good while ago, about ten years back. He used to come to the harbour every day for a month or so and just sit and watch. He used to talk a lot, just out loud, talk about all sorts of things. Things he said he had done, where he had been, experiences…you know."

"So what happened?"

"During one particular summer, we had a problem with the boat. Engine problem. We couldn't get out to sea and some of the more casual crew wanted to move on. They needed the money," he indicated. "I have a permanent crew of three now, myself and my two sons," he said for clarity, "but at that time when I lost a couple of the *hands,* I needed to replace them. It was a busy time, and it was…is.. our livelihood so with the boat being out of action and needing some help fixing it, I took him on."

"To do what?"

"Clean, polish, sew nets, fix pots, a whole bunch of things."

"How long did this last for?"

"He worked with us the entire summer, though he would often disappear. Sometimes for days, sometimes for a couple of weeks."

"Did he say where he went?"

"No. We tried to find out, but he never said anything. He would disappear one day and be back the next."

"What happened at the end of that summer then? I assume you would continue fishing into the autumn, the winter. It is your livelihood after all, so what did Hedge do?"

"I don't remember as it was a long time ago, however, he stayed with us for a good while longer than expected. He had learnt from us and we had gained confidence in what he was doing, on the boat and out at sea." Henderson said. "Then one day he just disappeared. He didn't arrive to go out on the boat, and we didn't see or hear from him for months."

"Until he arrived back...?"

"Yes. Out of the blue, about six months later. He pitches up, walks along the moorings says hello, and asks if he could work on the boat again."

"What did you say?"

"I told him to clear off! I told him that we didn't need him, that he was unreliable."

"Did he say anything?"

"Yes. He said he been to visit a sick relative interstate and that he was sorry about his leaving without telling us."

"Go on.."

"As you can imagine, we went through the same issue. Eventually, due to his complaining, we took him on again."

"And he did the same thing."

"Several, no *many* times! He went up to Colac and we found out later that he had somehow managed to get various jobs up there. With Vets, some of the trainers and others. Basically, he was just erratic, fickle, unreliable. He was up there for over four years before he came here again. We couldn't keep up with his antics. Eventually, we couldn't be bothered with him."

Having heard what he had, Bruce asked, "what happened when he came back the third time?"

A crease spread across the fisherman's face. It was clear from the frown that Hedge had upset a lot of people at some point.

"We heard..."

"We?"

"The *community,* those with small businesses, the small farmers around here. We do have a chamber of commerce here in the 'bay you know. We run our businesses extremely well and we do communicate, share information," he said. "*We* heard he was back in the area but decided it was best that no one give him a job. Eventually, he pitched up at my door again. Figuratively speaking."

"Looking for another job?"

"Yes."

"And you told him, *no thanks.*"

"Yes."

"What happened?"

"He did the same thing. Hung around."

"Until…?" Bruce said encouraging Henderson.

"Until we told him to bugger off."

"And let me guess," responded Bruce, "he didn't."

"No Inspector, quite the contrary. He disappeared. Was gone for at least another year."

Bruce was surprised. He thought back to what he had heard previously, seen in relevant statements. Had Hedge gone somewhere else other than Colac? And if so where?

"Did you ever see him again before he ended up dead?"

"Oh, yes indeed,"

"Where? When?"

Henderson turned and walked towards the tower of boxes against the wall. They were sitting on a pallet, rows of ten by ten boxes, stacked, and ready for collection. Water dripped from their sides onto the cement floor. It was obvious that the contents had been covered with ice before the box had been sealed. Bruce followed slowly behind.

Stopping at the pallet, the fisherman said, "This is our business. This is what we do. I've been doing this for thirty-six years, working out of this harbour," he stated, nodding at the closed door of the co-op as it rattled from the wind outside. "It's been my life" he went on, "and I've been lucky. Timothy Hedge," he emphasized, "was a nuisance because he stuck his nose into areas he shouldn't have."

Bruce felt a surge of excitement run through him as Henderson spoke. He hadn't expected much detail but it seemed now that he was getting an insight into what had happened with Hedge.

"What do you mean. Areas where he shouldn't have?"

The fisherman considered his answer.

"He used to hang around…at night…listening to conversations. Somedays he would hide, all day, sitting in the bush just behind us. Listen to people on the golf course, in the shops. He heard lots of stuff and he used it."

"Used it?"

"Yes, made-up stuff. Pretended he knew more than he did."

"Why?" asked Bruce, trying to understand what was being suggested.

"To take advantage, to try and blackmail people."

"Blackmail?"

"Yes.."

"Of doing what?" asked the policeman incredulously. "I thought you said very little happens here?"

Henderson smirked. "Very little *does* happen here, but occasionally we have our little scandals as all places do. Affairs, thefts, Council fights. the *usual*," he said.

"Hardly reason for murder," Bruce responded.

"That's true," came the reply, "which is why I can't say how he ended up in that truck. I don't know and frankly, I didn't care then, and I don't care now," he retorted.

"But you think there was a reason?"

"I assume there must be. But I have no idea what it is."

"Other than Hedge must have crossed someone?"

"Crossed. Upset, pissed off. I guess any of those words would apply, Inspector. Unfortunately, I don't know who...nor indeed why," he said casually. "I'm not sure."

The two men faced each other for a few seconds. Henderson showing no emotion on his face. He had said plenty and Bruce had gained much.

"Any reason why this didn't come out when you were first interviewed?" asked Bruce.

"No, Inspector...no reason. Two years ago, I had other things on my mind, my business was going through a rough time," he said. "We were looking at losing everything due to issues with the boat. I had been through some health problems as well. Timothy Hedge was just an irritation. He hung around the town spruiking rubbish and pretending he knew a secret of sorts. Something big. Something he had uncovered. Something valuable to him."

"Any ideas?"

"No, I think it was just a made-up story. Something he traded on."

"Resulting in his murder."

"Possibly. I don't know. As I just told you, I didn't care for him then and I have less interest in him now. On the face of it, he pretended to be a loner, but deep down I think he was callous and conniving. A ratbag, a real bastard."

CHAPTER 27

"How well did you know him?"

She thought about it for a second before replying.

"I knew him reasonably well," she replied, " We worked together for a little while when I first moved to Colac. Max had been one of the longest standing Vets in the area at the time, so I worked within his practice until I went on my own."

They were standing in the Vet's room within the stable block on Pete's farm.

Outside the wind from the cold front from the west continued to push the clouds around a sodden sky. Rain then sun, then rain again interrupted the day. Shadow, then darkness, then bright sunlight shone through the half-opened door at the back of the facility.

Cannon had heard from Pete that Deb Ryan was visiting during the day to look over all the horses, particularly *Flimflam* who was due to race in the next couple of days in readiness for Warrnambool.

He was keen to get her view and her observations on the fitness of the horse as well as that of *Wings of Dawn* who had been cooped up in his stall for the past day or two. Even though there were other options about how best to keep his horses fit, Pete and Cannon had agreed that *Wings* in particular would be nurtured very carefully. He would be trained *for* the Grand Annual and how that played out was the subject of long discussions between them. They concluded that it didn't make sense for Cannon to come all the way from the UK to help Pete with his plans for the horse and then they change them just because of what happened to Optin. Cannon himself wasn't sure if the murder of Optin had anything to do with racing anyway, but he kept an open mind.

He watched as she continued to work on one of Pete's flat horses, a small bay.

"*Centrefold,*" she said, changing the topic. She lifted and stretched the horse's legs, feeling for abrasions and noting if the horse showed any signs of injury. "She's a mare that's been around the traps here for quite a while. Due to run again in the next two weeks or so. I've looked after her since she first arrived as a three-year-old. I think she's raced over twenty times already. Won twice or three times from memory. Won about 45,000 dollars all up."

"About 32,000 pounds," he replied, "not too shabby."

"That depends. The owner races her for fun. He's a nice guy," she said.

Cannon noted her eye's glinting. He caught her stare and there was an uncomfortable pause between them. He cleared his throat then turned and looked towards the partially opened door.

Smiling to herself she held the horse's head, then rubbed a hand along it's back feeling for any sign of strain. He remained silent, though he enjoyed watching her work.

"Once she's finished on the track I hope she ends up in a paddock somewhere and lives a long life," she eventually said, walking the horse towards the sliding door. He watched her lead the horse outside, feeling the icy blast as she opened the door fully. A stablehand, who had been standing out of the wind under a canvas cover to protect herself from the rain as she smoked a cigarette, took *Centrefold* from Ryan and led her away, back to her stall.

Cannon smiled. A Vet passionate about her job was something he was happy to see.

"Well where were we?" she asked nonchalantly, picking up a bucket and a spade and proceeding to collect the manure left behind by *Centrefold*.

"Max Optin, his murder, what do you make of it?"

"Pretty gruesome I hear," she replied pouring the contents of her bucket into a larger tub.

"Yes, it was," he replied. "Gruesome is probably a good word for it. I've seen much worse in the *past* but you never really get used to it, no matter how many murders or accidents you get involved in."

She noted how he emphasized the past.

"You were a policeman, I believe?" she said.

"A Detective Inspector, a DI…" he let the acronym float on the air. He didn't want it to sound precocious. "A long time ago," he continued, a soft smile on his face.

"Is that why you are asking me about Optin?"

"No, not at all," he answered, "I'm just curious. The police were asking Pete about someone called Timothy Hedge when we were at Terang a week or so ago and obviously it meant nothing to me, but when I heard about Optin somehow it sparked my curiosity. I guess I can't run away from what I've experienced for so many years, no matter how long I train racehorses."

"I understand," she said.

"So, any ideas…" he asked, "about Optin? Why would anyone want to kill him?"

"No idea," she replied. "As far as I know he pretty much kept to himself after his wife died some years ago."

"Kept to himself?"

"Well, the rest of us *Vets* in Colac knew that he had stopped looking after larger animals and concentrated on domestic pets. As a consequence, clients would talk about the various practices at times and after a while, we all got to know each other's business."

Cannon nodded. *Small towns*, he thought, *the same the world over*.

"And that includes your personal life?" he asked.

She blushed before answering.

"Some parts of it," she answered, "but that's no one's business other than mine is it?" she stated. "Anyway, regarding Max, he basically became a homebody. I hardly ever saw him out in the town, so I personally had no idea what he was up to or who he would have been dealing with. In fact, it has been several years since I last caught up with him."

He was about to ask a further question of her when the sound of hooves could be heard, a contrast to the wind that still blew fiercely outside. *Montego Girl* was led by her stablehand into the room.

"Ah Wendy," Ryan said, "how are you doing?"

"Good thanks," replied the girl, "how are you?"

Cannon stood back as Ryan took the reins from the girl, leading the horse towards the middle of the room. "I'm fine," she replied, "leave her with me and I'll give you a shout shortly after I've had a look over her. Mr. Cannon here can help me if I need," she said, a smile lighting up her face.

The girl nodded, then walked through the internal door into the stable block itself. "It'll be warmer," she mouthed, as she closed the door. Cannon watched her through the glass window as she headed towards the Tack room.

Ryan worked on *Montego Girl* as Cannon continued to ask her about Optin. She shared what she knew but she had nothing significant to add from that she had already told him.

"We saw you at Pakenham, the other day," he stated. "Pete and I, we were watching the racing from there," he clarified. "It was pouring with rain at one point."

"Oh, yes. It was a bugger of a day, to be honest."

"Yes, it looked like you were pretty busy."

"Umm," she replied. "Yes, I had several horses that needed *vetting* that day. It's funny," she continued, "somedays there is nothing to do, the next day it's a flood."

"And Pakenham was a flood?"

"Almost literally!" she responded. "I was surprised they waited until the last before abandoning the meet. I did let it be known to the stewards about how dangerous the track had become but that call wasn't mine to make. Eventually though they saw sense."

Cannon nodded. "I see *Royal Mint* didn't run particularly well."

She thought about it for a second, remembering the horse from the last race before the abandonment.

"To be honest there were a few that didn't do as well as expected on the day but given the circumstances, the weather, the track, I wasn't surprised. You know how it is, that's the joy of racing," she stated. "Sometimes these animals decide to race and at other times, like humans, they decide to focus on other things."

He knew what she meant. What she implied. Cannon watched her for a few more minutes. He hadn't anything else to ask. He decided that it would be unfair to get in her way as she continued with her work, her regular look over each of Pete's horses. They agreed that she would give him a call at the house about the health of *Wings of Dawn* and *Flimflam* later that evening and he left her alone to carry on.

CHAPTER 28

"The police have been asking questions about Hedge," the skipper of the *San Marino* complained into his mobile phone.

"Yes, I heard," replied the voice from down the line.

"What do you think we should do?"

"As we agreed last time. We need to take things a little easier. Leave it with me. I'll take care of it. I've already stopped the shipment due in the next two weeks."

"And what about Optin?"

"What about him? He's dead."

"I know. Did you....did..."

"Did I kill him?"

Silence.

"No, I didn't," the voice said finally.

The connection was broken.

CHAPTER 29

Walt Grovedale was a gregarious man and on the face of it, a man who loved to tell stories. He liked to hold court in his local pub, the Union Club Hotel on Murray Street.

He had been away in Queensland over the past few days and had come back to a police enquiry, the murder of Max Optin.

Bruce and Cromwell had interviewed him during the day.

Once they had left, he had made a call to Pete to find out *what was going on?* They had agreed to meet in the pub and discuss it further.

A murder across the entire region, the wider area was unusual. A murder in their backyard and of someone generally well known in the community was shocking. The last murder that had taken place had been eighteen months earlier and that had been a domestic violence matter. Before that, the last one was in Apollo Bay, *Timothy Hedge*.

The fact that the burnt-out car had been found on Grovedale's land had upset him.

He was quite a small man but had a huge personality. His flame-red hair, coloured through regular treatment, confirmed to others a vanity he thought acceptable. He had a mild ruddy complexion typical of his ancestry. His parents had been Irish immigrants and had settled in the area during the early 1950's. At that time, Colac and surrounding regions had been nothing more than paddocks but had developed over the years through the industrialization of forestry and dairy. It became a town in 1948 with a population of 10,000 and declared a city in 1960. Grovedale's family took advantage of the regional development by buying land and developing their business. They bought into a sawmill and over the years added additional services, becoming the leading distributor of wooden frames to the housing sector. Grovedale had inherited the lot. Fortunately for him, he wasn't one to rest on his laurels. Others would have put their feet up and lived a life of the multi-millionaire, but Grovedale was much more sensible, much more cautious. He had worked hard, growing the business over the years, and becoming a recognized figure in the community. On his early retirement, a few years earlier many of the staff were visibly upset, almost treating him with reverence. His outgoing nature allowed him to enjoy the attention at the time, but he knew it was just how life went. *You look after people, they will look after you*, he had always believed.

In his last speech to his staff at a party thrown for him by his board on his 'going away', he had declared that *retirement* was *just a word*. He had plans to live life to the full now. He had secured the business through a series of trusts keeping 51% of it. His two sons and daughter had been given 30%

and now occupied some of the senior roles, including Finance and Production. Grovedale had, over the years, hired others into the remaining Executive Management positions, most of whom had now been with the company for over ten years. He felt secure.

They were at the bar, the three of them, Pete, Grovedale, and Cannon.
Pete formally introducing Cannon on their arrival.
Cannon had been told that since retirement Grovedale had become a feature at the pub and every Wednesday he would come and spend some time at the hotel. While the others stood, Grovedale sat half on and half off his seat due to his back, the pain he had suffered for years due to a bicycle incident which meant he had to keep shifting around on the chair. He was not quite a *jack-in-a-box*, but his constant movement almost seemed to enhance his personality making him seem even more upbeat and out there than most.
Despite the pub being relatively quiet, it being mid-week, there were enough patrons in the gambling room and in the bistro to keep the owners happy. Now and again a customer would pass Grovedale as they came in and out of the building and either say *g'day* and move on or spend a few minutes chatting with him about the affairs of the day. Grovedale loved it. Cannon and Pete watched on, staying silent unless they were introduced.
The manager, David Tussoch, who had owned the place for the past fifteen years, loved the fact that there was a local personality in Grovedale who was happy to be part of the community, someone who others could flock to, circle around. It was his regulars like Grovedale and those who came out on a Wednesday night that kept him in business.
"Another *pot*?" he asked.
"No thanks mate," Grovedale responded, "I'm driving. Don't want the cops pulling me over."
Tussoch nodded, asking the same of Cannon. He declined.
Now that they had finished their drinks, it seemed a suitable time to talk about the real reason they were meeting.
"So, what's been going on?" asked Grovedale. "I heard from the police a little about what happened to Optin. They didn't tell me much but said he was found dead over in your neck of the woods."
Cannon guessed that Grovedale was just pretending to be dumb about the Optin situation. It was obvious to Cannon that the discussion with the police would have ensured that he knew exactly where things were at.
Cannon allowed Pete to speak.
"Yes, it seems he was run over."
"Run over? The police just told me that he had been found dead and that his car had been torched on my land."
"Well, he was found on our jumps training area. One of our track riders

who was out early to get our fences set up found him and called me. The body was in quite a mess," Pete continued, re-imagining the scene.

"But why would anyone want to kill him?"

"Walt, I have no idea, but whoever it was seems to have been pretty thorough about hiding their tracks."

Cannon jumped into the conversation. In his own mind, he was trying to put a puzzle together. He needed to eliminate some of the pieces if he could.

"It may seem a bit of a cliché but Pete is right. The killer hiding their tracks is literally true. From what we've been able to glean from a couple of people I've spoken to since the murder, the killer or killers got away on a bicycle or bicycles after they torched Optins car."

"A bicycle?"

Cannon nodded.

"The police didn't mention that to me either," Grovedale said.

"And they shouldn't have unless they thought it was relevant to you. It's knowledge that they have and need to keep quiet about. They can use it as and when…. "

"So how come you know so much about it, Mr. Cannon?" retorted Grovedale.

Cannon shrugged. "Used to be a DI," he said. "Spent years in the force in the UK and can't seem to ignore what goes on around me. For some reason, I keep asking questions, and the ghosts from the past keep showing their faces."

Grovedale nodded a curious understanding.

"A bit like business," he said. "I can't let go of it either…sometimes I wish I could."

Cannon looked into Grovedale's eyes, then looked at Pete. He made a decision.

"To answer your question, it was Deb Ryan who told me about the bicycle."

"The Vet?"

"Yes, we had a chat yesterday and she mentioned it."

"She's a ripper girl, is Deb. A real beaut and she does a good job." Grovedale said.

"Couldn't agree more,' Cannon replied. He waited a few seconds before continuing, asking. "Mr. Grovedale?"

"Walt."

"Walt…" echoed Cannon. "Just for my curiosity, the track that Optin's car was burnt out on, on your land, is there any significance to it?"

"What do you mean?"

"Well I understand you used to ride in races at one point, is that correct?"

"Oh yes, many years ago, but I haven't had a chance to ride a bike since my operation, my accident."

"But you love the sport?"

"Yes," Grovedale replied. "When I was younger I rode as much as I could. It kept me fit, gave me energy and it was a good outlet for me to have a laugh with my friends. I rode a lot around here, including the tracks of Forrest. In fact, I helped set out some of them, you know. So yes, it was, and in fact to some degree still is, a big part of my life."

Cannon nodded. He hadn't expected Grovedale to reveal much, but what he had said was useful.

"Thank you," Cannon replied.

CHAPTER 30

"Then give me a quick update!" Thatcher stated.

He was on the phone calling from Melbourne.

Seth Cusscom had sent him a message about the lack of progress on the Hedge and body-in-the-bush cases. Bruce, it seemed had become less engaging with the locals once the Optin murder occurred and despite Cusscom having provided two resources, Alworth and Bossin, he was still in the dark about things. He wasn't happy at being left out of where things had gotten to.

To be fair, Bruce had tried to meet with Cusscom several times, but his approach was either ignored or meetings cancelled at the last minute.

Initially, Bruce had decided to leave written reports, short updates on progress concerning all three cases, however after a while he realised that nothing was being read so he decided to stop.

The games people play, he thought at the time. It had only been a few weeks but now felt like a lifetime since he had first been asked to work on the Forrest and Apollo Bay cases.

Yes, progress had been slow, he admitted. In fact, in the one case, there had been no progress at all. Bruce needed a breakthrough.

The fact that Cusscom was feeling a bit left out was no surprise to Bruce and frankly, he didn't care. The politics of local and metropolitan or state policing continued to annoy him. Petty issues and disputes about inconsequential policies, procedures, and engagement just got in the way.

Unfortunately, he found that he needed to swim through them at times. Thatcher's call was one example of needing to keep his head above the water and not sink in the political mire around him.

"Well Sir," replied Bruce, "regarding the Hedge murder, I think we are making progress."

"How so?" asked Thatcher cynically.

Bruce cleared his throat. Fortunately, Thatcher had called while Bruce was still in his hotel room. He had been five minutes from leaving, so he had the element of privacy as he spoke.

"It seems he had upset quite a number of people especially down in Apollo Bay and as such he had become a nuisance with all his antics, a *persona non grata*. It appears that many of those he had previously been able to work with were antagonistic to him., shunned him."

"One normally doesn't end up dead just because you upset or piss-off someone. There must be more to it than that?"

"Agreed Sir. I think he must have gone a bit too far, pushed the wrong buttons."

"Any thoughts?"

Bruce felt the time was right….. "One of the people I spoke to yesterday raised the issue of blackmail."

"Blackmail?!" A splutter from down the line. It sounded to Bruce that Thatcher had swallowed his coffee down the wrong way. He allowed his boss time to compose himself. Once he had done so he said, "Bloody oath AB, I'm not sure what you think has been going on, but blackmail? Seems a bit extreme doesn't it?"

Bruce let the barb pass. "We are still investigating Sir. Once I get a better picture I will advise."

"And don't forget Cusscom."

"Yes Sir, I'll have a chat with him if I can during the course of the day."

"Okay," Thatcher said, then carried on with what was on his agenda. Bruce knew his boss well. He was nothing if not organized, focused. "The body in the bush. Any update with that one?"

"No Sir, nothing as yet."

"Any ideas?"

"The only one we have so far is that there was *no* crime. We think maybe the man was a tourist or a worker somewhere who had an accident or a medical episode resulting in him falling or collapsing where he was found. Being hidden in the bush on the furthest off-road cycle track from Forrest, it's possible he was never found because those riding through on the track would have done so at speed. If he was covered by bush then it's likely that he was effectively invisible."

"But you didn't find any clothes on him, did you?"

"That's correct Sir, he was found naked."

"So how does one explain that?"

Bruce sighed. He was beginning to get a headache. He needed another coffee himself.

"We think, and this is just a *theory,* Sir," he said, highlighting that what they had considered still needed to be tested, "that he may have been found by someone and all his belongings stripped from him. Clothes, any ID, etcetera, and then covered up again."

Both policemen had been around long enough to have seen many things over the years. What was on the table between them now wasn't as far-fetched as it seemed. Thatcher knew not to discount what Bruce had said. Eventually, he said, "I suppose it's possible. I assume the DNA evidence about his likely origins hasn't helped?"

"You mean the fact that he was definitely not born here."

"Yes."

"Well, not really Sir. All it has done is given us something to think about. We are still looking into that," he lied.

Bruce knew what was coming next.

"Optin? A murder on *your* watch," said Thatcher unfairly. "What's the latest? And please make it quick, I have a 9 am meeting."

"Again Sir, not much to tell. Though to be fair it is a little early on in the investigation. The SOCOs and the forensic teams are working through the evidence they have already collected, though I don't hold out much hope they will come up with anything useful. They have some ideas but in relation to the who and the why, we have a lot of leg work to do around here."

Thatcher eventually showed that he was feeling sympathetic towards Bruce and that he appreciated his efforts.

Despite the lack of progress on all fronts, Thatcher knew he still had the best man on the job.

"OK AB thanks for the update," he said. "Take care of yourself and don't forget to keep Cusscom informed of what's going on. I'll let him know that we have spoken and for him to expect a report, either verbal or in writing, your choice, during the day."

"Thank you, Sir," Bruce said, listening to the line buzz as Thatcher disconnected. He picked up a jacket and his coat. It was still raining, and it had gotten colder overnight. He needed that coffee.

CHAPTER 31

"How often do the trials take place?" he asked.

"They take place almost every two weeks during the season," Pete replied. They were sitting in the lounge. The TV was on, but the sound was off. Cannon noticed it was an old episode of *Fact or Fiction* that was showing. Michelle and Emily had been wrapping up presents in the dining room ready for Stephanie's birthday party over the coming weekend. It was just after 10 pm. Stephanie was in her room. Emily was not sure if her daughter was keeping quiet deliberately or had already gone to sleep. With the soft lighting and no sound coming from under her door, Emily decided to wait until later to check.

"I assume the trials are for fitness and capability?" Cannon queried.

"Mostly capability, to be honest."

"In what way?" asked Cannon, intrigued.

He had assumed that like in the UK there was a path that horses in the National Hunt game would go through. In Australia, due to the smaller population of horses and the limited number of races and states they could race in, horses were able to race in any type of race provided they met certain criteria.

Cannon had read the rules before but went through them again. He wanted to ask Pete a question, but before he did, he read through the eligibility requirements.

Prior to a horse participating in its first official hurdle trial, it must have schooled to the satisfaction of a Steward over three (3) approved hurdles.

For horses new to jumps racing, they must complete two hurdle trials to the satisfaction of the Jumps Review Panel prior to being able to accept for a hurdle race. One of these trials must be over 2800m (10 obstacles).

To get a horse qualified for steeplechase races, it must already be qualified for hurdle racing, then complete the course in at least two starts in hurdle races, before completing one steeplechase trial over 2800m (10 obstacles) to the satisfaction of the Jumps Review Panel.

To re-qualify a horse for the current season (if that horse was qualified in a previous season), they must have at least one trial over a minimum distance of 2400m (8 obstacles) to the satisfaction of the Jumps Review Panel, prior to accepting for a race (hurdle or steeplechase) in the current season. Horses can use a steeplechase trial to become re-qualified for both hurdle and steeplechase races.

"I guess you're right Pete, they seem pretty straight forward to me," he said, thinking again about the UK model. In the UK there were point-to-point races and *bumpers*, in addition to the novice races, all the way up to the classics. Trainers used these races to help give confidence to their horses over time. Many of the most successful runners were often eight years old and upwards and were taken up through the grades quite systematically. It seemed that locally in Australia, the horses in jumps races were on average much younger and raced across both disciplines.

After he had re-read the rules, he said. "From what I can see it's pretty easy to get a horse into a race. *Wings* and *Flimflam* seemed to have met the criteria easily and even some of your others are likely to have no issues either. Oh, and by the way, I've been reasonably impressed by the jockeys we saw the other day at Terang."

"Like Christian Counter?"

"Yes, Counter is a good horseman from what I saw. On the other hand, it's the guys on the training track that still bothers me a little."

Pete was a little taken aback. While he had asked Cannon for help, he was still a little sensitive to any criticism of how he went about things. After all, he had done reasonably well over the years with his jumps horses. What he wanted Cannon to do was to take him to the next level. Pete had made the best use of the staff available to him in the area. Sometimes he had the use of some of the more professional jockeys if they were available to school. At other times he had to call on those jockeys who were of lesser skill but were still small enough to ride for him and met the requirements he needed, be it their weight or their experience in jumping.

"Sometimes I have no choice."

Cannon noticed the slight vibrato in Pete's voice. He decided to tread carefully. He was there as a guest. He was there to provide advice, though in recent weeks he was clearly doing much more than that.

"I understand," he replied. "Anyway, I just wanted to point out on a positive note that up until the incident with the Vet, I think the jocks were getting to be a bit braver and it was translating to the horses. That other horse of yours, the one running for the first time during the carnival…"

"*Holdthephone?*"

"Yes, *Holdthephone,* I think he could do well."

Pete seemed pleased.

"Well we'll trial him again at the next meeting at Cranbourne, and that should give us a better picture of any improvement, thanks to you," he said. "Then it's up to him whether he runs during day one of the carnival."

"I assume you have nominated him?" asked Cannon.

"Yes, he qualified at the first attempt. The owner is a local businessman, Ed Morley and he's keen to race him."

Cannon smiled. *Owners were the same the world over,* he thought.

The two men stayed silent for a second. They could hear laughter coming from the kitchen. Emily and Michelle had obviously broken out the red wine.

"Fancy a drink?" asked Pete.

"No thanks, but please don't let me stop you."

"I'll give it a miss as well," Pete replied. "I have to get up early again tomorrow. Milking never ends."

"Umm, I hope the police have finished their investigation at the training facility. I'd like to jump all of the horses tomorrow that still need to trial if that's possible? Cranbourne is only a few days away."

Pete nodded.

"In addition, we have the final race for *Flimflam* to get through before the carnival."

"Yep, as I keep saying, *no rest for the wicked*," he replied, suddenly yawning and needing to stretch.

They heard laughter again and loud voices coming from the kitchen. Pete smiled just as Emily came into the lounge offering them both a nightcap.

"Coffee for me, please," accepted Cannon.

"Just plain English, for me love," Pete said.

Once Emily had disappeared Cannon asked the question he had been dying to ask all evening.

He had thought about how best to phrase it and hoped it didn't sound too melodramatic.

"Pete, there has been something bothering me now for the past few days and I was wanting to get your view."

"Oh?" Pete replied, intrigued.

"Yes. It's about the carnival. Well perhaps it's more widespread than that, but let's stick with that meeting for now."

Pete shrugged. Cannon needed to make himself clearer.

"I'm talking about cheating. Horses being *got at*. The Grand Annual is worth a lot of money to the winner, don't you ever worry about it?" he asked.

Pete smiled. "You've seen how little security I have here," he said, "and that's because we trust people in the country. I'm sure in the city, or like you in the UK, you are a bit more cautious, but for me, I'm reasonably happy in the way we do things here. I'm not naïve but I don't believe it's a big problem. There is too much at stake and……"

"Despite the recent Optin issue and the police coming back to you about the Hedge matter?" Cannon interrupted.

"Yes, I think so," he considered. "The Optin murder has shaken me up a bit but it took place well away from the stables, and just happened to be on my land. It hasn't really been an attack on the horses, more the person. It's unfortunate but I can't see how it relates to the actual racing."

Cannon acknowledged Pete's logic with a nod.

" Concerning Hedge, given he was killed two years ago in Apollo Bay, the only involvement and linkage to the farm and the horses that I can see is that he worked here at different times, and I've told the police all I know."

Before Cannon could respond, Michelle and Emily brought in the tea and coffee, placing a tray down on a small, side table.

"Anything else we can help you with?" asked Emily, her cheeks flushed a rosy red.

"Nothing for me thanks," replied Cannon, noticing a few biscuits on a small plate on the tray.

"Okay, see you in a while," Michelle said to Cannon. "We've nearly finished so I'll see you in bed soon."

"No problem," he answered, kissing her on the cheek then reaching for the tray.

"Anzac biscuit," said Pete as he bit into one of several options from the plate, a loud crunch rent the air as he did so.

Cannon had stuck with a chocolate digestive.

Once they had polished off the plate between them, Cannon said. "What do you think of *Chesterman's* chance for the Grand Annual this year?"

"He's a good horse, and Sormond trains him well. He's won both his races this season. Won them easily."

"I see," Cannon noted. "Do you reckon he'll be the favourite?"

"Unless something else comes out of the pack, then yes I think so."

"What if he gets injured before the race?"

"Mike!" said Pete sitting up in his chair, "what are you getting at?"

"To be honest, I don't know. It's something that's bothering me a little. It's just a feeling."

"Care to share it?"

The cogs churned inside Cannon's head, before he said eventually, "I think the torching of Optin's car was a message."

"A message?" Pete responded.

"Yep, a message. But I'll be damned if I know to whom and about what, however, something is going on and we need to be careful."

"And you think that someone may be out to get at the horses. Possibly *Wings?*"

"Possibly…" Cannon said, leaving the thought with Pete.

CHAPTER 32

"What time is it there now?" asked Cannon.

He was sitting in bed. Michelle was sitting up next to him but wearing earphones and listening to her music on her iPad. She was trying to read at the same time.

"It's just after two in the afternoon," answered Rich. "I guess it's just after 11 at night there?"

"Yes, and it's bloody cold. It's been wet and blustery all day."

"Well, it's not much better here Mike. It's been cold but dry, thank God."

They were talking on Skype and Cannon could see that his Assistant was wearing a warm short sleeve corduroy jacket over a heavy shirt.

"How are things otherwise? Any news?"

Telside hardly ever used email, so most of his communication with Cannon was via the phone or Skype. Occasionally he used FaceTime, but mostly Skype whenever he needed to stay in touch.

"Nothing really other than we have had a few enquiries from a couple of owners who are looking to put their horses with us. I've made some time to catch up with them when you get back. Overall, it looks very positive. Getting more horses in than leaving will hopefully give us the opportunity of building up the business even further."

"That's great news Rich," replied Cannon.

"Too true Mike,' Telside replied. "Plus, a couple of the horses that we *may* get are of a better class than those we have currently."

"Oh, go on," Cannon answered. He could sense Rich was excited. Hopefully not prematurely.

"Well, it seems that a couple of the owners are unhappy with some of the big trainers that they have their horses with. From what they tell me, some of them are finding that despite their horses being at a successful stable the focus is only on the top six or so runners in those stables, you know the ones that get on the TV? Some owners think their horses are missing out and want to move them elsewhere. Does that make sense to you?"

"Yes, I guess so."

"So I think some of them are looking for a change, looking at other trainers, those that will give their horses more attention and not just have a stablehand or a stable jock look after their wellbeing."

Cannon understood what Rich was saying but didn't want to slag off his fellow professionals. He kept quiet, allowing Telside to continue.

"I think what happened in the National has seeped into the collective consciousness, Mike, and it would appear that some of the owners are happy to give us.....you..."

"Us..." smiled Mike down the connection.

"Us..." Telside repeated, "a chance to take on some of these better horses."

Cannon was pleased with what he was hearing.

"I tell you what Rich, if we just pick up a couple of these better horses, it will be great for the stable, for the business. I can't wait to get home."

"Me too Mike. Looking forward to planning the new season."

Cannon nodded.

"And how are things going there, anyway?" Rich asked.

Cannon filled him in on the progress he believed they were making, then they discussed the murder of Optin.

"That's shocking," Telside said. "How horrible. I guess the police are investigating?"

"Yes, they are but there is something that's bothering me," he said. "It was something that was said to me that didn't make sense at the time, but it has sparked something in my head and I can't seem to work out what it is, and it's beginning to bug me."

"Can't you drop it? Leave it to the local coppers?"

"I wish I could," Cannon answered. "I wish I could."

During the night, Cannon dreamt. He tossed and turned, trying to scare away the ghosts, the faces that came to interrupt his sleep, to chase him into the next day. He woke up sweating, Michelle sitting up with him. It was just after six am. Rain was hammering at the bedroom window. Was it the sound of the rain that had woken him? He couldn't remember what was in his dreams, however, there had been many faces.

CHAPTER 33

"Who could he have been blackmailing, and about what?" asked Bruce. It was a question put into the room without warning.

"It could be anybody, Sir," replied Bossin. "If Hedge was creeping around, and suddenly pitching up without warning, he could have overheard or seen anything that he thought was worth making something out of."

"Umm," Bruce replied, "that's possible. However, if he *was* blackmailing someone, as Henderson suggested, then one assumes there must have been a quid in it for him? Let's have a look and see if he had a bank account and see if he was putting money into it at the time," he said. "We know he normally worked for cash only, but he may have had something hidden away somewhere? Maybe under a false name? I'm surprised nothing was identified or considered in any of the reports put together at the time, though to be honest, I didn't think about blackmail then either."

"I don't think anyone did Sir," Bossin replied.

The comment didn't make Bruce feel any better, but at least it was something to go on.

"Let's have one more look at all the statements collected during the initial investigation and those we took the other day and see if we can find anything inconsistent. The only new line of enquiry we have is this possible blackmail issue. I'm surprised that it had never been mentioned before, but now that it has, I've had a thought." Turning to Cromwell has said. "Sam, can you look at the Forensics' report again and check for me whether there was anything significant about the way Hedge's body was handled before it went into the truck? If he had been working on a boat or around the harbour say at the time of his death, I would have thought there would be some evidence of that? Perhaps we missed it or didn't think much of it at the time? Anyway, could you have another look? If he was blackmailing someone, it has to have something to do with the harbour. All the other stuff about affairs etcetera seem to be a smokescreen for what could really have been going on. Those sorts of domestic issues are generally too immaterial for someone to be murdered," he hoped.

As Bruce spoke, he realized he was beginning to talk himself around to the blackmailing theory. He hoped their further investigation would confirm or refute it.

"Okay, I'm off to speak with Cusscom, to keep him updated," he said, leaving the room.

CHAPTER 34

The trials in advance of the Warrnambool carnival were scheduled a week before the actual meeting.

The Grand Annual with *Wings* had been their goal all along, however Cannon and Pete had hoped to see improvement in *Flimflam's* form, especially over hurdles. Any improvement before the trials began would be ideal.

The horse had been nominated to race in a two-mile hurdle at Casterton, 300 km plus away from Melbourne, as a lead up to the *Galleywood* Hurdle. That race on day one of the carnival was worth $150,000 over the same distance.

It had been a long drive from Colac. Cannon and Pete watched through their binoculars as the field circled around at the starting gates. Christian Counter sat upright in the saddle, the all-salmon colours that Pete owned stood out against the other seven runners who silks consisted mostly of blues, reds, and blacks. The rain that had pummeled the area over the past forty-eight hours had stopped. The track was heavy, but racing was still going ahead. Cannon and Pete were thankful, as the drive had taken longer than anticipated. *Thank goodness the horse float taking Flimflam to the track had left a good few hours before they had*, Pete thought.

The horses were slowly called into line, and before long were sent on their way by the starter.

It wasn't long before Cannon realized that the horse was in trouble. The tactic had been to sit at the back and wait until the last four hundred metres of the race before Counter was to make his move. Fitness wasn't an issue despite the interruptions with Optin's death. After the police had given the go-ahead, Cannon was able to give the horse more attention before the Casterton meeting, and even Debra Ryan had said after inspecting the horse that it was fit and without injury. It was noticeable now, however, that even before the very first hurdle something was wrong. *Flimflam* was over racing, throwing his head around, and not concentrating on what he was there to do.

Counter struggled to keep his mount straight, barely clearing the first. The horse was racing wildly, sitting on the speed in second position. Cannon thought back to Ryan's comments a few days before. *Sometimes they have minds of their own.*

At the second, Counter could not control the horse anymore, and as they reached the hurdle the horse shied away to its left, sending the jockey hurtling to the ground, straight over the fence. He landed on his left shoulder, a sickening crack sounded as he hit the ground, but it quickly faded like a shout in a desert as *most* of the field negotiated the hurdle in a quarrel of noise. Expletives filled the air as the horse directly behind *Flimflam* was interfered with. *Flimflam's* refusal to take the jump resulted in that horse's jockey being similarly dislodged.

As the remaining six horses continued racing, Counter slowly unbundled himself from the protective ball that he had curled himself up into, standing up stiffly and trying to move his arm in a windmill fashion. The paramedic in the ambulance that had been following the field quickly made his way to Counter. He noted that the other fallen jockey was walking around easily, cursing his bad luck. It was Tony Carey.

"I'm alright," Counter said to the ambulance man, "just a knock, another fall. Part of the game."

"Either way mate, let's get you off the track and back to the rooms. We'll have a better look at you down there."

Counter knew he couldn't argue. He jumped into the ambulance.

Carey joined him. He was still cursing his luck as they drove back to the steward's rooms for the necessary briefing.

Cannon and Pete stood in front of *Flimflam* after he had been caught and brought back to his stall. They were disappointed as the horse had been well fancied by them both *and* the market. He had started as second favourite. They were trying to work out what had gone wrong.

After the race, they had caught up with Counter once he had become available and tried to get to the bottom of what had gone wrong.

"The horse was uncontrollable," Counter said, "right from the off. He seemed like he had his mind was elsewhere. Not sure what it was but it was a different horse to normal. He didn't want to settle at all."

Cannon listened as Pete sought the necessary answers. "Anything obvious Christian?"

"No, not really. He seemed alright during the warm-up."

"Okay, maybe just a bad day?"

"Maybe." Counter replied.

"Well we need to get to the bottom of it, before the carnival, we can't have him racing like that down there," Pete said. "If he's not right through the trials then I'm going to scratch him."

Cannon could not argue with Pete's logic, but he sensed the horse was not itself for other reasons, not just having a bad day. He couldn't yet work out why, but his suspicions were beginning to solidify.

CHAPTER 35

When they got back home, it was dark. *Flimflam* was still being driven home separately in the horse float, none the worse for wear for his ordeal.

They had spent most of the trip back trying to understand what went wrong. Cannon had decided to keep his thoughts to himself.

Pete parked his car and Cannon went inside the house. It was still very cold, but the leaden sky had kept the temperature from falling too low. Overnight it was expected to remain in single digits.

Cannon took off his coat as he entered the house and was soon engaged with Michelle and Emily in wishing Stephanie a happy birthday for the following day.

A party had been arranged for her with her friends the next day, but Emily had decided to have a special family dinner the night before where they could give Stephanie the presents they had bought for her.

Pete spent the next hour supervising in the milking shed before he walked through the door. By the time he did so, everything was ready for dinner. After he cleaned himself up and changed, Emily brought out the gifts she and Michelle had bought for her daughter. The clothes they had chosen and the money they had put into a birthday card were well received.

As they lay in bed after dinner, Cannon and Michelle reflected on their respective days. One had been through a disappointment, the other not so. Eventually the conversation turned to Cassie and her plans to go to South Africa. Cannon expressed his concern. Michelle agreed, but as with Cassie's move up to York to study, she highlighted to him that Cassie was no longer his little girl and that she had grown up. She had to make her own decisions.

Cannon reluctantly accepted what Michelle said, but would still raise his objections next time he spoke with his daughter. He knew he couldn't stop her going if she made up her mind to do so, but he would try to convince her otherwise if he could.

Slowly their conversation waned and while they talked sporadically for a while longer, the gaps between each sentence became longer. Gradually each drifted off to sleep. No ghosts came to him in the night.

CHAPTER 36

"Engine Oil," she said, "under his fingernails."

"Specific type?" Bruce asked.

"Generally, the same type you would find in any engine. Engine oil in trawlers may be slightly different to other boats especially if they are diesel, but the oils are now all synthetic and it's only their features that highlight the difference."

"Features?"

"Yes, things like Viscosity, or an ability to remove carbon from the engine. Mostly things like that that are not easy to establish. In fact, the oils used in boat engines are very similar to those used in normal car engines."

"And that proves what exactly?"

"It proves that it was missed, as a clue, two years ago."

"Missed?" echoed Bruce.

"Yes, given the report didn't specifically state the oil *could* have been related to a boat, it wasn't seen as relevant. I think the focus was on something to do with a car. The oil type just proves now that he was around a boat. Not that he worked on one at the time of his murder."

Bruce thought about it for a second. "So far it's only Henderson who has mentioned that Hedge worked with him on his trawler. So perhaps the oil under the fingernails was picked up when he *did* work on the boat?"

"Perhaps, but didn't Henderson also say that Hedge was kicked off his boat sometime before he disappeared?"

"Yes, he did. The question is, however, whether Henderson is telling the truth or whether Hedge was actually snooping around the harbour and got the oil under his nails just through picking things up? Most of the nets and floats have oil on them when they are sitting on the quayside. If Hedge was trying to keep himself hidden he could easily have picked up anything."

"Agreed," Cromwell said. "But it does prove he was in the area not long before his death. He hadn't gone walkabout as some have suggested. So someone knows where he was, someone knows who killed him and why."

"Maybe another visit to our skipper is needed?"

"I guess so, Sir," she answered.

"Oh, by the way?" Bruce asked, "any update regarding Hedge's bank account?"

"No Sir," she answered. "It seems that he *did* have an account with the *Bendigo Bank,* but it was nearly always empty. In fact, it had bugger all in it, so if he was blackmailing anyone, whatever he got from them was likely to be in cash. Perhaps that's how he survived after he lost the income he was getting from the odd jobs that he was doing? Maybe he was living on the

blackmail monies?" she said.
Bruce considered her comments.
"Maybe Constable," he replied, "maybe..."

CHAPTER 37

"What do you think went wrong?" she asked.

They were standing in front of the stable. *Flimflam* walked around at the back occasionally stopping to munch on a bale of fresh hay that the stablehand had placed in a metal basket halfway up the wall of the stall.

"I'm not sure," Cannon said. "He seemed a little distressed during the race, but soon calmed down after his fall. The jockey said he never settled at all."

"That's odd," Deb Ryan replied. "As I told you after I looked him over the day before the race, he seemed perfectly fine. Fit and pretty much raring to go."

"Yes, it does seem odd."

"He seems okay now," she continued, nodding at the horse.

"Yep," replied Cannon. "Let's hope he trials okay down at Warrnambool. He needs to do well there first to have any chance on the big day itself. It's huge prize money. I had hoped that I had been able to help Pete, but now after what happened, I'm not so sure."

"Is he travelling down there with *Wings?*" she asked.

"No, we've decided to send them on separate floats. He'll travel down with *Holdthephone*. *Wings* will travel on his own, just in case..."

"In case of...?"

"One of them needing to stay down there," he replied. "Especially if either of the pair falls or injure themselves. Also, *Holdthephone* will keep *Flimflam* company on the trip. Hopefully, keep him calm."

"That's probably a good idea," she said, "but let's just hope nothing happens to any of them."

"I hope so too," Cannon replied. "After the trials, we'll try and taper off their training. Give them a break, keep them fresh for their respective races," he said.

CHAPTER 38

"The police have been back to see me again. They think I may have had something to do with Hedge's murder."

"How did you work that out?" asked the voice.

"Just the way they were questioning me. The things they were asking."

"And did you?"

"What?"

"Have anything to do with Hedges' death?"

"Of course not."

"Then you can relax."

CHAPTER 39

Cannon called Bruce.

"I think there is a message in where Optin's car was torched."

"What makes you think that Mike?" Bruce replied.

The fact that he had three investigations going at the same time was not lost on him. He knew that progress was slow and interference from Cannon was not what he had expected. The last thing he needed now was a conspiracy theory.

"After Pete and I caught up with Walt Grovedale, something sparked a thought."

"Do you want to share it?"

"That's why I am calling Inspector. I think it's worth a more detailed conversation."

"Are you able to come to down to the station on Queen Street later today?"

"Yes," replied Cannon. "I'll be there after two if that's ok? We've got a few things to do down here first and then I'll drive down."

They sat in the same room. Cannon, Bruce, Cromwell, and the two Constables. Bruce was keen to move quickly if Cannon's *theory* had merit. He doubted it, though.

"So Mike, what message do you think was sent with the torching of Optin's car?"

"It was a warning."

"To whom?"

"Grovedale himself."

"Grovedale?" repeated Bruce. "For doing what?"

"I don't know yet, but …"

"Sorry Mike," interjected Bruce, "but if you've come all this way just to give me an unsupported theory, then I'm sorry to say that I think you've wasted our time and frankly I am disappointed." He looked around the room, each of his team nodded in agreement.

Cannon shrugged. He had been a policeman himself for long enough. He knew his instincts. He couldn't yet provide proof to Bruce, but he believed he was right in his thinking.

"I'm sorry you think that way, Inspector."

The policeman remained silent for a second, thinking about Cannon's response, the strength of commitment in what Cannon was saying, proposing. Bruce didn't want to reject the theory out of hand, after all, he had been quick to dismiss that of Cromwell and she had proved him wrong. "If you believe it was a warning to Grovedale, what do you think it relates to?" he asked.

Drawing on his own experiences Cannon said, "Most warnings are either concerning something that has happened in the past and the person or persons issuing the message is threatening to *reveal* it. Or the warning is a message that something is about to happen *to* the person receiving it."

"And which of those two do you think Grovedale has been advised of?"

"I'm not sure," Cannon responded. "It's more a gut feeling at this stage but given where the car was torched, I think it relates to the past."

Bruce looked at Cromwell and the others for any input or views in response to Cannon's comments. They all stayed silent.

Sighing, Bruce said, "Mike, we haven't been able to uncover anything untoward about Mr. Grovedale when we went through our records. He is a respectable member of the community and has been for years. In addition, there is no information anywhere that would associate him with anything that would constitute a crime of any sort. No scandal, no gossip," he stated. "From what we know he has run a very successful business here in Colac all his life, and he continues to be a part of it today, albeit as a shareholder only. Other than the odd parking and speeding fines, there is nothing to suggest any wrong-doing on his part that we can see."

"That may be true, but it doesn't mean something didn't happen. It just means it wasn't reported."

"That's true, and it's a possibility," Bruce agreed, "however what makes you so confident about this…this theory?"

"Timing, Place. Something has happened for someone to kill Optin and somehow there is a link to Grovedale."

"Okay, let's assume your *theory* has merit, which I'm personally not convinced of," Bruce said, "allow us to do some more digging about Mr. Grovedale, and I will come back to you if necessary. In the interim, I'll meet with him as soon as I can and see what he has to say, what his thoughts are on the matter. In the meantime, thanks for your input."

"No problem," Cannon replied somewhat cynically, "glad to be of help."

Bruce wasn't sure if Cannon *was* actually helping, but he kept that thought to himself.

CHAPTER 40

The floats arrived as expected. There appeared to be no concerns about any of Pete's horses as they were unloaded at the track, ready for their trials. If everything went according to plan all three would be heading back to Colac later that day, as the trials were expected to be concluded by late morning. Cannon had been asked by Pete to act in his stead as an official representative of the stable.

George Sormond was also in attendance. He was keen to see how *Chesterman* trialled, but he also wanted to keep a keen eye on *Wings* and *Flimflam,* particularly the former.

Wings and *Chesterman* trialled over the same distance of 3200M but at different times. Both easily won their races, but that meant nothing to the likely outcome of the Grand Annual. Other runners nominated for the Grand Annual also trialled during the morning in different heats and finished their races in different times. The times taken to conclude each trial was dependent upon how keen some of the other triallists raced. Accordingly, it was difficult to gauge which of the runners nominated for the big race were the main threats. With twelve runners likely to face the starter it was expected that at least six would have a chance of winning. The previous year's winner *Salt of the Earth* had been retired from racing due to injury, so the big prize for winning the race was up for grabs to any number of horses and trainers. It was the first time in a couple of years that the previous year's winner had not come back for a second bite of the prize money, the winner's cheque.

During the final trial of the day, Christian Counter took a tumble. He was riding a horse in a hurdle race when the horse fell. Counter did not get up as easily as he had done at Casterton and stayed down way longer than he should have. The resulting review of the fall revealed that the jockey had broken his arm after landing on the shoulder that he injured when he had fallen from *Flimflam* the previous week. In addition, it was subsequently confirmed that he had also damaged a couple of vertebrae in his back. His carnival was over. Cannon realized it as soon as he saw Counter fall from his mount, and it was confirmed by the sight of the jockey staying down on the ground and the medical attendants working on him for an extended period. Cannon hoped it wasn't the end of a career as well. He had seen many a fall and many jockeys never recovered. He hoped Counter did.

Cannon relayed the news to Pete, calling him at the farm on his mobile.

"I'll try to get Carey," Cannon said, "to partner *Wings* in the Grand Annual.

I heard from a couple of the other trainers here on track that he didn't have a mount after his own was scratched. I think he'll be pleased to have another crack at the race."

Pete was delighted with the thought of getting Carey to replace Counter if that was possible.

Cannon went off in search of the jockey to lock him in for the ride. The only concern Cannon had was the fact that Carey had never ridden *Wings* before.

CHAPTER 41

Bruce and Cromwell sat with Grovedale. The house was quiet. It was a large Federation style home with a balcony that effectively surrounded the building. It was the first time that Bruce had been to the place. Previous conversations with Grovedale had been on the phone.

They were inside a lounge room warmed by an ornamental gas fire. The white stones inside the heater were licked by the blue flames of the gas. Outside the wind had dropped but the threat of rain that had held off over the past twelve hours remained. The grey sky continued to darken as the afternoon wore on. The temperature hovered just above thirteen degrees.

Inside the house the thermostat has been set at just over twenty degrees, it was extremely pleasant. Bruce and Cromwell had removed their coats and sat on plush leather sofas. Grovedale was a very wealthy man and his vanity showed in the type of furniture that was set out in the lounge. On the floor were expensive rugs and on the walls, paintings in oils, chalks, charcoal, and watercolour. The variety of colour and style of the pictures were not something that Bruce had encountered before. They were evidence of a lifetime of someone collecting without thought. The pictures were varied. There was no theme. Money didn't always bring class, Bruce thought. He guessed that if he was to explore the rest of the house he would find similar quality throughout and perhaps again see mismatches of style. He didn't envy anyone trying to collate things and organize them more sensibly. Bruce pitied Grovedale's wife.

"How can I help Inspector?" Grovedale asked. "You said you had a couple of questions for me."

"Yes, and thanks for your time Mr. Grovedale," Bruce replied. "We just have a couple of things we wanted to clear up with you if we may?"

"Fire away."

Bruce took a deep breath. He was taking a chance and he knew it. Cannon had put an idea into his head, and he needed to get to the bottom of the theory. It wasn't totally without merit and it was all they had to go on. The investigation into what had happened to Optin had not yet resulted in any significant developments and indeed they had run into a roadblock. Follow-ups on the cycle track imprints found in the immediate area of the burnt-out car had come to nought. It was soon discovered through talking to the owner of the local bicycle shop, *Bike Guru* on Murray Street, that the population of users in the area using bicycles with the type of tyre found at the scene was way too numerous to even consider investigating with any seriousness.

The investigation was stalling. Cannon's idea at least gave them something to follow up on. Bruce got straight to the point.

"We have a view that there was a message being sent when Mr. Optin's car was burnt-out on your property."

"A message? To me?"

"Yes, Sir. A message. Perhaps a threat of some kind?" Bruce asked.

Grovedale sat back in his chair, crossing his legs as he did so.

He pondered the statement for a few seconds then sat forward, leaning towards his visitors.

"Inspector, I'm not sure what this is all about, but I can assure you that there is no reason for anyone to threaten me. I have nothing to hide and have nothing to be fearful of," he said. "In the *good old days* when I was in business and a business rival was wanting to *have a go* at me or my company then he and I would meet formally to try to address the issue, man to man, and we would resolve it. There would be no *subtle* threats as you are suggesting now, everything would be put on the table. So, as I have already indicated, there is no reason anyone would want to threaten me. I haven't ever done anything to warrant it," he stated.

Bruce stayed quiet. It was clear that Grovedale had more to say.

"As far as I can tell this case is about poor Max Optin. The fact that his car was burnt out on my property while I was away, is to my mind irrelevant to me personally, so I can only assume that you are seeing things which are not there Inspector," he said. "I think you could be jumping at shadows."

"Maybe Sir, but we do have some questions that need answering and perhaps you could help us?

"Go ahead," Grovedale replied, folding himself back into his chair.

Bruce recalled how he felt when Cannon had posed the question, the theory about the car and where it was destroyed. Bruce hoped that Grovedale couldn't tell that he was fishing for answers, that he was not convinced by Cannon's theory.

"Well despite what you have said Mr. Grovedale, the question that we need an answer to, is why Mr. Optin's killer set the car alight on that specific track? As I indicated before, we think that there is a message in it," he continued. "We know that you used to cycle for many years and despite your inability to participate as much as you used to, cycling was and still remains, a passion of yours. Accordingly, we want to know whether that specific track means anything to you? Anything at all? Particularly as we understand it was a track that you built."

"Yes, you are right Inspector I did have a lot to do with that track's construction, but that was years ago. Since my accident, however, I haven't been anywhere near it," he said. "So as far as your question is concerned, I'll repeat my answer. I can't see that there is any relevance or linkage as to where Mr. Optin's car was destroyed and a threat to myself."

"Very well, Mr. Grovedale, we will leave it there. If there is nothing that rings any bells then we have nothing else to bother you with," Bruce replied.

"Thank you. I can't think of anything that would justify you spending any further time looking into my background but if you want to, please go ahead, I have nothing to hide."

"No worries," replied Bruce standing as he did so. "Senior Constable Cromwell and I will see our own way out."

Grovedale nodded in acknowledgement as the two policemen left the room.

CHAPTER 42

The silence of the night was only disturbed by the hiss of bicycle tyres as the cyclist pushed their way across the sodden road. The gate to Pete's property had been left open, as it always was. It was easy to cycle into the place. There was no need to climb over any fences around the property or lift a bicycle over a gate. As Cannon had mentioned to Pete, security was pretty limited. The cyclist took complete advantage.

The road up to the house and beyond towards the stable block was like the slippery back of a dark snake. The cyclist had no lights, but the rider was able to negotiate a path to the stable block using the moon that was slowly on the wane, heading across the sky towards the horizon and ultimately dawn. Silvery fingers of light shone through broken clouds that had already dispensed their rain adding to the peripheral light that was coming from the house.

It was a little after two-thirty am. Pete, Emily, and Stephanie had been asleep for hours. Cannon and Michelle had stayed up until just before one am to have calls with Rich and for Michelle to talk with Cassie.

Both were now asleep, though Cannon still tossed and turned as his mind wandered.

The cyclist walked into the stable block. *Wings* stood and watched as his stable door was opened. The cyclist wearing gloves smiled then turned to walk down the centre of the block, opening the doors to the boxes of all the other horses. The intention was not to hurt the animals, but for the animals to hurt themselves. If *Wings* could be injured and be unable to race at the carnival, then it would give George Sormond a much better chance of taking the big prize on offer for winning the Grand Annual.

The only issue was that the cyclist had done exactly the same thing just an hour earlier at Sormond's stable. Opening the door to *Chesterman's* stable before opening all the others.

It was the noise, the whinnying of some of the first tranche of horses that had gotten loose and were now free from their stalls that woke him.

Cannon and Pete rushed to the front door of the house almost simultaneously, both wearing housecoats over pyjamas.

"What the hell..? said Pete, turning on the inside, then outside lights to the house.

Silhouettes of several horses could be seen walking and running towards the main road. Pete and Cannon made a beeline towards the stable block. They wanted to see how many of their horses were now out of the stable block. The outside lights helped, but it was impossible to know how many horses, and which ones, were roaming free and which were still in the stable block. They found that four of them were still standing in their own stables, the balance had managed to *escape*. One of the four was *Wings* who clearly wasn't interested in making a break for it. The other three did not include *Flimflam* or *Holdthephone* who were now roaming the property somewhere and had no way of getting back to their stable. Herd instinct was driving the horses in a single direction, towards the open road and freedom.

Cannon called out to the stablehands, their sleeping quarters only a short distance from the actual stables. He banged on windows and doors trying to get them awake so that they could help with the round-up.

Within minutes a group of small men were dressed and went in search of their charges. It was now nearly four am, the time when most jockeys or stable riders were usually getting up and readying for the day.

The final tally when everything was completed, the horses collected and returned to their stables was two horses lost, another two hurt in one way or another and thankfully the rest being retrieved uninjured.

Flimflam had damaged a tendon by kicking against a wall. The door to his stable had not been opened fully by the intruder and it had become stuck, partially ajar. A small piece of wire used to keep the door locked while feeding or cleaning out the stall had held the door in place and as a consequence *Flimflam* had become agitated, kicking out until the door was open and he could roam free. In the process, he had badly damaged his leg.

"Shit!" Pete shouted. It was the first time Cannon had seen the other side of his host. "What a bloody mess! What a bloody mess!" he repeated.

"Yes, agreed," said Cannon, "thank God we didn't lose *Wings* through all this. That *would* have been disastrous!"

"Umm," Pete replied. He was really agitated, frightened, Cannon noted. "But we have lost *Flimflam*. I just hope *Holdthephone* can do us proud next week," he said. "Notwithstanding that, *Wings* is safe. I think we dodged a bullet overall."

Michelle and Emily were now making tea in the kitchen. They had spent the last couple of hours watching nervously from the front door as the horses were recovered and brought back into their stables.

Cannon's thoughts turned to possible suspects. Who would do this? Who would try and nobble Pete, and put his racing livelihood in jeopardy? For what reason?

Despite the early hour, he picked up his phone to call Bruce.

"I know," said Bruce before Cannon could even speak. "I've just got off the phone from George Sormond, he's had the same issue."

"What, someone opening all the doors of his stable and letting the horses run free?"

"Yes, I'm assuming you are calling for the same reason?"

"Exactly," replied Cannon. "Though it looks like it was done this way to avoid the real reason. As if the person concerned is making sure that we don't know who they are targeting. One thing is clear though," he stated.

"What's that?" asked Bruce.

"That whoever is behind this, is determined, *and* clever," he replied.

The rest of the day was a blur to Bruce. It wasn't really his domain. He had called Thatcher to fill him in on what had happened at Pete's and Sormond's farms and had subsequently discussed the issue with Cusscom. Bruce now realized that Cannon was right. Somehow, what was going on was linked to Optin, but what was it and how did it tie in with Sormond, if at all? He spent the day moving from one stable yard to another and finding out exactly what had gone on. Sormond let it be known his complete displeasure at what had happened. He sought police support to protect *Chesterman* in particular, but the request was denied. Bruce advised Sormond that there were very limited resources available to him from the local Colac police station, and he already had the majority of them in Alworth and Bossin. In addition, the only crime committed that they could think of concerning the matter was trespass and breaking and entering. It wasn't *murder* and accordingly with everything on their plate, they needed to focus elsewhere. Sormond was livid but Bruce advised him that given the lack of any CCTV at either property they would be guessing as to who was responsible for the break-in. They would continue to investigate it, but they needed to prioritise their cases. Bruce did not want to admit anything, but at this point, they had no idea who could be responsible.

It was now only five days to the carnival. The horses due to race at the meeting were now supposed to be on a reduced regime. They were fit, knew how to race, how to jump.

CHAPTER 43

The body in the bush had taken a back seat. No one had even thought about it. The focus was on Hedge and Optin. Bruce tried to work out how, or if their deaths were connected in some way but could find no evidence to that effect. In addition, if there was any link between Optin and Grovedale, but again he hit a brick wall. He could find nothing.

The only matter that at least seemed to make sense was that someone was trying to stop some of the local horses from Colac, particularly those of Peter Brownlow and George Sormond, running at the upcoming Warrnambool carnival. It wasn't what he and Cromwell were in Colac for. They were there to solve murders. Unfortunately, they were not getting very far. He picked up a coffee cup and drank the cold remains before asking her.

"What I still don't understand," he said, "is why Hedge was dressed up as a jockey when he was dumped into that rubbish bin? What's the significance?"

They were in the situation room, just the two of them.

"Because Hedge was trying to blackmail a trainer, perhaps?" Cromwell replied.

"With regards to what?"

"Drugs? Enhancements?"

"What type of enhancements?"

"I don't know Sir. I'm no expert, but I have heard it mentioned in the past that some trainers have used methods that are deemed unfair, cruel, or even downright dangerous in order to get a horse to run faster."

"Perhaps we need to call in someone who could tell us all about it? How it works?" he asked.

"That could be useful," she answered.

Bruce rubbed his chin, thinking, before saying. "The only problem I have with learning more about this game is that it *still* doesn't tell us who Hedge *could* have been blackmailing or even if it's relevant. In fact, at this stage, we still don't know if he was up to anything at all."

"True Sir, but once we have a better understanding of this racing game, maybe things will become a little clearer? Also, perhaps what Cannon was highlighting was right, maybe the murders of Hedge and Optin are linked somehow? The question we need answers to though, is the why and the who?"

CHAPTER 44

Walt Grovedale was a worried man. He hadn't thought about the incident in a long time. Was there a threat to him? He knew who could have issued such a warning but was unsure as to why now? He thought the matter had been resolved - a long time ago.

Cannon watched as Deb Ryan looked over *Wings*. The horse appeared to have taken all the drama of the past few days in his stride and had done well. Nothing seemed to have phased him and the stable riders had continued with the horse's prep for the Grand Annual. His stride into the chase fences had improved. Also, the control he now showed when turning around to begin a second run over the four training jumps had been so much better than when Cannon had first schooled him. This would be crucial during the race when the field charged along through the figure of eight course of the Grand Annual. It was a unique experience for a horse and as such any horse competing in the race needed to be prepared for it.

"I think he's done very well," she said. "No sign of anything bothering him at all. He appears to be rock-hard fit, thanks to you, and he seems to be a settled horse. Very relaxed, very professional" she said. "I'm sure Pete is delighted."

George Sormond had been focused on winning the Grand Annual since *Chesterman* had been the runner up the previous year. This was going to be his year. He owned the horse, after all. It was his time.

Sormond had been training horses for a very long time, but the big prize of the Grand Annual had always eluded him. He had decided to take a chance. Someone had found out. Was he being targeted because of it?

CHAPTER 45

"I think we were both lucky," said Cannon.

He was sitting with George Sormond in Sormond's house. Cannon had decided he needed to visit the other local trainer alone. He needed to do some more digging.

"I agree, mate," Sormond replied. "If *Chesterman* had been seriously injured, or worse killed, then I would have been really, really, really angry! As it is, I'm both pissed off and furious, especially at the police. I have thirty-odd horses in my stable and anything could have happened that night. Fortunately, *Chesterman* is okay, but I know it could have been a lot worse than it was."

"What was the final outcome?" enquired Cannon.

"I *lost* three of the flat horses to injury."

"Shit," Cannon replied. "I'm sorry to hear that."

Sormond sighed, resignedly. "The good news is that I own one of them outright, the other two are partly syndicated but the owners are not happy. They've asked me to install more security now."

"I would agree with them," Cannon replied.

"Yes, but it's expensive to buy, install, maintain….not to forget all the passwords or codes I need to remember for the alarms themselves."

"But it will keep you and the horses safe. It's a good investment. Money well spent," Cannon replied tailing off. He had questions to ask but he needed the timing to be right. He needed to control his impatience. Both men sat back for a few seconds, each contemplating what the other had said.

Cannon silently sipped the tea that he been offered by the house-keeper Mary when he had first arrived. Sormond was drinking his regular rum and coke.

Cannon finished his drink then put the mug down on the arm of his chair, he continued to press Sormond about the recent intrusion.

"Any other losses or just the three?" he asked.

"No, I had more," Sormond said. "I lost a few of my jumpers. Four of them will never race again due to the injuries they sustained running down into the road. I've already had to have three of the four put down due to their injuries. A fracture of the humerus in one case, another due to badly chipped knees and a third due to tendon and ligament damage."

"God! What do the owners say?"

Sormond sighed. "We haven't been able to get hold of them yet. Well, I tell a lie we did manage to get hold of one of them. They were very angry about it," he said, "and it was me they were angry with. Not the perpetrator."

"I'm sorry to hear that," Cannon replied.

Sormond looked into his glass. He swirled the brown liquid around, then in a single gulp drank the remainder. Cannon watched the man closely. He looked downtrodden almost defeated. Cannon wasn't totally convinced that was the case. He decided that it was time to ask what he needed to.

"George, is there any reason at all that you can think of, as to why you were targeted?"

Sormond sat silently for a second, his mind churning. Eventually, he said.

"No, there is no reason at all for anyone to do what they did! I don't think it was very sensible, and no way to get a message across. You may not be aware but a couple of years ago we had all sorts of drama. All sorts of protests. Given the timing of the carnival coming up, I think it was likely to be those crazy greenies, the same ones as before. They seem to protest about everything to do with racing…bloody idiots!" he concluded.

"So, you don't think there was any linkage between this, you…and what happened to the Vet, Max Optin?"

"Why would there be…?"

Cannon watched the man closely. Throughout his career in the police force, he had met, negotiated with, cajoled, argued against, fought, and talked with many, many people. He had learnt to watch for subtle signs about their behaviour, how they spoke when under stress, how they gave away their true feelings through the odd scratching of an ear, or of rubbing a face. Cannon saw Sormond give something away. It wasn't a confession, just a brief glimpse that Cannon noticed. It told him Sormond was lying about something.

He decided not to push the point. What Sormond was hiding would come out sooner or later.

CHAPTER 46

"I think George Sormond is hiding something," Cannon said.

He and Pete were sitting in Pete's kitchen. The glow from an overhead track of spotlights shone against the dark of the windows. Outside, soft fingers of rain caressed each pane. The winter mornings were not dissimilar to those in the UK, Cannon thought. They could see their reflections in the darkened windows.

"Why do you say that?" Pete asked.

"Call it experience, intuition."

They sat in silence for a few seconds, both men drinking coffee, enjoying the warmth inside as they ate breakfast.

"Do you have an idea what it is, what it could be…or even why?"

"I'm not sure," Cannon replied, "but I have an idea it is something to do with *Chesterman*. I have a couple of thoughts but I'm not sure which is correct, and I don't want to say anything just yet, in case I'm wrong. I'd look a fool if I did that, plus I hardly know the man really. He's been very kind to me while I've been here and he's obviously quite impressed with what you've done yourself over the years with just a small number of horses, the jumpers in particular," Cannon said. "So, before I put him on the spot, I need to find out more."

Pete nodded in agreement. "Makes sense Mike, I just hope that this mess can get sorted out sooner rather than later. With the carnival just a few days away it's been nothing but a distraction," he said. "I'm so thankful for your help and getting *Wings* much better prepared than I could ever have done. He seems to be thriving. It's just a pity about *Flimflam*. If I get my hands on the bastard that opened those doors and let those horses roam, I'll fucking murder him."

Expletives were not Pete's thing, but Cannon could understand the frustration.

The two men continued to talk for a while. Pete had arranged for an assistant farm manager to look after the milking and other duties around the farm for part of the morning, leaving him free for a few hours. He was keen to learn more from Cannon, noting for example how the work that went into *Wings* before the carnival was slowly being reduced, giving the horse more time to recover from its training. It was hoped that by the time the big race came around in just a few days any exertions, niggles, or tweaks would have been noticed and hopefully addressed. The last thing they needed was the horse to be lame or carrying any other injury.

The race itself would soon sort out who had put the miles into their training and who hadn't.

The light of the morning started to permeate through the windows and the darkness outside slowly dissipated, the reflections in the windows disappearing like ghosts.

"Let's get going," Cannon said, "we've got work to do."

They watched as the track riders took *Wings*, along with *Striped King*, around the long circuit of just over a thousand metres and then jumped them both together over the four steeplechase fences. *Striped King* wasn't as fluid as *Wings,* nor as skilled, but he had replaced *Binge-Eater* as a racing companion.

"Looking good," Cannon said to Pete, "*Wings'* stride into the fence is perfect. His rider certainly has become a lot bolder over the past couple of weeks. It makes for a better combination and ultimately a better result."

Pete was pleased with what he was seeing. The stable rider turned *Wings* around once he had cleared the jumps, the horse blowing slightly but that was more about clearing the *cobwebs* out rather than fitness. After the incident in the stable yard, the horses had been kept in their boxes for twenty-four hours while the investigation by the police as to what had happened continued.

"Take him around the track for a couple more laps," Pete said to the rider, "we want to make sure that when the Grand Annual heats up over the last half mile that *Wings'* fitness can carry him through."

Cannon agreed, adding. "We also need to get some pace into him as well so that when he needs to sprint at the end he can. I suggest you take him around quietly, say half pace the first couple of times, then gradually increase to three quarters on the penultimate lap and on the last lap, let him stretch out in a sprint for the last four hundred."

The rider touched his cap acknowledging the instructions and went off to do what was requested.

Pete asked Cannon if he would mind staying to watch, while he went off to check out the rest of the farm activities.

Cannon was only too happy to oblige. He knew he had done all he could to help get the horse ready for the big race. He just hoped nothing would happen to prevent that from happening.

CHAPTER 47

"So, you think Sormond is hiding something, Mike?"

"Yes, I do Inspector," Cannon replied. "I have a feeling that he knows more about what happened to Optin than he is letting on."

They were sitting in the lounge of Pete's house. Pete having vacated the room to allow Cannon the opportunity to share with Bruce and Cromwell his view about Sormond.

"I think the *attack* if I can call it that, on his stable compared to the *attack* here at Pete's stable was a bit of a ruse, a smokescreen."

"How do you mean?" Bruce replied.

Cannon took a deep breath. He didn't want to lose credibility with Bruce. He wanted to ensure that what he was saying, based on his gut feeling had *some* semblance of truth.

"I think Pete was the real target and that Sormond's horse *Chesterman* was never intended to be harmed. I think the fact that both stables were broken into using the same method was intended to throw the police off track. To get you to think that the attacker intended to *get at* some horses, particularly those involved in the Grand Annual, *Chesterman* and *Wings*."

"And you don't think that?"

"No, I don't," replied Cannon. "I think the break-in is one thing and the murder of Optin another. As I said, I think Sormond knows more about the Optin situation than he is letting on. If I'm right then I think Pete's place was an intended target but as I said, Sormond's place never was."

"Why do you say that Mr. Cannon," Cromwell said jumping into the conversation.

"Because of what Sormond said to me and how he said it. He claimed to know nothing about Optin's murder, but I think whoever did murder Optin knew that Sormond was up to something and is using it against him."

"Such as….?"

"I think he's been up to something and he has been for a while. I think Optin knew what it was and threatened to reveal it. I think that the man Hedge also had an idea about what was going on but decided to keep it in his back pocket until he was able to use the same information for his own purposes. Unfortunately for him he never got to use it. He was too busy blackmailing someone else."

"And how do you know about the blackmail?" Bruce asked.

"It's an educated guess, to be honest," replied Cannon. "I can't see how else Hedge would have operated. I gathered from what you've said previously that he moved around a lot, was always paid for any work he did in cash, and then he suddenly disappeared. Seems like he did that a lot until he was found dead in a garbage truck. Murdered. People are not murdered just like that. He obviously upset someone." Cannon concluded.

"And what's your view about Sormond then? What do you think he was or is up to?" Bruce asked.

"I think he's been using some kind of a *motivator* on some of his horses and I'm sure Optin had known about it for a while. Remember the Grand Annual is an obsession now."

"So why didn't Optin say or do anything about it?"

"Because I think he was being blackmailed himself."

"By who?"

"Hedge initially," replied Cannon.

"Sorry I'm confused," replied Bruce. "You are telling me that Hedge was blackmailing Optin as well as someone else?"

"Yes," replied Cannon, "and I think that the second person killed both of them."

"Why?"

"For obvious reasons," replied Cannon, "to make sure neither Hedge nor Optin revealed what was going on."

"But if Optin knew what was happening, then why did he not just come out with it. Let the police know? Also, Hedge was killed a couple of years ago so Optin couldn't have been concerned about him anymore."

"Well that's true but he would also have had to reveal that he was being blackmailed himself and I don't think he was willing to do that. At least not at the time he was killed."

"Okay, okay," answered Bruce, still not sure where this was all leading. "If you say Optin was being blackmailed by Hedge or someone else, what was it that Optin was hiding?"

"I'm not sure but I think it was something big. I think Optin was part of something and Hedge found out, I think it's been going on for a while."

"But you don't know what it is?" asked Bruce.

"No, I don't," Cannon replied.

"So, let me get this straight," Bruce said. "According to you, Max Optin was into something big. Hedge found out about it and blackmailed him?"

"Yes."

"Hedge was then murdered, but you have no idea by whom?"

"That's correct," replied Cannon, somewhat sheepishly. He wasn't sure why he felt that way. It wasn't his case. It wasn't even his country. He was on holiday. Yet somehow death had found him. Almost always followed him.

Bruce carried on with his assessment of where things were at.

"And Optin was then murdered, and you think it relates to something that Sormond was or is engaged in?"

"Yes."

"But again, you don't have any evidence to that effect?"

"No, just a feeling," Cannon answered.

"Based on…?"

"Based on the conversation I had with him. I think that he was somewhat relieved that Optin was no longer around to reveal what he knew."

"That Sormond was using an enhancer or something similar on his horses to get them to race differently, better?"

"Or worse…Yes."

"But someone else knew?"

"Yes," replied Cannon, "and I think that person was also involved in the same thing that Optin was. I think Optin was finally going to reveal what it was to the police, but the other person or persons had other ideas. They murdered him before he could talk."

"But why?"

"Because it's likely to be still ongoing."

"And you think it relates to Sormond?"

"No, I don't. The Sormond matter is something entirely different. I think Optin became aware of what Sormond was up to and realized that someone else was also involved. I think this other individual was or is part of the bigger picture that we just talked about, and Optin was going to reveal that as well."

"What makes you think that?"

"Remember Optin said he no longer dealt with horses anymore. I think once he found out that this other person, someone he trusted, was involved with Sormond, he decided to stay away, initially turning a blind eye. It was only when he finally decided to reveal what the other person was involved with that he had to be silenced."

"But why now?"

"Perhaps he'd had enough of the subterfuge? Perhaps he just couldn't carry on with it?' I'm not sure but I just think he'd decided to say something, and he'd let whoever killed him know what he was about to do and that signed his own death warrant."

"Quite a story Mike," Bruce replied.

Cannon wasn't sure how to take the comment. He stayed quiet.

Bruce considered what he heard. He looked at Cannon, then Cromwell.

"If Mike is right," he said, "we have a killer somewhere in our midst who is cold-blooded enough to murder at least two people. Obviously this someone could easily kill again. I think we need to have a chat with George Sormond and quickly."

CHAPTER 48

They were sitting in George Sormond's house. The view from the building across the paddock to the stables where *Chesterman* was housed was blighted by the low cloud and rain that continued to soak the area. Sormond had hoped that the rain would stop soon, or at least that it had stopped in Warrnambool. *Chesterman* didn't mind soft ground to run on, but heavy ground was not his favourite. It was also highly unlikely now, based on the last few days of weather and lack of sun, that the Grand Annual would be run on a *good* track.

Bruce got straight to the point, the reason for their visit, arriving at the house unexpectedly.

"We think that you may be in danger, Mr. Sormond," he said.

The trainer considered Bruce's words before asking. "Why would that be Inspector and if true, which I doubt, who am I in danger from?"

He waited for Bruce to answer.

The policeman decided to be careful. Not to reveal too much but to get Sormond to think that Bruce knew more than he did. Bruce hoped that Sormond would inadvertently fill in the gaps in their knowledge, would provide missing detail that would help in their investigations. They still had two murders to solve, one of them at least two years old.

"Well as far as the *who* is concerned, we don't yet know, but I think you do."

Sormond laughed. "You think someone I know, wants to kill me?"

"Yes, as I mentioned before, we think that to be the case."

"But I still don't understand Inspector, why and for what reason?"

Bruce sat back in his chair. He looked towards Cromwell who had silently turned on her phone to record the conversation. She had not advised Sormond when she did so and she knew she was in the wrong, but they needed the evidence to progress. The game was on.

"We think that you may be involved in something your industry does not support and someone has been helping you perpetuate the practice."

"And what is this practice that our industry rejects?" Sormond retorted, "And who is this other person you are referring to?"

Bruce decided not to answer the questions directly. He took a more obtuse approach.

"Tell me Mr. Sormond, why do you think Max Optin was killed?"

"I'm not sure I can answer that Inspector. Perhaps you should ask the killer if you can find him."

"What if I told you that I think you are lying Mr. Sormond? That I think you know more than you are telling me."

Sormond began to get angry at the assertion. His patience wearing thin, he didn't need lecturing.

"Inspector!" he responded. "Are you here to tell me that I need to be careful and that *someone* is out to get me, or are you here to accuse me of something? Either way, I wish you'd let me know what you think is going on?"

"As I mentioned before, we think Max Optin was murdered because he knew what you were up to…" Bruce replied.

"And I murdered him?" replied Sormond. "Laughable!"

"No Sir, we don't think you had anything to do with that. We think that someone who was aware of *what you have been* doing killed Mr. Optin."

"But what *is it* that you think I have been doing?"

"Helping them, help you."

"To do what, Inspector?"

"That's something we are still trying to resolve," replied Bruce, trying not to give away the fact that the police still had little idea what Sormond was involved in other than the theory propagated by Cannon. The theory that he was affecting his horses' chances while running in races. "In *your* case, we think that you have been using something to improve the chances of your horses winning their races, and we think Mr. Optin found out."

Sormond's face went white. He tried to hide it, but he saw that Bruce was quick to see that he had hit a nerve. He tried to deflect his concern.

"If you believe that's what I am doing, have you contacted the racing authorities to advise them?"

"No Sir, we are not here to do that. In due course the practice we think you are employing will come out, but what *we* are trying to do is to solve a murder, that of Max Optin. Our job is about policing the community, not the horse racing fraternity."

Sormond's face quickly reverted to its normal state. His bravado and confidence returned.

"So, tell me, Inspector, if you think that I need to be careful can I ask you again, who of, and for what reason?"

"The person we believe is helping you."

"And that person is…?" Sormond asked, knowing full well that Bruce's accusation could not be supported.

"As I mentioned previously, we don't yet know, but we do know that the person or persons killed Max Optin."

"Because Optin supposedly knew about an alleged practice you say I am involved in?"

"Yes."

"So why did he not do it earlier? Why did *he* not tell the racing authorities if he had suspicions?"

"We don't think *he had suspicions,*" Bruce replied. "We think he knew for sure."

"And yet did nothing about it?"

"Correct, because he was involved in something else. Something *much bigger* and it was ultimately that something that got him killed. That's why we are here," Bruce said. "We are here to help you."

The taste of the statement did not sit well in Bruce's mouth, but he had needed to say it.

Sormond rubbed his chin. "To help me...?" he said, mockingly under his breath.

"Yes, Mr. Sormond as strange as it would seem. We don't need another death or murder. We need to find the killer of Max Optin.

"And you say Optin was involved in something much bigger than what you believe I am guilty of?"

"Yes."

"And what is that?"

Bruce did not want to reveal anything, primarily because he didn't yet have an answer.

"Let's just say Mr. Sormond that we believe you know the answer to that question. That you are using that knowledge to protect yourself against the person or persons involved in Optin's murder. In return, your actions concerning your horses are being supported somehow. It is almost a case of at least two parties having a hold over each other. A gun to each one's head." Bruce said accusatorily. "I'm sure you realise that withholding information from the police is an offense?"

"Yes, Inspector I do, but I'm sorry I can't help you anymore. I don't know what you are talking about when it comes to Max Optin's murder. All I know is what I've told you."

He could see that Sormond was lying, but Bruce had little to go on with. He had tried to highlight to Sormond that he was potentially in danger, and it was because he was hiding something or someone. Someone who could kill him.

CHAPTER 49

The last of the exercises were completed, the horses washed down, and their boxes were made ready. It was nine am, two days before the Grand Annual meeting would start. The actual race was on day two of the carnival. *Wings* would be transported down to the course tomorrow. Cannon watched as Deb Ryan gave the horse its final check-up. She was methodical in her approach.

"He's come through the past day or so without anything obvious. If anything, he looks stronger than ever," she enthused. "I think you've done a great job, Mike. He looks a million dollars."

Cannon smiled. "Thanks, Debra," he said, "I'm glad to have helped. I just hope that it's all worth it in the end. Pete and Emily have been very generous to Michelle and me, and Pete has given me much more freedom with *Wings* here," he nodded at the horse, "than I could ever have expected."

"Pete's a good man," she answered, "I'm sure he's happy with what you've done."

"Thanks."

She turned back to the horse rubbing his face then called for his stablehand who had been standing outside vaping on a small pipe to come into the Vet's room and take the horseback to the stable. The rain had stopped the previous afternoon and overnight a wind from the north had begun to dry out the wet ground. It was what Sormond wanted, Cannon thought, it was not what *Wings* would prefer. A softer landing was his preference.

Once *Wings* had disappeared, had been taken away, Cannon asked, "How well do you know George Sormond?"

She considered the question before answering. "Extremely well. I have known him for years. Why do you ask?"

"Do you see him as a potential cheat?" he asked, her question answered with one of his own.

"Cheating? How? With regards to what?"

"His horses."

"To achieve what?"

"To win the Grand Annual. I understand it's been an obsession of his to win the race and to be the first local trainer to do so for quite some time. Twenty-five years I believe?"

Cannon and Pete had talked about it when they had sat in Pete's kitchen discussing the attack on the stables. It was one of many subjects that they had touched on.

"I guess anything is possible," she replied, "I'm sure many people have *obsessions* as you call it, but cheating on a horse race, that's a bit singularly minded."

"That's true, but it is worth quite a bit of money. The winner earning about $200,000?"

"That's true, but I don't see George needing the money. He's a very wealthy man already."

"So, you think perhaps it's the prestige he's wanting?" he asked, "to show that a local trainer can win the race if he had the right horse?"

"Could be. Have you asked him?"

"Not really, but I was interested in your view."

"I don't have one," she replied. "I look after the horses, I don't train or bet on them."

"But you do like to attend race meetings?"

"Yes of course, whenever I can. I love it," she replied. "I wish I could attend more often. It's just that the travel takes so much time and I have my practice to run, so I'm limited as to what I can do and when."

Cannon smiled his understanding.

"Tell me," he said, "what do you think about Max Optin? His murder?"

"I'm sorry?" she queried, "what about it?"

"Well do you have any idea who would have wanted him dead?"

"I'm not sure what you are asking Mike, but why do you think I know anything about his murder or who want to kill him?"

"I don't," Cannon said. "I just know that you worked with him previously and that he may have mentioned something, anything, to you that he may have been worried about? However unlikely."

She stared at him as if to say that she was very disappointed that he would think that she would know anything about Optin's death. Cannon took the glare at face value. He apologized.

"I'm sorry," he said, "I didn't mean to offend you…"

"But you have," she interrupted. "And if you think that I was involved in Max Optin's murder then you are mistaken!" she replied, her voice rising. "And frankly Mike, I'm surprised you would even think that. I don't know what you believe I would gain from Max's death, but I can assure you that there was nothing to be gained. Certainly not by me!" she exclaimed.

She began to cry. Cannon didn't know what to do. He had assumed something, drawn a conclusion and now he felt that he had made the wrong one.

He tried to mutter another apology, but she walked out of the room, outside and into the cold, ignoring him. He watched her go. Without hesitation, she climbed into her car, and without looking in his direction drove off towards the road.

Cannon knew that he would need to straighten things out with her once the carnival was over before he returned to the UK. He knew Pete relied on her, so he would need to talk with Pete as well to ensure he hadn't broken the relationship between Vet and friend. The day had started well, but it had turned to shit now. Cannon hoped that the next two days would be much better. They needed to be.

CHAPTER 50

"How are you feeling?" Cannon asked. "Nervous?"

Pete and he were at the dining room table. Dinner was being prepared by Emily, Michelle, and Stephanie. They had gone to a lot of trouble asking what the *boys* really wanted.

Only two nights out from the start of the carnival and three nights until the big race meant that time had caught up with them. They knew that there was very little else they could do now. It was a time of waiting. The training was complete, the transport booked, the jockey on board. The horse was in magnificent order.

"Extremely," Pete answered. "I'm not sure I can eat anything at all, between now and the end of the race."

Cannon smiled. He knew the feeling. Had experienced it before himself.

"I think the most important thing is to enjoy it, whatever happens," he emphasized. "I'm personally looking forward to it and I know Michelle is as well."

Pete nodded towards the kitchen where voices and laughter could be heard. "I think the *chardy* or the *shiraz* is going down well," he said, "looks like *Em* will really miss Michelle when you guys go home. I think they've had a good time together these past few weeks."

"I agree," Cannon replied. "I hope we can get you over to our place at some point in the future. To reciprocate the hospitality that you've shown us."

"It's nothing really mate. To be honest I think it's been more of a break for *me* than anything else. You've done all the work with the horse. I'm just the beneficiary."

Cannon raised his beer glass that was sitting on the table and offered a toast. "I hope this isn't premature," he said, "but here's to you, and *Wings,* and not forgetting Emily for giving Michelle and I the opportunity of experiencing a wonderful spectacle with you in a couple of days. Let's hope everyone has a great day and whatever happens, we are all able to enjoy it."

The two men clinked glasses, then sat back silently in their chairs. Each had their own thoughts.

Cannon wasn't solely focused on the upcoming race, he was also trying to rationalize some of the questions in his mind.

"Penny for them…?" Michelle asked as she came into the dining room, carrying a casserole dish.

Stephanie followed with a tray containing large bowls of rice, carrots, and peas. Emily immediately behind her daughter carried a new bottle of red wine. "For the table," she said, smiling.

Cannon reached for the bottle, setting it down in front of him.

Over the past few days, they had been unable to eat like this. With the police investigation going on with regards to Optin, the *break-in*, and the need to keep the farm and the training going, having dinner together had been difficult. To be able to do so now was a privilege, something that Cannon and Michelle were extremely grateful for. He decided to put his thoughts to one side. Now was not the time.

He answered Michelle's question. "Oh, it's nothing," he lied, "just enjoying the moment."

She looked at him, turning her head slightly as if to say she didn't believe him. She knew him well enough by now and knew when it was time to discuss things and when it was time to stay quiet. She decided to let the subject go. If he wanted to discuss it, he would.

"So nice to hear," she answered enigmatically.

CHAPTER 51

He decided to make the call. It had been playing on his mind since the actual incident. He used the phone that he had been given. The one he had been told to use once and once only.

"Was it you?" he asked.

"Me what?"

"That burnt that car out on my land?"

"What do you think?"

Grovedale considered his answer. "Yes, I think you did."

"Then you have answered your own question and I have no reason to answer it for you then, do I?"

"But why? I thought we had agreed a solution, came to an arrangement," he said, his voice cracking slightly. "I thought it was over, sorted!"

The voice on the other end of the line went silent, it unnerved Grovedale. For all his wealth, he still knew that he was liable, responsible for what had happened. Money couldn't buy protection from his conscience.

"I've changed my mind," the voice said eventually.

"What do you mean?"

"Exactly that…I need to tell the police what happened. I'm not going to carry the secret anymore."

"No!" shouted Grovedale down the phone. "Please…" he said, his voice a plea for mercy. "Please let's discuss it first. Maybe we can come to another more suitable arrangement?" he queried. "Maybe there is something else that I can do for you? If it's money you need then …"

"I don't need any money…" the voice interrupted, issuing the words through gritted teeth.

"So, what do you need?" Grovedale asked.

The disembodied voice on the line responded. "I want justice."

'For whom?" Grovedale replied. "For you?" he said, laughing as he did so, trying to portray some bravado that he didn't really feel. "Or for *him*?" he suggested. "It's a bit late for *him* now, isn't it?"

"Is it?'

"Look, don't play games with me," he replied. "I want us to resolve this amicably and I want to do so sooner rather than later. However, if we can't come to a deal then things may get ugly. I'm sure neither of us wants that."

The line remained quiet. There was no response. He thought he could still hear breathing.

"Hello! Hello!," Grovedale shouted into the receiver, "Are you still there?"

"Yes."

"So, what do you want to do?"

"We'll meet." the voice said. "I'll be in touch."

CHAPTER 52

They sat in the Marble Dragon Restaurant. It was the first time that Bruce and Cusscom had had the opportunity to have dinner together. Bruce intended to give an update to his *de facto* boss.

He wanted to bring him into the loop more than he currently was, particularly as the investigation gathered momentum. While there wasn't too much more to report on since they had last spoken, Bruce felt that things were becoming a little bit clearer. Also, it was politically expedient to ensure that Bruce had addressed the gaps in the relationship between Cusscom and himself. It would help both Bruce and Thatcher in the long run if the *locals* were happy.

Bruce looked around. The restaurant was busy with takeaways being collected but was generally quiet inside. The phone at the reception desk seemed to be ringing constantly, its low tone just enough to be heard by the few seated patrons. Pink lanterns with long black tassels connected to the bare ceiling with a dark plastic-covered wire swayed in the air throughout the room. The movement was caused by the reverse cycle air-conditioning unit that blew warmth onto the patrons.

Bruce had removed his coat, the cold outside long forgotten. It lay draped across the back of his chair. They sat at a table for four, a plastic lazy susan sat between them on top of the table. Blue and white bowls, with Chinese writing and images of dragons floating across rivers painted on them, stood empty beside them. A white cotton tablecloth completed the table layout.

They had ordered a beer each and red wine to go with their meals. Both men having chosen spring rolls and prawn toast as starters followed by honey pepper beef. Their *hors d'oeuvres* had already been served.

Cusscom took a bite of his toast as Bruce said, "I apologise, Seth, if the team has been less than engaging on the Optin case but we've been trying to understand the landscape around here. It's been challenging at times. Some of the folk we have been talking too haven't always been as accommodating as we would like."

Cusscom wiped his mouth with a napkin before answering. "Are you surprised?"

"Well…no…umm…yes, yes, frankly I am surprised," he replied. "I would have thought a murder of a relatively prominent person in the community would have set tongues wagging, got people thinking, even scared some of them into action."

"Because…?"

"Because of what we are. As a community. It's something unique to us I believe, especially out here," he said, waving a hand in the air. "It's what

Aussies do."

Cusscom swallowed another piece of toast.

"It's what we *used* to do," he replied. "Things are a little different now. I think the world has changed and I think the people of Colac have done the same. Changed… I mean."

"When I was here two years ago, " Bruce said, "when we started the Hedge investigation, everyone I met was willing to help, to do what they could to help the police find out what had happened to the man. How he ended up in a garbage truck. Now it's just….well…"

"Yesterday's news?" interjected Cusscom.

"Yes, and it seems that it's the same with Optin."

They both sat silently for a second. They knew they were right, that the general public seemed to have become immune or inured to death, murder, or tragedy. They saw it every day on their TV, phone, or media devices. No wonder they didn't want to get involved. Nor indeed it seems, did they want to remember anything either. Perhaps looking ahead was much better than looking backward?

A waiter walked silently up to their table and poured them both a glass of water from a bottle he was carrying, subsequently decanting wine into their glasses. He then politely asked them if they had finished their starters before removing their plates. Nodding, he turned and walked off towards the kitchen.

"So where are we now then?" Cusscom asked eventually.

Bruce considered his words.

"We have an idea that …."

The mobile in Bruce's coat pocket began to ring loudly. The sound piercing the relative quiet of the restaurant. Embarrassed at the noise, he held a hand up to his boss seeking understanding in not replying as he desperately dug inside the coat pocket for the phone.

He looked at the writing on the screen. *Cromwell.*

"Yes?" he said once he had been able to tap the answer button and put the phone to his ear.

"Sorry Sir to interrupt your evening," she stated, "but I think you'd better get down here quickly."

He was confused. She had said nothing, but he knew she would not have contacted him without a reason.

"Why, what's up Constable?" he asked, his face stern as he looked across at his *boss.*

He wasn't expecting the answer he received.

"It's Walt Grovedale Sir."

"What about him?"

"He's just been found dead. Down here by the lake," she replied. "Looks like murder!"

CHAPTER 53

The white lights that had been put up by the forensic team blistered the darkness. A tent had been erected over the crime scene, and the body of Walt Grovedale lay under a sheet. The crystal clear night accentuated the stars that spread across the sky from east to west. It was cold. Walt Grovedale, however, was not feeling any of it.

People dressed in forensic gear, blue coveralls on their shoes, paper suits as needed, moved around quietly, professionally, taking pictures, taking samples of grass from the ground, searching for clues. Blue and red lights from police cars and an ambulance flashed quietly in rapid succession, the colours disappearing into the night sky.

They stood forty feet from the water and moonlight glinted across the lake's surface. The silence that spread across the huge expanse of water enveloped them, just like the vapour that steamed from their mouths as they spoke quietly to one other.

"How long?" asked Bruce.

"According to our forensic friends over there, no longer than about two hours, at least until he was found," Cromwell replied.

Bruce was thinking out loud.

"So, you called me at around eight, which means he'd been dead by around six," he said. "That would have been just after sunset, which is a bit of a dangerous time to be committing a murder don't you think, especially here?"

He looked around. They were standing near a picnic barbecue facility that was now empty. It hadn't been used since the weekend, but it had been cleaned, the dull metal of the barbecue shining in the powerful lights that lit up the area. A grassy bank ran towards the water and a couple of the forensic team slowly edged down the slope as they inspected the ground for footprints, taking photographs as they did so.

"How is the kid doing?" he asked.

"Under the circumstances, I guess she's holding up pretty well. She's in shock obviously, but at least she is back at home now. I'll go and see her later. Maybe even wait until morning."

"Umm, I think that's a good idea," Bruce responded, thinking about the young girl who had found the body. She had been walking her dog and had been on her way back home when she came across it. Grovedale's body had been lying on the grass in almost complete darkness. The young girl had nearly tripped over it.

The interruption to dinner with Cusscom was frustrating, Bruce thought. It had been a chance to mend bridges and he had felt that he was just about getting back on good terms with him before the call. That would have been something positive to report, something that Thatcher would have been happy with, pleased about. Now, however, he had more bad news.

When he had received the call from Cromwell he hadn't expected to be standing in the dark and the cold. He hadn't expected to be looking at yet another victim, yet here he was with *another* body, another mystery to contend with. As he stood quietly contemplating the next steps in the investigation, he questioned himself. What had he missed?

He walked over to where Grovedale's body was lying, carefully standing on the rubber mats that were strategically placed on the ground allowing the relevant teams to search the area and collect any evidence they could without disturbing or contaminating the immediate environment.

Grovedale's Mercedes had been found in one of the car parking spots that overlooked the lake. The doors were unlocked.

Bruce pulled back the sheet with a gloved hand and noted Grovedale's empty eyes staring up at him. He was surprised that the plastic bag that had been used to kill Grovedale still covered his head.

"Not a pretty sight is it, Sir?" Cromwell asked, looking through the clear bag at Grovedale's face. The grimace, the saliva around the mouth, the lolling tongue, and the bulging eyes. Murder by suffocation is such a callous *cause of death* she thought. Cruel.

"No," he replied, "it's not. But it's also very unusual. I haven't seen a murder like this for a long time. No gun, no knife involved…yes very unusual. It seems like whoever did this has thought it through. It's not very efficient, but it is effective and it's quiet," he continued.

"The forensic guys have noted that there are signs of a knock to the back of the head."

"That would explain a few things."

"Like no sign of a struggle?"

"Yes," he replied. "It looks like he must have been meeting someone and was ambushed, then killed. Given the timing, if around six is accurate, then there would have hardly been anyone around at that time of night. Most people would be at home, staying warm."

He looked around again. Having been at the site of the body for a few hours and wandering around as the various teams worked, Bruce realised that he had lost all sense of distance and of his immediate surroundings. When he checked, he noticed that the site of the body was at least thirty metres from where Grovedales' car had been parked. The car park itself was roughly fifteen metres higher than the lake, and the slope down to the water was quite severe, at an angle of more than 60 degrees. The contour of the land where the body lay and where Grovedale was likely to have been attacked, to the car park itself meant that if anyone had been in the general area of the cars they would have been unable to see anything at all regarding the attack.

Bruce also considered the possibility that Grovedale may have been killed *inside* his car and the body dumped where it now lay. He would check when he could with forensics to see if there was any blood or other DNA evidence inside Grovedale's car that would indicate it. Bruce considered all options, but his initial conclusion was that Grovedale had parked his car, was walking towards the picnic barbecue facility, and was attacked from behind. As the investigation continued, he noted that there was evidence of the footprints on the grass around the body having been interfered with somehow. It appeared that there were signs of a rake of sorts having been used to excoriate the ground. He also expected that whatever had been used to hit Grovedale from behind was likely in the dark waters of the lake by now.

"Let's have a look in the car," he said, and they walked up the slope towards the vehicle.

Under the dull glow of the car park lighting and with small torches held in the mouth or their hands, Bruce and Cromwell spent the next ten minutes examining Grovedale's car, careful not to touch or remove anything. Forensics had already looked at the vehicle briefly but intended to do a more thorough analysis once they had removed it from the scene. A tow truck had been arranged to move the Mercedes to a police impound yard just a short trip away on Queen Street. Inside the car's glove box Bruce found an iPhone. Using a pen from his jacket he pressed a few buttons on the device but noted that the battery had died so he had no idea whose phone it was. He assumed it belonged to Grovedale. Any detail that they might be able to glean from it could be vital in the investigation, he thought.

By four am, he had had enough. While technically the murder could have been taken up by the local murder and robbery squad, Cusscom had agreed to allow Bruce to run and lead the investigation. Yes, it was a murder and yes it had happened where it did, but both Bruce and Cusscom believed the killing of Grovedale was somehow linked to the deaths of Optin and Hedge. When Bruce hit the mattress of his bed just before five am, he was exhausted. It had been a long day and an even longer night.

Still fully clothed, he closed his eyes and as his head hit the pillow, it didn't bother him at all.

CHAPTER 54

"Dead?" repeated Pete, "Oh my God Inspector, what the hell is going on?" The six of them stood together in Pete's kitchen. It was just before ten am. Bruce had slept for a couple of hours only. He was tired and looked dishevelled. Cannon understood why.

Bruce had found it necessary to explain the status of the investigation surrounding the death of Grovedale. He wanted to ensure that everyone in the house excluding Stephanie knew that they would need to give a statement about their movements the previous evening. When Bruce and Cromwell had first arrived at Pete's house, Cannon and the others had no idea about Grovedale. Cannon had been down at the stables checking on *Wings* and the other horses while Pete was off somewhere managing the farm operations.

Despite the murder having taken place the evening before, Bruce had managed to keep all of the details about the who and the how, out of the media other than to advise them via a *statement*, that a body had been found the previous evening near Lake Colac.

While Bruce was busy elsewhere, Cromwell had spent part of the morning talking with Grovedale's family, his sons, his daughter, and his wife.

She had arranged for their statements to be taken by Alworth. She doubted that they were involved in their father's/husband's murder but the investigation into everyone's whereabouts during the previous evening would require them to provide details of their movements. She noted that it was odd that Mrs. Grovedale had not raised the alarm about her husband not having returned to their house by the time she went to bed but was told by her that he often stayed out late catching up with friends. Sometimes he even went into Melbourne without her and stayed overnight.

She advised them that as part of the investigation they would also be required to provided details of their individual financial positions and their personal relationship with Grovedale.

Insurance beneficiaries, shareholdings, wills, and all possible financial outcomes that would arise from Grovedale's death would be looked at. Fortunately, this would be done forensically, using a team of resources in the City. All these elements of the case would take time.

Bruce and his team were under pressure. It was less than twenty-four hours since the murder and already he was stressed. Phone calls and lengthy conversations starting just after six in the morning were taking their toll. With Optin's murder still unresolved, the body on the track case that everyone had forgotten about still up in the air and now Grovedale's death, it was enough to make anyone quit the job. Cromwell hoped, however, that Bruce would see it through, that he was made of sterner stuff.

Cromwell knew that it wasn't impossible that a family member had killed Grovedale, but on the face of it, it looked highly unlikely. It appeared that he had a steady family, a family that stayed together in business, a family of long-standing, and a family that was a large part of the local community. A check of individuals' movements the previous night would be made. Statements would be taken, checked, and double-checked. Alibis verified, confirmed, where possible. She knew that where some people had been out and about, travelling around the time of the murder, it would be more difficult to verify as Colac did not have a comprehensive or coordinated CCTV system across the region or in the town itself. It was country after all!

Cromwell reflected on the fact that they would need to ensure that every possible angle was followed up. With such a small team and limited resources, it was a task that would take much longer than it would normally do in the City. All this would be adding to the pressure, she thought.

She reflected again on what they had noticed at the crime scene. She guessed that Grovedale wasn't expecting any trouble from whoever he was meeting and the gash on the back of his head indicated that he was likely struck without warning. He had clearly misplaced his trust. When you *know* the person you are meeting, she thought, you are less alert, more casual, and less aware of any danger to yourself. Grovedale should have been more cautious especially when meeting someone at night in a dark area, especially when it was well away from the public areas.

The point was moot now though, he was dead.

Cannon asked the obvious question.

"How?" he said.

"I'm not really at liberty to say," Bruce replied, "but what I will say is that I think the person who you believe issued a warning to Mr. Grovedale, has now carried out that threat."

"My God, Pete," Emily said dismayed and frightened. "This is Colac, not bloody Melbourne or London. This type of thing doesn't happen here," she exclaimed.

She turned to look at Michelle who was holding on to Cannon's left arm. Emily's face reflected a sense of sadness and disappointment. She had invited a friend to stay with them, to holiday, to travel thousands of miles across the world and it appeared that death was always there sitting on someone's shoulder. To Cannon, it seemed that death was now a constant visitor, an unwelcome visitor at that. In just a few weeks since they had arrived, death had visited way too often. Through the putting down of a horse after it broke its leg, to the murder of a member of the local Vet community, and now the death of a neighbour.

Pete's face remained stonelike, his expression hiding how he felt inside. Bruce acknowledged Emily's response by asking all of them to remain calm and stating that he didn't think any of them were in danger.

"How do you know that?" Cannon asked, somewhat brusquely. He knew from experience that the police could never guarantee anything. Could never rule anything out.

Bruce knew where Cannon was coming from. He had hoped that his own words would have soothed Emily and he had hoped that Cannon had been able to accept and support what he was trying to convey - as one policeman to an ex-policeman? He decided not to respond immediately and tried to deflect answering Cannon's question.

"How are the horses now? he asked. "Have there been any further problems since the other night's break-in?"

Pete answered. "No there hasn't been," he said, "but I think it's because we've taken action already. Whoever it was who broke-in would struggle to do the same thing now. I've engaged a security company to provide short term cover through on-site guards each night until a security system, which I think will be a network of cameras and alarms, is installed on the property."

Bruce realized that they had now taken the need for improved security very seriously, he was pleased that they had.

He let Pete continue with his explanation of the actions he had taken so far. "The network that I want will secure the stables and the house plus the milking shed, the storerooms, feed areas, and fridges. I'm getting a couple of quotes at the moment," he said. "Given what happened the other night, I wish I had done it ages ago."

Bruce nodded his understanding.

For a few seconds, there was silence between them, the gravity of what had occurred with Grovedale overnight finally having hit home. Bruce asked Cannon to join him and Cromwell in the lounge. "If you don't mind Mike?" he said.

Cannon looked at Pete and Emily who were now seated at the dining room table. Michelle remained standing next to Cannon. He had his arm around her, comforting her. He looked into her face as she turned towards him. She smiled sadly, then nodded. A brief acceptance of where they now found themselves.

They sat together in the lounge room, the three of them. They had waited until Emily and Michelle had brought them tea. It was now just before lunchtime. Cannon was concerned about *Wings* and the exercise the horse needed in order to be fresh for the big race in less than forty-eight-hours-time. He had requested that one of the senior stablehands ensure that the horse was taken around the exercise track. Providing detailed instructions about what he wanted done, he hoped that by doing so the horse would continue to show that it was ready for Warrnambool. Cannon intended to follow up with both the rider and the stablehand later in the afternoon.

"The last time we spoke," began Bruce, "we thought that George Sormond was in danger. Obviously, we got that wrong."

Cannon sat motionless. He waited for Bruce to continue.

"And now I have another body on my hands," he said exasperatedly. "So, my question to you Mike, is given Grovedale's death, do you still think Sormond is at risk?" he asked.

"Yes I do," replied Cannon.

"But you have no idea as to the reason why?" he asked.

"I have a gut feeling but I can't prove anything just yet."

"A view that he's been cheating. That he's using methods on his horses that makes them run faster."

"Yes."

"And that someone knows this and that puts him in danger?"

"Yes."

Bruce decided to lay his cards on the table. He now had no alternative. The murder of Grovedale on *his* watch was yet another crime he needed to solve in addition to those already on his plate. He was under stress and aware of the impact the current state of things was having on his reputation. He needed a breakthrough.

"Mike," he said. "I wouldn't normally ask this and its highly irregular, so please understand that what I am about to say could get me into serious trouble."

He looked at Cromwell. He hadn't discussed it with her, but he believed that she would support him, given the circumstances. He hoped that she would get on board.

Cannon shrugged an acceptance. "Go on."

Bruce chose his words carefully. "Given last night's murder and all its implications, I'm sure you realise how things have changed for Cromwell and I over the past couple of weeks?" he said. "What started out with the two of us being sent here to provide support to the local police team to try and solve the mystery of what had happened to Timothy Hedge has now become much more than that, and after what happened last night it seems that we are potentially at risk of even more killings."

"That's correct," Cannon replied, "and it's possible that anyone could be the next target."

"And that's precisely why I need your help."

"To do what?"

"To be my eyes and ears over the next few days. While we continue our investigations into what happened to Grovedale and the others," Bruce emphasized. "In particular, I would like you to be aware of George Sormond's movements. Where he goes and what he does."

"Because like me you think he's still in danger?"

"Yes. After last night he must be."

"What about the rest of us?" Cannon asked. "After the break-in, the other night, which I think was specifically intended to frighten Pete and his family, how do you want to address that? Pete's family and my wife were really affected by it, and I'm concerned for their safety."

"I don't have an answer, unfortunately. I have limited resources myself, so the only thing I can suggest at this stage is to let the guards that Pete has hired be your first line of defence, especially tonight. If there is a need to leave the property at any point, then I'd suggest you go in pairs at a minimum, plus keep a phone handy."

Without a PC standing at the door all night, which often happens in the UK, Cannon knew that Bruce was right. They needed to be vigilant but also needed to take some personal responsibility. The police couldn't protect everyone, all the time.

"Okay," Cannon said, responding to Bruce's request, "is there anything that you think is worth me being aware of? As an example, you haven't told me how Optin died, so am I dealing with a gunman or someone more cunning?" he asked. "It's important to know, as over the next forty-eight to seventy-two hours our focus will be on Warrnambool. We'll be concentrating on the horses, the Grand Annual, so I'm not sure how I can help while I'm there."

"By being aware…." Bruce replied.

"Of?"

"What will be going on around you."

"Because you think that something will happen at the carnival?"

"I'm not *sure* about it," Bruce replied, "but I have a feeling."

Cannon smiled at him. Just a few days prior, Bruce had castigated him for having a *feeling*, now Bruce was offering his own. Cannon let it go. He picked up his cup and drained the tea, he used the few seconds of silence between them to make his decision.

"Okay," he said, "I'm pleased to be able to help."

CHAPTER 55

The pressure was beginning to drop. The *low* weather system that had begun to push into the region was expected. The clouds from the west had built up overnight, the waves across Bass Strait had begun to swell. Whitecaps began to appear, and the storm front would have made any pick-up much more difficult. The decision to cancel it was a good one. It shouldn't have happened anyway, as it had been agreed to slow things down for a while.

The Captain of the *San Marino* watched as the tanker cruised past his own boat. It was heading westwards into the mouth of the storm. The *San Marino* however was staying where it was. The fish in the area were still plentiful. The catch he and his crew would make would justify their existence. What they caught today would be sold, or packaged for sale, by evening. It was a living. Sadly, it was the other cargo he collected and concealed that allowed him the extras.

The morning sun was rising now. Long fingers of light spread across the grey sky, filtering, and shimmering. The crew continued with the tasks at hand. They had all seen spectacular sunrises before, during their time at sea. They had become blasé about such things now. They didn't even watch the sky at all.

As light reached the boat, the swell was compounded by rain. Initially, it was just like sea spray, fine and soft. Within fifteen minutes, however, the rain began to pour down. The wind was blowing almost parallel to the sea itself, sending sheets of water across the ocean and the deck of the *San Marino*.

The Captain moved to the wheelhouse. It would be a few more hours before they were safely back in the harbour at Apollo Bay. He had been given the news, a text had been sent to him. The police still wanted to talk.

CHAPTER 56

"Was it necessary to kill him?"

"What do you think?"

"I don't know, I'm asking you," the Captain said.

"He was going to tell the police. I had no choice."

The Captain stayed silent for a second.

"So, it *was* you?"

"Yes."

The sailor stayed quiet, he was thinking. Eventually, he said, "I think we need to re-evaluate things. It's gone much further, much better than we could have possibly imagined, but I think we may have reached a milestone now."

"Like what?!" the voice sounded angry to the skipper.

"The amount?"

"The amount? What do you mean, the amount? Are you thinking of giving it up, quitting?"

"I'm considering it."

The Captain heard the voice take a deep intake of breath at his comment. It was obvious to him that the very thought of stopping was anathema to the party on the other end of the line.

The voice continued. "I think it would be best if you *consider* whether you prefer your freedom or whether you would prefer a jail cell," the implication, the threat obvious. "I agree that we need to slow things down a little, but to suggest that we stop altogether is out of the question. You've done very well out of *the arrangement* so far."

The Captain sighed. "I'm getting older you know. I've just turned sixty and I won't be able to run the boat forever. I will need someone to take over at some point."

"I agree, but not now!" responded the voice, who then proceeded to end the call.

CHAPTER 57

"It would be so much better if this bloody rain would stop," Cannon said. They were slipping and sliding in the mud that had somehow managed to congregate near the horse loading bay. The carnival was starting the next day. The Grand Annual was just over forty-eight hours away. The rain was both a curse and a blessing. Softer ground would help *Wings* but would not be to the liking of *Chesterman*.

Pete's staff had prepared the horsebox for him, but he and Cannon were going to give it the once over. They didn't want to leave anything to chance. The break-in had heightened their concern. The death of Grovedale had put them on edge.

Despite Cannon's reservations, everything seemed to be going as planned. The drive down to Warrnambool would take longer than usual due to the wet weather. They needed to take their time on the roads, but both Pete and Cannon were optimistic about *Wings'* chance in the big race, so going slower and getting there in one piece would be a victory in itself. A victory over their nerves.

"Ummm, yep," Pete replied in answer to Cannon's observation about the rain. "With luck, this storm will blow out over the next day. I can't see many people being *on the hill* if it's raining as hard as this."

Cannon had heard about the *hill* and had looked at images of it on his computer. He had wondered if it was possible as a trainer to get to the top of it before the race began and then get back down again after the race was over, in time to welcome back his horse into the parade ring? *Preferably it would be nice to welcome him back into the winner's enclosure,* he thought.

They continued preparing the horsebox, checking everything inside and out. Tyre pressure, door bolts, rain guards, the padding for the horse's head, leads, rubber matting, and even the brakes on the vehicle. They conducted a thorough check before they felt comfortable.

Finally, they loaded the horse. The sight of such a powerful animal, who appeared so relaxed as he clambered up the ramp into the box, stirred Cannon. He didn't own the horse, he had no direct connection, but he felt that after all that had happened, there was a lovely connection between them. Cannon hadn't expected when he had first arrived at Pete's place that he would be given a free rein to do what he liked with the horse's training. He appreciated the trust he had been shown and the freedom he had been allowed. He knew that because of the support he had been shown, he had gotten much closer to *Wings* than he ever would have if he was a visiting trainer *into* the UK. He was extremely appreciative.

With *Wings* safely aboard, he closed the door at the back of the box and gave two taps on the side of the vehicle.

The engine of the SUV that was going to pull the box roared into life. The driver was aware of the contents of the box he was pulling. He had been Pete's regular driver for several years now. He had transported *Wings* previously but had never seen Pete as nervous as he was now. He gave a wave and slowly pulled away, rain and mud spat from the rear tyres as the rain continued to fall. While the rain continued, it appeared to be slowing slightly. Ideally, they wanted it to stop completely. The driver was oblivious to the spray that covered the road behind him as he pulled away. They watched as, despite the slippery conditions, the SUV and horsebox were expertly driven from the stable yard down to the main road before turning left and heading towards Warrnambool.

"I'll see him later," Pete said.

"Are you still insisting on staying with him tonight in his stall, as well as tomorrow night?" Cannon asked.

"You might think I'm crazy, but this is so important to me, I'll do anything to protect that horse," Pete said, pointing in the general direction of where he thought the horsebox would now be as it travelled towards Warrnambool.

Cannon mulled over what Pete had said. Eventually, he responded, "…and so would a couple of others like to do the same…" he said, before letting the thought drift into the ether.

Pete did not reply, he had his own thoughts…. and tonight, they were all about protecting *Wings*. He hadn't considered for a moment that he may need to protect himself.

CHAPTER 58

The death of Walt Grovedale, a murder victim, could not be contained from the public. Bruce believed it was necessary to issue a statement quickly. He hoped that someone knew something.

Within hours of the information having been released, the press began to hound the police. The local press and the city scribes were relentless, the local press in particular, keen for a story. Cusscom and Thatcher tried to shield Bruce from the scrum that was developing. They tried to use a media consultant as a mouthpiece. It was unsuccessful.

Bruce was thankful for the support, but he remained under pressure. The hierarchy needed the crimes solved, not just reported on.

The fact that Optin and Grovedale were both locals to Colac and both knew each other began to spark a concern within the community that the killer or killers were targeting people who had a linkage to the horse racing industry, both men having had at least some association.

In addition, a rumour was started in Forrest and Apollo Bay that a killer from the past had returned to the area. The rumour was that the killer had never been caught, that he had killed at least two people previously, and that he was hiding out somewhere in the bay.

Bruce had no idea how the rumours had started, but he could guess.

CHAPTER 59

"He seems to have settled in nicely," she said. Deb Ryan had been waiting at the track for *Wings* to arrive. It was just before six pm. He had arrived just after four, Pete had arrived an hour later.

After finding the box number that *Wings* was going to stay in over the next couple of days, the horse was taken from the trailer and safely ensconced in his stall. "He has eaten up already as well, a good sign," she said.

"Are you here for the whole carnival now Deb?" Pete asked.

She smiled. "Yes, I've been very lucky, I've been given the gig as Vet for the entire three days of the carnival. It seems the original choice, a Vet from New South Wales, couldn't make it due to illness, so the Stewards have asked me if I was willing to take over? Given I live much closer than an alternate from the City and there is no one available locally for all three days, I guess it was an easy ask?" she stated. "Also, I am a regular attendee at country meetings nowadays, so I know all the protocols and processes already."

"And it was an easy acceptance for you?"

"Yes."

"I'm pleased," Pete said. "I'm sure Mike will be as well. I'll give him a call shortly to let him know."

CHAPTER 60

"What the fuck!" Bruce shouted. "How is it possible? What the f….!" he nearly repeated. He was exasperated.

In his hand, the initial report covering Grovedale's murder suggested that the evidence the forensics team would be able to glean from the scene was likely to be of limited value. He threw the document on the table scattering the polystyrene cups that they had been drinking from. Bruce was standing, gesticulating, Cromwell and Alworth remained seated, silent, watching.

The DNA evidence that had been collected had been looked at by a local lab. According to the report, the information/evidence that they had been able to extract and collect was almost worthless. So far, the lab technicians had not been able to find any match from the site to their databases. It would suggest that the killer or killers had never been swabbed previously for any DNA matching or collection. So, like any other normal citizen, there would be no DNA detail on any official database that could be found that could link them to the scene. Clearly, the killer or killers had been very careful, very cunning in how they had murdered Grovedale. A thick plastic bag held over the head of a barely conscious man tied with a cord was not difficult to execute. If held on the head while wearing plastic gloves, the DNA evidence available would likely be even less. Fibres from clothing or DNA extracted from saliva were possible to match, but one needed something to match it against, and at this stage of the investigation that was not possible, for the reasons mentioned in the report. Bruce soon realized that unless they were lucky, it *could* become another unsolved case. His copybook was really being blotted, he thought. Even the analysis and inspection of Grovedale's car had produced nothing of value that could be used.

While he knew the report contained just the initial findings, it was apparent that Bruce was not going to be presented with too many answers.

"I just don't get it," he said, "we have *all* these tools and all the technologies, yet we can't extract anything of value from the crime scene down near the lake? Why the…."

Cromwell knew that her boss was extremely frustrated and tired. It was late afternoon and he had been dealing with the press and other social media enquiries throughout the morning, up until lunchtime.

She tried to intervene, calm him. They had worked together over the years, and they had been successful in solving many crimes. She had faith in his leadership.

"Sir," she said. "Maybe it's time for you to take a few minutes. Have a seat. My God, even have a nap for half an hour! There is a spare room that you can use just along the corridor," she indicated. "If you feel like it?"

Alworth added his support, giving Bruce something to consider.

The afternoon had turned much colder and the light was beginning to fade outside. It had stopped raining again, but for how long? An uncomfortable night lay ahead of them. The *situation* room was going to be where they would cocoon themselves as they reviewed the evidence, the information that they had gathered so far. The death of Grovedale had confused their thinking. They still had no clue about Optin. The mystery behind Hedge and the body in Forrest was even further from their minds. They needed clear heads.

"Perhaps you're right."

She smiled weakly. "Even if it's just an hour, I'm sure you will feel better after that. Much sharper," she went on. "I'll arrange for some dinner to be delivered and Alworth and I, along with Bossin, will collate all the information we have, and then we can work through it all together. There must be something in there somewhere that we've missed?"

Bruce slumped into a chair, his entire demeanour showing defeat.

"I'm fucked," he said, "totally…"

CHAPTER 61

"Pete said that the horse had arrived safely," Cannon announced, "and that he's getting ready to bed down with it."

Emily smiled.

They were in the kitchen putting away the remnants of dinner.

"Do you think he'll be okay?" Emily asked.

"I'm sure he will be," Cannon replied. "It's a bit odd but given the circumstances, the authorities seem to understand the concern. He's in a stable block just off the course and as long as he stays away from the track, he should be fine."

"I am worried about him," she responded. "He's going to be all alone and it's going to be very cold tonight."

Michelle put her arm around her friend, giving her a brief hug. "He's got his phone with him, he'll have lots of blankets and there is the additional security that the course has brought in for the meeting, so I'm sure he'll be fine."

"I do hope so," Emily replied, "I'll sleep much better when this is all over."

"I'm sure we all will Em, but I'm glad the police have taken it seriously," Cannon said. "After everything that has happened, it's the least they could do in their support of the trainers. Allowing them to keep a watch over their horses tonight by staying with the horse in its stall is a great initiative. I don't know how many have taken up the offer but with the carnival starting tomorrow I'm sure the last thing the Warrnambool Racing Club needs is an attack on the horses or on any of the trainers. It would be a PR disaster."

Cannon guessed that his words didn't help Emily much, but she slowly began to appear less nervous. By the time they had cleared away everything and had finished their evening teas and coffees, she seemed to be back to normal. Once they had said their goodnights Michelle and Cannon found themselves alone. It was just after 10:30 pm.

"I'll quickly send a text to Pete, to see how he is doing," he said.

She nodded agreement, then indicated that she was off to the bedroom.

"I'll be with you shortly," he continued as she walked away down the passage.

Cannon drafted a quick SMS asking Pete if he was okay and to reply with a simple 'Y' to verify that he was. He hit the send button.

He waited for a response. Nothing.

Cannon walked towards his room. His stomach churned. "C'mon Pete. A simple yes is all I need," he said to himself. As he entered the bedroom the phone buzzed. He looked at the screen. The text wasn't from Pete. It was from Cassie. "Please call me," it said.

Pete did not reply.

CHAPTER 62

It was just after eight-thirty pm. While Cannon, Michelle, and Emily were discussing Pete's safety, Bruce and his team were reviewing all the evidence they had been able to collate so far. Empty take away noodle boxes and half-finished trays of rice and prawn crackers were dotted about the table along with coffee cups, coke, and other soft drink bottles. The place looked like a bomb had hit it. It was no place for neatness.

Four deaths.

"Hedge."

"Optin."

"Grovedale."

"Mystery man in Forrest."

Bruce pointed to a pile of statements, reports, and various pieces of information that had been compiled during the investigation to date.

"Any ideas?" he asked.

"Sir, surely there must be a link between some or all of them?" Bossin said, "it's not possible that we can have four deaths in such a short period without there being at least *some* connection. This is Colac for God's sake!"

"I agree Constable, but what the hell is it?" Bruce replied. After he had slept and eaten, Bruce felt more human, much better. Just a few hours of shut-eye had helped. He knew they may be grasping at straws now, but he also knew that somewhere the answer they were seeking was in right front of them.

"Look, what we are missing is motive," he said eventually. "Why would someone kill any of these four? Once we know that, we could look at potential suspects. What is really pissing-me-off though is that we can't see any reason why Hedge was killed other than he *may* have been blackmailing someone. But who? I can see a link between him and Optin and Grovedale, as he did work for them at times, but even if Hedge had something on both of them, he was killed two years ago. So, who would murder a Vet and a retired businessman like Grovedale now? For what reason?"

"Is the timeline relevant, Sir?" asked Alworth?

"In what way?"

"Well is the two-year gap meaningful?"

"You mean did anyone move away from the area for that period?"

"Yes Sir."

Bruce looked at his notes. "Not that I can see," he said. "The only person who used to *disappear* for any length of time was Hedge."

"What about Optin and Grovedale specifically. Is there any linkage there?" Cromwell asked.

"Again, nothing obvious."

"But Optin's car was burnt out on Grovedale's property?"

"Yes."

"And we still don't think it's relevant, even though Grovedale is now dead?" she asked.

Bruce didn't respond immediately. He hadn't totally dismissed the idea when it was first mooted, but the more he thought about it, perhaps Cannon was right. Perhaps it was a warning, despite Grovedale's protestations at the time.

Even so, who had sent the message?

"I'm still not sure," he replied.

"And what about our *mystery* man?" Cromwell asked, holding up a thumb and forefinger of her right hand before combining the two into a circle, a zero, to emphasise the total lack of progress. "We seem to have forgotten about him," she reminded them.

She picked up the forensics report and scanned its contents. She had looked at it several times in recent days but she hadn't focused on it given the attention they had placed on Optin's murder.

"Small boned, aged approximately mid-twenties, emaciated, possibly Asian," she read out aloud. "Starved to death."

As she read the words, something stirred in her memory. What was it?

She mulled the words over again in her head.

Bruce was speaking. "We may need to visit Apollo Bay again…"

"That's it!" she shouted. "Apollo Bay!"

Bruce, Alworth, and Bossin all looked at each other.

"That's it!" she said again.

Bruce asked the question. "Sorry Constable, but *what* is *it*?"

"The linkage," she responded.

"I'm not with you."

"Sir, wasn't Hedge found dressed in jockey silks?"

"Yes."

 "Well isn't that the connection?"

"What is…?" he said, still unsure what Cromwell was referring to.

"Horse racing," she answered.

"How do you…?" he began, trailing off.

"The *mystery* man," she answered. "I'm guessing he was a jockey or someone used in that capacity," she answered. "See here," she pointed excitedly to the words she had been reading. "Small boned…emaciated…."

"But it still doesn't…" Bruce tried to argue.

"It doesn't prove anything directly," she said, "but if you add the fact that Optin and Grovedale were killed only after the body on the track was found, then it can't be a coincidence."

They were becoming excited, animated. Bruce remained cautious.

"We still don't have a motive for any of the murders, though," he said.

"Agreed Sir," replied Cromwell. "But we do have a link to something else."

"What's that?"

"Grovedale."

"Grovedale and…?" he asked, searching for the answer.

"The track. The bike track," she said. "Cannon was right, Sir. The car was burnt out on the track that Grovedale used to ride on for a reason. It *was* a warning. When you add that to the body in Forrest being found on that bike track, there is a connection."

"Somewhat tentative, I'd say Constable, but I'm happy to go with it", he replied. "But where does Optin fit then? What's the link there?"

She was bold. She needed to be. Having made the linkage in her own mind, she was happy to stretch her thinking. "The bicycle," she answered, "and the place the car was destroyed," she continued.

He looked at her dubiously.

She continued. "How clever for the killer to ride off from where the car was torched. On a bicycle!" she stressed. "The clue was staring us in the face. Plus, Optin was killed at the training track near the jumps circuit. It *has* to mean something. Everything points to a horse racing connection."

He hadn't expected things to develop so quickly.

"And what is the biggest thing around here currently?" Bruce asked rhetorically.

"The Grand Annual," Alworth said, "two days from now. Worth $200,000 to the winner."

"Is it worth killing for?" asked Bruce.

"Some people are obsessed with winning it," she replied, "so it's not impossible. We know from our previous experiences that people have killed for less."

Bruce asked them to look through the statements again. Checking for dates, times, check for anything that would support their thinking. Did what they have now provide them with a motive?

He needed to make some calls. One of them was to Cannon.

CHAPTER 63

They needn't have worried. Pete answered the phone straight away, apologizing for not returning Cannon's call the previous evening. Cannon gave him an update.

"The police called last night," he said, "apparently they've had a breakthrough". It was eight am, Cannon was already dressed and would be leaving for the course at nine.

Pete had been awake most of the night. He had been unable to sleep, hearing every creak, every sound that permeated the darkness of the stable block that housed the horses that had arrived early for the carnival. The wind from the west had intensified over the past twelve hours but fortunately, the rain had stopped. If the breeze continued it would result in a drying track, Pete thought. If the wind eased, however, and it ends up being a soft track then he knew that *Wings* would love it. There were thirty-six hours still before the race, a lot could happen before the off.

Pete responded to Cannon's news. "That's great to hear," he said, "did they provide you with any detail?"

"Nothing specific, nor would I have expected them to. They need to follow up on a few things, but they believe they have an idea who has been behind the killings of Optin and Grovedale. Also, they think they have a motive."

"So, did they say what their next move was?"

"Well, they have to be careful. They need to formalise their evidence and then they will arrest the person concerned. I guess it's similar to what I used to do in the UK, but I could be wrong."

"But they haven't said yet who is it?" Pete asked.

"No," replied Cannon, "but let's hope they have got it right."

Pete agreed.

"So how are things there now?" Cannon asked.

"To be honest Mike, they are a little bit crazy. There are so many horses and people here now, it seems like organized chaos."

Cannon smiled. He could imagine the scene. He guessed that it would be like some of the UK meetings such as Ascot, Chester, York, and Aintree. From early morning, the carnival would be in full swing. Apart from the horses and trainers that regularly attend the Warrnambool races when there are only a couple of hundred people at the meeting, there would now be thousands of racegoers, media people, owners, food and drink suppliers, people in taxis and buses, all converging on the course. Many would have been setting up stalls from early in the morning, some even before Cannon awoke.

"And the horse?"

"He seems to be taking the whole thing in his stride. We took him for a stretch at around five-thirty. Tony was very happy to get onboard him. They had a run around the track and Tony was pleased with how the horse felt."

"And the horse is settled now?"

"Yes, he's back in his stable and he's eaten up ok. I've groomed him and Deb is coming to see him later. She's going to give him a thorough check-up, take blood, and all the necessary samples she needs to take."

"That's good to hear," Cannon replied. "Subject to traffic I should be there around midday to about one," he said. "I'm planning to leave by nine."

"No worries," Pete replied. "I'll see you when you get here."

It was just before 10 pm in the UK. Cannon was ready to leave but he needed to make another quick call. He dialled Cassie's phone.

"Is everything alright?" he asked. "Your text just said to call. Is there anything the matter?" he asked again, repeating the question.

"No," she replied. "I just wanted to wish you and Pete well for the race. In-person rather than by text."

"Oh, thanks," he said, a little surprised. She wasn't one who normally followed what Cannon was doing, how his horses were running or how much success, or lack thereof, he had. He knew she was focused on the future. She was her own young woman now. She had her own dreams.

He decided not to tell her about the recent developments, as he didn't want her to worry.

"The actual race is tomorrow, local time," he said. "About three-thirty in the afternoon. That will be around six-thirty am your time."

"I'll be awake by then."

"Okay, well I'll text you the result. If it's a good one, I may even call," he replied, with a smile.

"That would be great Dad."

They stayed silent for a second. While he could not see her, he could sense that she was waiting for him to ask about the trip to Cape Town. To see if she still intended to go. He decided not to ask. It was her decision. Finally, he said, "Well I'd better get going. I need to fight the traffic in order to get into the course," he exclaimed. "I believe it is going to be pretty horrendous. So many people apparently. Anyway, thanks for everything love. Take care. Love you. Speak soon."

It had been a while since he had told her that he loved her. He realized when he said it how infrequently he did.

"I love you too Dad," she replied.

CHAPTER 64

Bruce had given Cusscom and Thatcher an update. He had been advised to tread carefully. What they had so far was *circumstantial* and Thatcher in particular was a little concerned.

"Look AB," he said, "we need an arrest, yes, but what we *really* want is one that will *stick*. We don't want some fancy lawyer tearing us apart even before we get to court, so if we stuff this up, we could be seriously embarrassed. I agree we need to move quickly, but we need to do so carefully."

The use of the nickname, *AB*, was not lost on Bruce. He ignored it. He couldn't care less about flattery, and he thought it insincere anyway. Call him cynical, but he had been around the traps long enough to know when he was being duped.

His job was to solve and close the cases given to him, and that was all that mattered in the long run.

"Thank you, Sir," he replied. "I'll keep you posted as to how things go, but we hope to make an arrest in the next 24 hours or so."

"I'm pleased to hear it," Thatcher replied. "Good luck."

CHAPTER 65

The roads around the Warrnambool racecourse were packed. Punters of all shapes and sizes streamed along the roads towards the entrances. Most were dressed for the occasion, many men in suits and coats, the women with cotton dresses, high heels, and hats. Many of the women showed too much flesh. Some because they could, some because they wanted to and some who should not have tried. Bearing all seemed to be a fashion statement to them. To stay warm, some men were more practical and wore jeans and coats, along with *'bool* beanies of yellow and black.

The weather was cool. The sky grey, the wind moderate and still blowing from the west. The cold front was lingering but by the time racing was scheduled to start at around eleven-thirty the sun was expected to make an appearance. The rest of the day would be partly cloudy, and the sky would be a watery blue. The temperature would not exceed 15C on any of the three days.

The thousands of racegoers walking along the road were joined by buses that were ferrying people from the railway station a couple of kilometres away from the track. Taxis slipped along side-roads to beat the crowds if they could and get their passengers to the course as quickly as possible. The visual spectacle of a mass of bodies standing together on the lawns inside the course began to develop as the minutes passed. Well before the first race, and soon after ten am, champagne bottles were uncorked, beers were opened. Tables and chairs along with blankets were set up for the day in the enclosures. Thirty-five thousand people were expected to attend the carnival over the three days.

Cannon drove towards the entrance for trainers and jockeys. He had been fortunate, as the trip down from Colac had been relatively easy. He was on his own, neither Emily nor Michelle wanted to attend the first day. It was always on a Tuesday and both had expressed a desire to stay at home and watch the racing on TV.

"But we'll only be watching sporadically," Michelle had said. "given we won't have any interest in the flat races."

Cannon understood. He knew that the next day, day two of the carnival, both Em and Michelle would be a bag of nerves.

Deb Ryan was very busy.

Being the assigned Vet for the meeting she had been at the racetrack since five am. It was only day one and even before the gates opened to the public, she had supervised the extraction of blood samples from a random selection of horses that were due to race during the first day. These tests were done to ensure that none of the animals had been given any substance that could enhance or limit their chances of winning their respective races. The samples would be sent away for analysis with a committed turn-around time of twenty-four hours. This commitment was to ensure the integrity of the sport.

In addition, she had already attended the club's board meeting where the Chairman had thanked everyone for their contribution to the carnival and asked each board member to ensure a safe and financially successful meeting was had.

Ryan was also specifically thanked for accepting the role of on-course Vet for the carnival's duration as quickly as she did. She had acknowledged the thanks accordingly.

Forty minutes before the first race, George Sormond began to take down the gate at the back of *Chesterman's* box.

The trip had taken a little longer than planned, predominantly due to the crowds that had built up throughout the morning. Trying to weave his *Ute* and the horsebox through the crowds of people was very difficult, very challenging. While the local police on *road and pavement* duty tried their best to ease traffic through to the course, it was not always straight forward. Many of the crowd refused to move out of the way and get off the road, which was why it took some time before a sense of normality prevailed and *Chesterman,* amongst others, was settled in his box in the on-course stable block.

They wouldn't take any action on day 1 of the carnival. The case they were building needed to have evidence, proof. Bruce had decided to wait until Sormond was down in Warrnambool. He wanted access to Sormond's training facilities. He sought permission from the courts to raid the property. They would do so on day two of the carnival, as they knew that Sormond would be focused on *Chesterman* and the Grand Annual. They hoped they would find what they were looking for.

CHAPTER 66

He watched the racing from the Grandstand. Cannon had been given access to all the function rooms on the course as well but preferred to watch, seated outside, under the cover of the large stand. It was the atmosphere he wanted to experience. This was his first time in the country. It was his first time at the carnival. He may never be back here again, so he wanted to lap it all up. He was impressed by the organization, enthusiasm, and knowledge of the crowd. He found himself getting a buzz from being at the event.

He hoped that what he had been asked to do before coming to the country, he had delivered. He believed that the horse, *Wings*, had a really good chance of winning the race the following day, but Cannon was also realistic. There were fourteen runners expected to greet the starter and he knew a few of them were in with a very good chance.

The first two races of the day on day one were jumps races. Both were over hurdles. The steeplechases were the main events of day two. After the hurdlers had completed their races, the rest of the day would be flat racing.

Cannon watched both hurdle events. Both were over the same distance of three and a half kilometres. In each event there was a runner that bolted upfront almost immediately, stretching out the field of horses behind them, and in each case, the *bolter* was caught just before the penultimate fence by the race favourite. The favourite in both cases won easily. There were no fallers and no horse in either race was pulled up.

The victorious jockey in both races was Tony Carey, *Wings'* partner the next day. Cannon had watched the two races carefully. He noticed that Carey was a very neat jockey. He rode high in the saddle which was good for when he and *Wings* would be attacking the fences. Tomorrow though, the obstacles would be much bigger, taller, and wider and many more of them than those of today. Cannon knew that Carey had raced in the Grand Annual at least twelve times over the years, and he had never finished better than in third place. He hoped that Carey hadn't used up all his luck today.

They watched some of the other races from the stables. Cannon was impressed with the facilities. He was also surprised by the level of security around the stables, and how each horse was identified before it was allowed access. Any horse needing to be stabled before its race was only allowed entry once it had been scanned for a microchip that had been inserted into the horse's neck, to verify that it was the animal that it purported to be. The detail obtained from the scan was then matched to a branding mark on the horse's shoulder. These requirements, these protocols to race, were part of the process for all racehorses and had been set up by Racing Australia. The sport's integrity was paramount.

Inside the stable block, each stall was properly prepared for each horse. It included the animal's name, the race number that it was to run in, as well as the saddlecloth number that it had been allocated. Every specific requirement, including feed type, was already known, leaving nothing to chance.

The human contingent had not been forgotten either. Catering arrangements for those looking after the horses were extensive and well organized. They had been set up in a special enclosure away from the general public. In the same area were facilities to be able to watch the racing. A large screen as well as several TV *stations* were in place.

Cannon and Pete watched a couple of the flat races as they ate a late lunch. Occasionally they noticed Deb Ryan vetting a couple of horses behind the barriers, as and when required. She seemed to have a busy time. Almost every race had at least one horse that required her assessment before it was passed fit to run. Several times she was able to decide on the fitness of the horse just by having it trot away from her and then trot back. Other times she needed to feel a horse's leg or check for a muscle issue, normally in the back below the saddle. In most cases, the evaluation would end with a gentle slap on the horse's rump and a smile all round. Cannon watched, intrigued. He knew she was a good Vet, so he was keen to see how her assessment as to a horse's fitness reflected in the race itself.

CHAPTER 67

Cannon and George Sormond were sat at a table in the Quorum restaurant on Kepler Street. It was very elegant. It provided *a fine dining experience* according to its website, even offering afternoon tea.

Cannon and Pete had been invited by Sormond, but Pete declined. He wanted to stay at the stables on the course. His presence providing the additional security he thought was needed there.

"Deb should be here shortly," Sormond stated. "I'm glad she could join us."

"Me too," replied Cannon, looking forward to seeing her again. Somehow, he was drawn to her, enjoying her company much more than he should. "I think she's had a busy day," he said, "and I'm sure she will appreciate the surroundings here. Much better than the on-track food," he smiled, holding up a glass of gin and tonic.

"Absolutely," Sormond replied. "I've been coming to the carnival for over fifteen years now and over the past couple, I've always had dinner here the night before the Grand Annual. It's such a nice place and not so busy like some of the other places around town."

Cannon looked around the room. It was pretty full already. He guessed that most of the diners were racegoers as well, as the conversations he was able to overhear included hard-luck stories about the day's racing and lost bets. They continued to make small talk for a while. Cannon wasn't sure about Sormond's motives for the invitation to dinner, but on face value, there was nothing that Cannon could detect from the conversation so far that indicated a hidden agenda.

"Ah, here she is," announced Sormond, as Deb Ryan walked into the room approaching the table from behind Cannon. Both men stood. Ryan apologized for being *fashionably* late. She sat down at the table taking a chair between both men. Cannon on her left, Sormond to her right. As she settled herself down, she brushed Cannon's shoulder with her hand. Sormond asked her what her *poison* was, and she asked the waiter for a bourbon on the rocks, she then picked up the menu scanning the *specials*.

Cannon was a little transfixed. Each time he had seen her she was always wearing jeans and a jersey, with boots. Typical clothing for working with animals, especially horses. The last time he had seen her, she had ended up in tears. Today, tonight, she was wearing dark blue trousers, black high heels, and a simple white blouse. The whole outfit was accentuated with a fine gold necklace around her neck and several gold bangles on her wrist. Cannon noticed she didn't wear a watch. She had also done something with her hair. While it clearly hadn't been cut or styled recently, she had somehow managed to brush it differently, away from her face. She seemed to have a bigger smile.

Cannon had not specifically dressed for dinner, and apart from a pair of slacks being substituted for his jeans and a new grey polo shirt, he still had the same jacket and shoes that he was wearing when he had left for the racetrack that morning.

He had let Michelle know of the invitation to dinner once Pete and himself had been asked. He hadn't known at the time that Sormond had also invited Deb Ryan along. He was glad he had.

After they had decided on their meals and the orders were taken, Sormond asked for their wine to be decanted and then served.

"Cheers," Sormond said, raising his glass. "To the carnival!".

"To the carnival!" Cannon and Ryan said in unison before taking a sip of their drinks.

"And thank you for coming," Sormond continued.

His guests nodded their thanks and appreciation for the invitation.

Cannon turned to Ryan enquiring, "So a very busy day for you Deb. How are you feeling now?"

She replied without hesitation. "To be honest, I'm pretty shattered. It's been a very long day and I know I'll sleep tonight. I shouldn't really be here, as I'm afraid I might fall asleep in my dinner, but I was so appreciative of the offer I just couldn't refuse it. I hope you don't mind if I excuse myself earlier than is normal?"

"That's ok, I'm glad you could make it anyway," Cannon replied.

"Thank you," she smiled. "When George asked me if I could join you both after Pete pulled out, it was a no-brainer."

Cannon smiled back at her. She held his gaze longer than he knew they both should have.

"What did you think of the racing today?" Sormond asked, breaking into their thoughts.

"I think it was pretty good overall," she answered, blushing slightly.

"I see you had several horses that needed vetting during the day." Cannon jumped in. "We, Pete and I, watched a few of the races on the TV after the hurdle races were finished."

"Yes," she replied, "there was only the one horse that I had to scratch throughout the entire card. It was in the last race. It was lame in the off-fore. A couple of runners in other races had lost shoes and their action had gone out but once that had been sorted, they were ok."

"That's good."

"Yes, some days are better than others. Today was one of those."

Their meals arrived and as they ate, they made small talk. Cannon shared his view about the weather. *Much colder than I expected.* His thoughts on Victoria. *There is so much to see, it's a pity that I won't be able to see too much while I am here, but what I have seen is beautiful. I hope to get a chance to drive along the Great Ocean Road and visit the Twelve Apostles. With luck, we hope to spend a couple of days in Melbourne and maybe visit the Yarra Valley.*

Sormond turned the conversation to racing the next day.

"It's the Grand Annual tomorrow. How is your horse looking?"

"Oh, *Wings* you mean? Yes, he's fine. He's very fit. Raring to go!"

Sormond appeared to shrink into his chair. His desire to win the Grand Annual was unabashed. It was an unnatural obsession. Cannon noticed the change in Sormond's body language. Was this why he had been asked to dinner? To find out the status of *Wings*? It was only a horse race after all. It wasn't life or death....or was it?

People had been murdered and Cannon couldn't forget that. The sight of Optin's body would never leave him. In his mind, it was piled on top of the others that had haunted him over the years. He hoped that he wouldn't see anymore.

Responding to Sormond's question, Cannon asked the obvious.

"How is *Chesterman*? I see he's the outright favourite for the race."

"Ummm, I'm not surprised, given he was the runner up last year, but I think the odds at three-to-one are a bit skinny."

"I agree. I see *Wings* is at *seven's*. There are also a couple of other chances, it would appear, *Readabook* and *Send-her-to-me* are between our two horses in the betting. Do you know much about them?"

"Not too much, but I do know Danny Birchmore as a trainer, and they are both his. I expect them to be competitive, as Danny has won the race a couple of times and his owners I suspect will have high expectations."

They continued talking longer than they should have. Deb Ryan excused herself before they had dessert.

It was after 10:30 before Cannon called it a night and thanked Sormond accordingly.

When he arrived back at his room in the hotel across the road from the course it was just before eleven. He texted Pete to see if everything was ok. Pete replied that it was. Cannon found it odd that he was staying where he was, without Michelle. He understood Pete's motives but didn't think Pete needed to be so cautious. Sormond had confirmed what Cannon had already rationalized. It was definitely going to be a big day tomorrow.

CHAPTER 68

Cold, but clear. The sky was a bright blue and the sun was melting the frost. Dawn had broken with Warrnambool waking to a one-degree temperature. The expected high was seventeen degrees Celsius. No rain was expected. The prevailing westerly wind would be drying out the track. It would be a perfect day for racing.

In Colac, Bruce had organized his resources to *hit* Sormond's racing facility hard. He needed to find the evidence they required. With the permission of the courts, they were able to unlock or break open any cupboard, open any drawers they wanted. They would arrive at seven am.

It took less than an hour. They found several *jiggers* but most importantly they found a bloodstained hammer in the same container. Bruce expected that the blood on the hammer, once tested, would be that of Walt Grovedale.

It was like trams, Bruce thought.
Often things seemed to arrive in pairs. They had the hammer and then he took the call from the skipper of the *San Marino*.

CHAPTER 69

Pete and Cannon had been awake since five am. Cannon was a little worse for wear initially but began to find his feet after breakfast. Despite his early start, the hotel had provided an excellent spread which he found worked exceptionally well in settling his stomach.

He arrived at the track just after six forty-five. Pete advised him that he had had a much quieter night than the one before and he had managed to sleep for a few hours. The horse had also taken everything in its stride.

He let Cannon know that *Wings* would be undertaking some light exercise, arranged by Pete, during a fifteen-minute slot that he had been given by the track manager. It was to be at seven-ten am. Fifteen minutes was all they were allowed given the state of the track, which had cut up a little from use during the previous day. The time limitation had been set due to the large number of horses racing on day two. Everyone needed their exercise. The synthetic track which would normally have been used for exercise had ironically become waterlogged due to the recent downpours and was off-limits.

George Sormond oversaw the *blow-out* training run by *Chesterman*. The horse completed its work, just as Sormond's phone rang. It was his stable manager. He let Sormond know of the raid by Bruce and his team. He advised him of what the police had found. Sormond thanked his man then put the phone back into his pocket. He had no time to contemplate what he had just been told. He would address that later. What he wanted, and wanted it desperately, was to win the Grand Annual. He believed he could win it without his horse getting any additional motivation but felt the use of such *tools* would always be of help. Even though they were illegal….winning the race had become his goal, his focus, his *raison detre*.

Regarding the hammer that the police had found, he just shook his head.

CHAPTER 70

It was race six on the card. The start time three-thirty pm. They were thirty minutes away from the off. *Wings'* regular stable rider and stablehand had arrived at the course at ten-thirty. The latter had begun grooming the horse almost immediately, freeing up Pete to get changed and get himself ready for the day.

The horse had left the stable and was now in the parade ring, the number four on his saddlecloth blowing about in the gentle breeze. The sun, something most people believed the previous day had disappeared forever, now shone on its rump. Muscles, strengthened over time, moved with the horse's gait. The strength of a powerful backside, needed in racing and which powered the horse along, could be seen by those who looked for it. Pete and Cannon could not have done any more. They believed that *Wings* was ready for the test ahead of him. They hoped that *Chesterman* wasn't.

The horses had left the parade ring and the crowd had scattered to the Grandstands or had walked up Grafton Hill. The latter provided a spectacular view of the entire course. The Grand Annual at 5500m long and 33 jumps is the longest race on an Australian public racecourse and has the most jumps of any steeplechase in the world. The last part of the race is almost run in a figure of eight, with the participants racing to the finish in the opposite direction to the way they had run earlier in the race.

Fourteen runners were facing the starter. There were only five minutes before the scheduled *off* time. Deb Ryan stood behind the stalls watching the runners and the jockeys as they walked around in circles. Some of the jockeys had taken their mounts away from the stalls and made them stand well away from the other runners, trying to keep them calm.
The start of the race was just to the right of the main Grandstand. The excitement of the crowd could be heard and felt by those on the track. A sense of anticipation was building. The *hill* heaved with up to six thousand people standing on the grassy banks, beers, and wine in hand, all waiting for the stalls to fly back and get the runners on their way.

Cannon and Pete watched from the Trainers' enclosure. Everything that had happened over the past few weeks had come down to this. Cannon hoped that the race would be run fairly. He didn't doubt it, but he did worry about George Sormond's intent. Cannon had received a call from Bruce. They were on their way down to Warrnambool with an arrest warrant for Sormond for the murder of Optin.

Bruce had told him what they had found at Sormond's property. The hammer, which they believed was used on Walt Grovedale, as well as *Jiggers* and other items that they believed, had been used on *Chesterman*.

Cannon had seen *Jiggers* used in the UK some years ago but believed that they had been largely eradicated from the industry there.

Jiggers are illegal battery-powered shock devices which, if Bruce was correct, would have been used during the training of *Chesterman* before the Grand Annual and other races. Cannon was aware of the process when a *Jigger* was used on an animal. It involved classical conditioning designed to ensure that a horse anticipates the delivery of an electric shock following some kind of stimulus that can be applied during a race. The stimulus is generally applied to a horse's neck. The horse feels the pressure of the device before it discharges its shock, a pressure similar to that of the butt of a jockey's whip. The jockey then applies a similar cue in the same anatomical area of a horse on race day. Through such classical conditioning, the pressure cue means that the horse will anticipate a shock when it feels the butt of the whip during the race and as a result will run faster.

Cannon realized that if true, Sormond's jockey would also be in on the scam.

Despite what Bruce had told him on the call, Cannon still had his doubts.

Deb Ryan was called to look at two of the runners.

One of them *Simple Steps* had lost a shoe. After the farrier had re-shod the animal, the jockey was asked to trot the horse a hundred metres down the track and away from the crowd that had gathered along the fence near the starting stalls. She watched intently then gave the go-ahead to the starter that the horse was fit to race.

The crowd was beginning to get restless as the start time passed. The starter began loading some of the runners.

The other horse that Ryan was asked to look at was *Chesterman*. The horse was sweating quite badly, and the jockey was concerned.

Cannon watched the large screen TV that dominated the infield. The vision showed that some of the runners were still circling around while others were already locked away in their starting stall. *Chesterman* stood quietly in front of Ryan, dripping sweat from his belly. He watched as she reached into a bag standing on the ground next to her. Then she turned and ran her hands over the horse. She looked like she was feeling for something. Once satisfied, she appeared to ask the jockey to get the horse to jog away from her. The horse was turned around, *jig-jogging* as it did so, ran a hundred metres away down the track then returned to the starting stalls.

"Okay, to race," she said.

The starter acknowledged her and within seconds an announcement was made to the crowd that *Chesterman* had been passed fit to race.

"What did you expect?" Sormond said quietly under his breath to no-one in particular. He was watching from the Grandstand.

Cannon continued to focus on Deb Ryan on the screen until the vision changed to a head-on shot of the starting stalls.

The tension began to rise, all the horses were locked in their stalls. The starter pushed his button and the gates flew back allowing the field of fourteen runners to start their five and a half kilometre trip. Thirty-three steeplechase fences ahead of them. The crowd cheered in unison and an almighty roar split the air.

As the field of horses raced towards the first obstacle, the on-course commentary began. The crowd stirred, shouting for their favourite and calling out to their jockeys.

Chesterman sat midfield as the horses cleared the first few fences. His jockey, Jim Bezelman, following the instructions from George Sormond to the letter. *Wings'* jockey, Tony Carey, kept a strong hold of the horse and sat in last place.

Cannon and Pete were relatively happy at this stage of the race.

At jump seventeen and twenty-two there were three fallers. From jump twenty-five, the field had strung out to the extent that there were only six horses with a chance of winning the race. Some of the remaining runners had been pulled up.

Wings and *Chesterman* raced together in joint third place just a few lengths behind the leaders. At jump twenty-six, just after leaving Cox's Hill and Brierly paddock, Jim Bezelman made his move. He gave *Chesterman* a whack on the shoulder with his whip and the horse accelerated, moving onto the shoulder of the leader with ease. At jump twenty-seven *Chesterman* flew across it as if it wasn't there and landed in the lead. The horse extended his lead to three lengths by the time had reached fence twenty-eight and cleared it with ease. Sormond watched as his horse raced towards the next fence. The crowd issued a collective gasp as the original leader fell at twenty-eight. Tony Carey cleared the fence then sent *Wings* in pursuit of *Chesterman*. Now there were only three runners with a realistic chance of winning. The crowd grew even more excited as the leaders accelerated down the hill and raced towards the finish line. *Wings* began to close in on the two horses ahead of him. All three horse cleared fences twenty-nine and thirty. At fence thirty-one, the second horse, *Titanic Whispers* made a bad mistake unseating his jockey to a collective groan from the crowd. Now it was left to *Wings* and *Chesterman* to fight it out.

Wings was still a length behind as the two horses came to fence thirty-two. Cannon and Pete watched the in-field TV as all the training of *Wings,* the miles put into his legs and the improvement in his jumping, began to show through. As the two horses landed on the other side of the penultimate fence, *Wings* was just ahead of *Chesterman*. The crowd in the Grandstand roared even louder, those on the hill screamed. To see a battle to the line was they had hoped for.

Despite themselves, Cannon and Pete began to shout.

Both jockeys began to urge their mounts on, pushing the horses' heads forward in a rhythmic dance of horse and rider. They were six hundred metres from the finish line, nearly five kilometres behind them. They raced towards the last fence locked together, neither horse giving any quarter. As they came to fence thirty-three, the crowd held a collective breath before roaring even louder as the combatants leapt in unison, *Wings* landing slightly ahead on the other side.

Now it was down to fitness and the in-bred desire to win. Four hundred metres was all that was left. Both jockeys had their whips out, using them as persuaders on their mounts.

The crowd's intensity grew to a fever pitch. Owners and trainers could only dream that their horse had got to this point in the race. The grandstand erupted as every person leapt from their seat to cheer on their preferred horse. The on-course commentator screamed, his voice like that of a mad-man.

Chesterman began to close the gap on *Wings*. Carey threw all that he could at his horse.

Two hundred and fifty metres from home both horses began to wobble slightly, their legs beginning to slow, feeling the effects of the race. Despite this, they continued to thunder towards the line. The gap between them now just a few feet. The jockeys using one hand on the reins and the other holding their whips as they tried to steer straight courses. It was inevitable that they would clash. At a hundred and fifty metres from the line, both horses moved simultaneously off their lines, bumping and boring into each other, the jockeys nearly falling off their mounts. The boring continued for nearly one hundred and twenty metres, neither horse nor rider giving in to the other. Thirty metres from the line they separated, as the jockeys managed to balance up each horse.

Less than two seconds later they crossed the finish line almost locked as one. Despite the commentator's scream, he couldn't split them, Even the close up from the large screen TV showed that both horses had crossed the line together. A dead-heat!

The result stood. A dead-heat was officially declared. The photo of the finish confirmed it. In an attempt to win the race outright George Sormond requested an enquiry into the last couple of hundred metres of the race and formally lodged an objection to the result. The stewards were requested to watch the finish again. They heard the assertions from both camps, finally deciding that both parties in the race had been as bad as each other. Both jockeys were suspended from race riding for six weeks. They had been found guilty of *careless riding causing interference*. It didn't change the result, however.

Pete and Cannon were over-joyed at the outcome. Michelle and Emily had watched the race from the owners' bar. They had driven down to the course but had struggled with the traffic. They had arrived just in time to see the start of the race and had almost screamed themselves hoarse by the end of it.

The presentations were over. The trophy sat on the table. *Wings* had been returned to his box after he had been given a wash-down. He had eaten up and Pete felt that there was no need now to stay with him in his stable. Anyone who wanted to get at the horse was now too late. The horse had done what was expected of him. They would be taking *Wings* back to Colac tonight.

George Sormond came into the bar. Cannon and Pete were toasting each other, then began toasting *Wings* and finally they toasted the race itself. They drank apple juice as both would be driving home soon. They would celebrate there. Michelle and Emily drank prosecco.
"Congratulations again," Sormond said. "It was a great race. I think we all deserve to celebrate. Can I buy you all a drink?" he asked.
"Not for me," Cannon replied, "but thank you anyway."
Pete declined initially but finally accepted a rum and coke. Emily and Michelle accepted another glass each of prosecco. Sormond ordered a whisky.
As they waited for the drinks to arrive, they chatted amongst themselves. Sormond was initially disappointed at the race result as well as the outcome of the objection he had laid, however, he eventually, reluctantly, accepted that he would not be able to reverse the decision.

The sun was slowly dropping towards the horizon. It was almost five pm. Long black fingers stretched across the racecourse, creeping towards the grandstands and the stable yards. Day two of the carnival was over. The crowds had almost gone.

Pete and Cannon, along with Michelle and Emily had become much too comfortable forgetting about the trip ahead of them, back to Colac. Eventually, the darkening sky outside reminded Cannon of the need to get going. He stood up from his chair.

"I think we need to get on our way," he said, stretching as he did so.

Pete nodded. "Yep, let's get *Wings* sorted out and into the horsebox and be on our way."

As both men offered their wives their hands to help them up from the chairs they were sitting on, Bruce and Cromwell came into the bar, walking straight up to Sormond.

They had met the crowds around the town and those leaving the course and had taken five hours to do a three-hour trip. Bruce was not in a good mood.

"George Sormond, I'm arresting you for the murders of Walter Grovedale and Max Optin. You have the right to stay silent but anything you say can and will be used in evidence against you in a court of law. Do you understand?"

Cannon watched the process unfold and shook his head. Pete, Emily, and Michelle stood in silence, stunned at what they were witnessing.

Sormond said nothing. He was led away by Cromwell to an awaiting police car.

CHAPTER 71

Sormond was given bail. Two days after his arrest he was back at home.

Bruce and Cromwell were sitting with Cannon.

"I just wanted to thank you for all your help with this case," Bruce said. "I think that without you we could well have struggled to close it," he said. He drank some of the tea that he had been offered. "Oh, and I also wanted to say well done, congratulations on the Grand Annual result. I saw the closing stages on the TV last night, What a great race, a great achievement."

"I just helped out a bit," Cannon replied modestly. "That's what we came here to do."

"Well, you achieved it, so well done," Bruce said.

"Thanks again."

"No worries."

Cannon felt a little uncomfortable. The past two days had been difficult for him. He had thought it over several times. He didn't like what he had concluded. He didn't know how to broach the subject, either. It wasn't his manor, his jurisdiction, he wasn't a citizen, he had no standing in the country. He was just a visitor.

He had shared his concerns with Michelle and then with Pete. Pete advised him to share his thoughts with Bruce. Now was the time.

"Inspector, if I may, I'd like to share with you a few thoughts about the Optin and Grovedale murders."

"Sure," replied Bruce. "Go ahead. But before you do, I can tell you that through his lawyer, Sormond has said that he knows nothing about the murders and doesn't have any idea why he was arrested. He may be out on bail, but the provisional hearing is set down for less than two weeks' time. I'm sure that by the time we get to court he will have changed his tune."

"That's a maybe," Cannon said, 'but…" he hesitated. "I think you've got the wrong man."

Bruce wasn't sure if he heard correctly.

"Sorry?" he replied.

Cannon repeated his claim. "I don't think Sormond has anything to do with Optin's or Grovedale's murders."

"What?" said Bruce somewhat bemused. "What do you mean, had nothing to do with their murders? We found the hammer with Grovedale's blood on it hidden away at Sormond's place. Who else would have hidden it, if not him?"

"It was planted," Cannon replied.

"Planted?" Bruce looked at Cromwell. He was almost incredulous at what he was hearing. "By whom…?" he asked.

"The real killer…" Cannon replied.

"And who might that be?" he asked.

"I'll fill you in first, then introduce you…"

CHAPTER 72

They were standing in the room. It was empty of horses but had the right people.

It was the weekend and Cannon would be leaving to go home, back to the UK in just over five days. He was looking forward to getting back. He had spoken with his Assistant, Rich Telside, the previous evening, after Bruce and Cromwell had heard what he had to say. There were some new horses in Cannon's stable. The season was still a few months away, but it was beginning to shape up to be a good one. He hoped he wouldn't be going back with his tail between his legs.

He looked at her. She seemed nervous. It was not like her.

They had managed to get her here under a false pretense. Pete had called and asked her to look at a particular horse. He claimed the horse was ill, possibly with colic. She rushed to his property and the Vet's room, only to find it empty. Empty except for Cannon, Bruce, Cromwell, and Alworth who followed her into the room.

"I'm sorry," she said when they had initially walked in, "but I'm here to check on a horse. So, would you mind leaving please?"

Cannon replied. "Sorry Deb, but we are here to see you. There is *no* ill horse. We just needed you here."

"Why? Why the subterfuge? What's this all about?" she asked.

"Murder," he answered simply.

"What?"

"Murder," he repeated, "the killing of innocent people."

"I don't know what you are talking about," she said, smiling nervously.

"I think you do."

She again rejected Cannon's assertion. She looked at him, holding his gaze. He looked away. This was hard enough as it was. He had been here many times in the past, but somehow this seemed personal.

"Okay," she said, picking up a chair and moving it next to a small writing table that stood to one side of the room, where she then sat down. "Go ahead, tell me what you know."

Cannon was taking no pleasure from this. He stood a few feet in front of her. Bruce and the others stood to one side.

"A few days ago, Inspector Bruce here got a phone call. The person who called him gave him some information. It was cryptic but useful. The Inspector gave me that same information and I've been wrestling with it since then. I couldn't understand its relevance and I couldn't work out how or why it had anything to do with Max Optin, that was until I saw you on the TV on Grand Annual day, vetting the horses."

"I'm still not sure of the relevance," she answered.

"I remembered what you did at Pakenham, with the horse's *Spirit Level* and *Royal Mint* when you were vetting them. You gave them gentle slaps on the rump."

"To encourage them..." she interrupted.

"Maybe with *Spirit Level,* but certainly not with *Royal Mint,*" he replied. "I think you were testing something on them."

"What?" she replied. "I'm a Vet for God's sake, why would I want to hurt a horse or even put a jockey in danger by doing such a thing? And what was it you are suggesting I was *testing* anyway?" she demanded.

"I don't think you wanted to hurt the horse. As I said, I think you were testing something on them, and I think you were doing so on behalf of George Sormond."

"Why?"

"Because you had made a deal with him."

"A deal?"

"Yes. He had found out what you were really involved in and he made you an offer you couldn't refuse."

"What do you mean?"

"That you would help him win the Grand Annual in return for him keeping quiet about your *endeavours.*"

"And how could I do that," she replied. "No one can guarantee success in the race."

"True," he said. "The race would need to take care of itself, but you could at least give *Chesterman* an advantage. As the Vet on the day, responsible for pre and post-race blood tests, you could quite easily manipulate them and *if* Sormond's horse won the race, you could quite easily ensure that the blood samples taken didn't show any abnormalities."

She did not respond.

Cannon carried on. "I think you took two samples from the horse *before* the Grand Annual. You provided them to the labs for testing as required, but the lab didn't know that the second one was taken when it was. It assumed the second sample was from *Chesterman* post-race. The second sample would show no sign of what you'd administered into the horse."

"Ummm," she answered. "And what would that be? And how did I do it?" she asked confidently.

"I'm guessing it was Clenbuterol or something similar. I saw you reach into your bag and get something out of it. I don't know if you used a spray in the mouth of the horse or gave him a quick jab with a syringe, but you definitely gave him something."

"And you can prove this.?"

Cannon did not respond. It was a theory. He took a chance, told a lie. "George Sormond has already confessed to the police that he knew about it. I think that will be enough proof."

She stared at him. Then she looked around the room. Tears welled up in her eyes.

"You killed Max Optin as well, didn't you?" he said. "Murdered him because he'd had enough of the lies and he was about to blow the lid. He was part of your group, wasn't he, but was getting tired of the secrecy? He knew about Hedge, that you killed him too!"

"No," she shouted, tears falling down her cheeks, "it's not true. It's not true."

Bruce and Cromwell looked at each other, they noted how Ryan began to appear uncomfortable sitting down. She seemed to be moving her hands under the table as if reaching towards something. A lower drawer perhaps?

Cannon continued. "Wasn't that why Optin said he no longer wanted to work with horses, because he knew what you were planning, what you were doing, particularly with *Chesterman*? And it got to him, particularly given what the group was doing?"

"And what was that?" she asked.

"The use of the trawler, the *San Marino*."

Ryan's face dropped. "How do you k…?"

"As I mentioned earlier, Inspector Bruce here received a call from the skipper on the day of the Grand Annual. It was cryptic but provided enough information for me to work things out."

"We were trying to help…" she said, tears flowed freely now.

"Yes, I understand," answered Cannon. "It was noble of you. Not just you, but the whole group."

Bruce was confused, saying so, "Sorry Mike, but what do you mean. The skipper said that there was a cargo collected by the *San Marino* on a relatively regular basis and that it was illegal. He didn't say what it was, but we assumed it was drugs."

Cannon looked at Bruce, then at Ryan. "It wasn't drugs Inspector. It was people. Refugees. People from Myanmar, China, Indonesia, some from the Middle East and other countries."

"My God!" exclaimed Cromwell. "People? I can't believe it."

"And that's why Hedge had to die," Cannon went on. "Somehow he found out about what was going on and decided to blackmail the group."

"The bastard deserved it…" Ryan said.

"I'm guessing you managed to trick him somehow, perhaps getting him drunk and used a drug on him to render him unconscious. Perhaps a tranquilizer or sleep aid? I'm sure if we ask the forensic lab boys to look again, they will find what we are looking for, won't they?"

Ryan didn't reply. She sat quietly, her tears now having stopped. Her world was unravelling. Her hands were in her lap.

"Your joke about dressing him in jockey silks was an interesting one and cleaning him totally to get rid of any possible DNA evidence was also clever. You must have thought it through very diligently," he said.

Ryan sighed. She turned towards Bruce, not wanting to look at Cannon anymore. It wasn't a confession, more an attempt to rationalize things. "We wanted to save the few refugees we could. We believed that this country wasn't doing enough to help those poor people. We're a rich country, a *lucky* country. These people needed our help."

"And so you brought them in, kept them close, used them as stablehands and track riders," Cannon said, remembering the staff that he had seen at Pete's and also at Sormond's place.

"Gave them a chance of freedom, of a living," she spat.

"And what about Grovedale?" Cannon asked, "Did he not deserve to keep living? Did he also deserve to die?"

"He'd known what was going on for a long time. He was going to tell."

"Just like Hedge?"

"Yes," she replied, "but not before I told the police about him."

Cannon was confused by her comment. He was convinced she had killed Grovedale because he was going to tell the authorities about the illegal immigrants. Cannon wasn't sure what Grovedale was getting for his silence, he was a rich man already. Money wasn't a factor. The warning she had sent to him by burning Optin's car on the bicycle track obviously meant something to both of them.

He let her speak.

"A year ago, a Tuesday it was," she said softly, "Grovedale raped me on *that* track. It was his favourite and he told me that he liked to ride it as often as he could. We are, were, both keen cyclists. He suggested we go for a ride on it one day. It was just the two of us. After about a kilometre he stopped and got off his bike, He said he had a puncture, but he was lying. I got off my bike to see if I could help him and that's when he forced himself on me and raped me. He raped me!" she began to sob uncontrollably.

Cromwell found a roll of paper towel in a cupboard and placed it on the table in front of her. She tore off a few strips and used it to clean her face. They all waited for her to continue. "He was a small man but fit and strong," she went on. "Afterwards as he dressed himself and I lay on the ground, I kicked out at him in anger and he fell. He landed on a tree stump and hurt his back. He never rode again."

"So why didn't you tell the police? About the rape?" Cannon asked. He felt a tinge of sympathy for her as the question left his lips.

"For the same reason, you wouldn't have. It was his word against mine and he knew about the immigrants."

"So, you made a deal?"

"Yes, but only once I got out of the hospital. We agreed we would both stay quiet. I was admitted for a week as not only had Grovedale raped me, but he *damaged* me as well. He took away my ability to have children. He tore my insides. He was brutal. I had to lie to the hospital staff about what had happened. Fortunately, they didn't ask too many questions, they just did their job. But I swore I would get even someday."

"And that day came when he told you that he was about to break the deal?"

"No," she replied. "I was the one going to break it not him."

Cannon looked at her, surprised. "Can I ask why?"

She turned to Bruce. "The man that was found on the track in Forrest," she said, "I put him there."

The room fell silent. Bruce didn't know what to say. The statement was completely unexpected. Bruce and Cromwell had not even contemplated that there would be any discussion about the *man on the track*.

Cannon let Bruce take over.

"How? Why?" Bruce asked.

"When Grovedale raped me and I ended up in the hospital, we had one refugee left who had not yet found work. All the people we brought in were kept in a lock-up on a small farm just outside Forrest until we could find them a job. We would take them food, water, clothing, and other things they needed fairly regularly. Sometimes it would fall to one of us including Max Optin amongst others, to take what they needed. If some of us were away, then one of us would hold the fort for up to a month if necessary. In this case, it was my job to look after him, but because of my being hospitalized for a week and subsequently needing additional treatment, by the time I got to the poor man, he had died. From starvation. We had left him a phone but in Forrest the signal can vary, and we didn't realise that he had no coverage. He couldn't leave the lock-up because he hardly spoke English and he had no idea where he was. He didn't really know us either. He trusted us. I let him down."

She began to cry again, softly.

Bruce stared into Ryan's face. Things now made sense, but he would never have connected the dots without her.

"And so you dumped the body on the track?" Bruce asked.

She began to shake, then she stood up. She seemed to need air, it looked like she was having a panic attack.

"I didn't know what to do," she began, her voice beginning to increase in pitch, trembling at the pictures in her mind. "I knew things would be quiet in the area. I remember it was a Thursday. I stripped him and used my car to transport his body to the parking lot near the tracks' end and then I carried him onto the track, pushed him as far as I could into the bush. I then covered him with what leaves I could find, then I left."

"And there the poor man stayed until he was found by accident," Bruce stated.

"Yes," Ryan replied weakly.

Cannon needed to know more. He had liked her. He knew there was something behind all this. He needed to know how things had started and why. He sought permission from Bruce to ask her another question. Bruce nodded, then left the room to make a call. Cromwell stayed behind.

Bruce was going to make an arrest, so he needed to let Cusscom and his boss Thatcher know the circumstances.

Cannon pressed her again, asking her the obvious...

"Why?" she said, "why?"

"Yes," he said. "I saw you as a good Vet and a lovely woman when we first met and you introduced yourself. Throughout my time here, I've only had the highest regard for you. I've seen you work, your caring nature with the animals, especially the horses, has been paramount. You clearly do love them. I didn't believe all the clues that were being dropped until now. I hoped I was wrong."

She gave him a sad smile. "You weren't."

"But WHY?" he repeated his earlier question, "Why the killing? Was that necessary?"

She responded immediately she had no qualms in doing so. She had her principles, her convictions.

"Seven years ago, I was married," she said. "My new husband and I flew to the Maldives on our honeymoon. Only I came back. Well, alive, anyway."

Cannon was shocked. He offered his sympathy which seemed shallow in the light of the current circumstances.

"My husband died on the third day we were there. He went diving in a group. From what I was told, one of the party in the group got into trouble. He tried to help but the individual panicked and pulled off his diving mask and his breathing regulator. My husband had a bronchial condition which we believed was under control."

Cannon realized the implication of Clenbuterol. It is often used within other compounds such as hydrochloride salt to help with breathing problems for those with chronic asthma.

"And it wasn't?" he interrupted.

"Well, it was until then," she said sadly. "He had an asthma attack. He drowned."

The silence between them all as they contemplated what they had just heard fell across them like a wet blanket.

Cannon looked at Cromwell, who despite being a police officer was almost in tears herself.

Without provocation or encouragement, Deb Ryan continued to talk, explaining her thinking, justifying what she had done and answering the very question Cannon has posed.

"In the hospital in Male where my husband's body was taken, I saw how poor many of the people were. I saw people who had hopes for a better life for themselves and their children. I saw the beggars outside in the street, those who relied on tourism or *throw away* dollars. I realized how many people across the world needed help. Help to find a better future. After my husband's funeral a few weeks later, I made it my objective to help the poor where I could. The poor not of this country, but from those that are down-trodden anywhere. I believed that they should have the opportunity to share in our wealth. If that meant bringing in a few people illegally then I felt it was worth it…."

Bruce came back into the room and decided to take back charge. Cannon accepted that he had done his job and with a simple nod, moved to one side and stood next to Cromwell. He noticed her wiping her eyes before quickly putting away a handkerchief in her coat pocket.

"I think the sentiment is very noble, Mrs. Ryan," Bruce said, invoking the formality needed upon arrest, "but killing people, no matter what the reason, is punishable under the law. So, Deborah Ryan, I arrest you and charge you with the willful murders of……."

She interrupted him by saying, "There is one other thing……"

Bruce stopped talking allowing her to continue, hoping though that she was not going to reveal another killing.

They waited as she composed herself. She looked around at each of them. Then she looked down as if looking at her feet. She moved the chair closer to the drawer. They waited.

"Go on," Bruce requested impatiently.

"My husband," she said hesitatingly, "…was Walt Grovedale's son! He was a champion mountain bike rider. It was he who took me to those tracks to ride on them. When I lost my husband, that left a big hole in my life. Something I could never replace or fill. A part of me was missing, but when Grovedale raped me, I swore one day that I would get even with him as he had taken away what was left of me. He left me with nothing!"

Before they heard the last syllable, before they could even react, Ryan reached for the top drawer of the table and pulled out a knife, a surgical blade used by Vets in operations, slashing at her own throat then plunging the knife deep into her chest. For a few seconds, chaos ensued. Bruce tried to catch her as she fell, and Cannon screamed for someone to call an ambulance. Ryan slumped to the floor blood gurgling from her neck and her chest. They tried to stem the bleeding as much as they could. They tried to keep her alive.

EPILOGUE

They were standing at the entrance, just before security. Once through, then it was on to passport control. Pete, Emily, and Stephanie had caught up with Cannon and Michelle the previous evening. They had enjoyed dinner together at the *Red Spice Road* restaurant on Queen Street in the city. After Ryan's confession, the days that followed had been a blur for Cannon. It had been necessary for him to meet with the police several times before finally saying his goodbyes to Bruce and Cromwell.

He was made aware, and he knew before they even told him, that he could be called as a witness at some time in the future if necessary. He was also advised that such a requirement would be done remotely, through the use of online tools such as Skype, Zoom, or any other option they may consider.

"There will be no need for you to come back over, mate," Bruce had said. Cannon was fine with that.

"Well, this is where we say goodbye Mike," Pete said.

Cannon offered his hand. "Yep, I guess so Pete," he answered, a glint of moisture appearing in his eye. Pete took his hand and the two men hugged each other. Cannon closed his eyes to hide his tears.

"I'll miss you, my friend," Pete said.

"Me too, thanks for everything."

They separated. Emily and Michelle hugged each other likewise.

Cannon turned to Stephanie. "C'mon little girl. Give me a hug then."

They each did the rounds, saying goodbye to one another.

"Right then," Cannon stated. "We'd better go."

Pete nodded. "Stay in touch."

"I will," Cannon promised.

"I hope you enjoyed your time in the City?" Pete asked as Cannon and Michelle picked up their hand luggage that had been standing at their feet.

"It was fantastic," Michelle said. "We had a great time this past week. We met some great people, saw some fantastic sights, and ate and drank some marvelous food and wine."

"I'm so pleased to hear it,"

"Yes, you really are very lucky," Cannon stated.

"I know," Pete said.

"Ryan was lucky too. If it wasn't for the speedy response of the paramedics in that ambulance I think she would have died."

"I agree. It was very fortunate that they were not too far away when we called…" Pete stopped for a second, thinking back to the incident. Was it really such a short time ago? Just a week?

Finally, he said, "It's just so sad that such good intentions led to so much pain. Even those on the *San Marino* who were doing something they believed in. They'll have to face the courts too."

Cannon nodded. Turning to Michelle he said. "Time to go home now, love. It's a bloody long way, but let's go."

ABOUT THE AUTHOR

An ex Accountant with a lifelong love of horseracing. He has lived on three continents and has been passionate about the sport wherever he resided. Having grown up in England he was educated in South Africa where he played soccer professionally. Moving to Australia, he expanded his love for racing through becoming a syndicate member in several racehorses.

In addition, he began a hobby which quickly became extremely successful, that of making award-winning red wine with a close friend.

In mid-2014 he moved with his employer to England for just over four years, during which time he became a member of the British Racing Club (BRC).

He has now moved back to Australia, where he continues to write, and also presents a regular music show on local community radio.

He shares his life with his beautiful wife, Rebecca.

He has two sons, one who lives in the UK and one who lives in Australia. This is his third novel.

Printed in Great Britain
by Amazon

86179120R00122